Bygones Be Damned

by

Jules Parker

The Wild Rose Press, Inc.
PO Box 708
Adams Basin, NY 14410-0708
Visit us at www.thewildrosepress.com

Publishing History
First Edition, 2024
Trade Paperback ISBN 978-1-5092-5613-6
Digital ISBN 978-1-5092-5614-3

Published in the United States of America

Dedication

To Kelley: Thank you for taking such good care of me.
Yes, you are always right.

Chapter 1

In the early fog of the cool December morning, Marcelina Page materialized out of the darkness. Bathed in the glow of post-season Christmas lights, she checked the numbers on a front porch and approached it. It was the plain, unadorned half of a modern duplex, clearly belonging to someone lacking the same holiday spirit as his neighbor.

Her chest heaved after the two miles she'd just jogged. Sweat dripped all the way from her thick, chestnut ponytail down to her running shoes, permeating her purple and yellow spandex outfit with hard-earned perspiration. Going straight for the front window, Marcelina peered through it. A lizard streaked across the screen, giving her a momentary, quiet jolt. A series of controlled breaths slowed her pulse before she raised her knuckles and wrapped lightly on the front door. When there was no answer, she reached down and tested the handle. It opened easily, a fact that surprised her despite all the "Neighborhood Watch" signs indicating this was a safe one to live in.

As she entered the darkened duplex, Marcelina closed the door softly behind her and waited for her eyes to adjust. Nothing of immediate interest stood out inside the great room. It was tidy, making the shadows boring and easy to identify: couch, chair, lamps, entertainment center…

Coffee table adorned with something intricate and shiny.

Her running shoes padded silently across the wood floors as she moved toward it. Somewhere in the back of the house, a rush of water was cut, bathing the place in silence. She stopped walking. Moments later a faucet turned on, and Marcelina knew her time was limited. But leaving didn't fit into her plans. Not until she'd gotten what she'd come for.

Identifying the intricate shiny thing as a brass model of the scales of justice, a smile curved her mouth. She reached into the pocket of her light jacket and placed a small figurine on one side of the scale. It tipped, lending an accurate depiction of which side she believed was winning.

Marcelina removed her jacket and threw it over a chair before proceeding to follow the sounds of a morning routine. At the end of a darkened hallway, a door was open, allowing a dim sliver of light to angle through and guide the way. Once she reached that room, she entered it to discover another sparse and orderly space. With the borrowed light from the attached bath, Marcelina scoped out the bedroom's dark, contemporary furniture with keen interest.

Bed. Dresser. Desk. Chair. Something out of place on the end table—a couple of files with a pair of wire-rimmed reading glasses placed on top. Magazine quality, as if a designer placed them on that small table to make the space look "lived-in."

How…boring.

At least the bed was unmade. Beside it, sheer curtains billowed from an open window letting in the cool morning air. With the days so hot, Marcelina understood the need to enjoy what pre-dawn had to offer. Southwest Florida was a humid place even in late December. But to open windows and then leave them without sufficient lighting was practically inviting trouble, even in a nice neighborhood.

The city of Naples itself was a sort of sultry grifter, offering a distraction in the form of a tropical paradise while at the same time emptying one's bank account. And people lost their minds when blinded by beauty—a human weakness Marcelina used to her own benefit. Like now, for instance.

The water was cut. Her gaze darted to the cracked bathroom door, which would open at any second. Though she knew she should leave, curiosity simply wouldn't allow it. So she instead moved over to the chair and sat down. Crossed one leg over the other. Waited.

The door swung wide. Out walked her naked lawyer, his face buried in a thick towel as he dried his hair and fumbled for the light switch. When he found it, the room brightened around him.

And there she was. Blinded by beauty. Marcelina drank him in, openly admiring the un-obscured view of muscular arms, a defined chest dusted with dark hair, and lean, powerful thighs. Her gaze lingered on the proud display of genitals between those thighs, making her fidget with an ache of appreciation. A moan escaped.

Walker Bishop stopped dead in his tracks. His freshly-shaven face popped out from behind the towel. As soon as he registered her presence, he let out a thick curse and covered his privates.

"I knew there was more to you than just a stiff suit," she teased.

He dove toward the walk-in closet. "Dammit,

Marcelina!"

"What?" She cocked her head, soaking in his sculpted posterior before the closet door closed and blocked her view.

"You broke into my house," came the muffled reply. "I'm pretty sure that's a crime."

"Your front door was open. Besides, I'm a criminal. It's in my file, which you probably haven't touched for weeks now."

"Get out of my bedroom!"

The anger in his tone had turned to annoyance, but Marcelina knew she was safe before walking through the front door. Her court-appointed attorney had a soft spot for her somewhere beneath that tough exterior. She'd seen it in his reluctant smiles, his annoyance and even his anger. It was the only reason he'd agreed to take her case when he clearly wouldn't win it, sullying his stellar track record.

With a sigh, she pushed out of the chair and approached the closet. "I'm not leaving, Walker. Not until we talk about my case."

A resigned sigh. "Wait for me in the living room. I'll be out in a minute."

Taking his naked image with her, Marcelina obeyed. *Damn.* The real crime was that he was completely off limits, bound by some canon of ethics that prevented lawyers from dating their clients. And, yes, he'd gone over his own strict rules of propriety, more than once since he'd had to remind them both of it a few weeks back when she'd responded to his lingering, appreciative gaze with one of her own. An undeniable attraction had grown between them over the last eight months, but he fought the idea with fierce conviction, so much that he'd avoided her since then.

Making herself at home, she turned on lights and scoped out the place while she waited. It was small but open, with curves and alcoves to break up the boxy feel. Light walls and throw rugs contrasted heavily with the dark floors and modern furniture that Walker favored. A black-granite-topped bar was all that separated the kitchen and its cherry cabinetry from the great room. A quick search of the cabinets yielded little food, meaning this particular part of the home wasn't used nearly enough. So, once the coffee was brewing, she made good use out of the last two eggs and a bag of shredded cheese. By the time Walker emerged from his bedroom, the whole place smelled like breakfast.

"That was completely out of line, Marcelina," he barked behind her. "Seriously, what's gotten into you?"

With her back still turned, she shrugged out a half-hearted apology. It was hard to be truly sorry when the rewards had been so worth the risk. "If it helps, I didn't mean to embarrass you."

"I'm not embarrassed, damn it. I'm pissed off and I want you to leave."

"But I'm making you some protein," she argued, fully confident in her abilities to sway him. "Oh, and the coffee's ready."

She could feel his glower on her back. Marcelina granted him an over-the-shoulder look of shame that had him rolling his eyes. Though his white dress shirt was properly buttoned, he'd forgotten the undershirt this time, allowing the outline of his solid pectorals to peek through, which danced when he attempted to put socks on while standing.

The man was clueless as to what that small oversight

did to her—made her want to drag him back to that bedroom and have her way with him despite his damned ethics. "Forgive me?" she asked.

He shot her a brief glance through dark lashes that were just as black and glossy as his still-damp hair. "I'm just wondering what happened to that model client you promised to be."

"I did knock first."

"And when I didn't answer, you helped yourself."

There was a thick Italian heritage in there somewhere, Marcelina thought. Something fiery to back his commanding nature, blue eyes, and fair complexion. When she realized she was fantasizing again, she cleared her throat and turned off the burner. "How else was I going to get your attention? You've been avoiding me."

"I haven't been avoiding you. I'm a criminal defense attorney which means I spend a lot of time in court."

The toaster popped. Marcelina added two slices to his plate of eggs then rounded the bar and set the food on the table next to his coffee and tub of butter. "Sit down and eat, Bishop." Her tone of voice told him to relax a little. "I swear I'll be good."

His cobalt gaze narrowed a bit, then slowly lost its chill. He sat down, looked at the food as he finished tying his shoes. "You didn't have to cook. I usually grab something on the way to the office."

"You're welcome." Amused, she lowered herself to a chair opposite his and drew a knee up while she sipped her own coffee.

Walker's mouth twitched as he finally sat down. It was a mouth that begged to be kissed, smoothed out from its strict, grim line. A square jaw added to a set of sharp features that were made for the courtroom…as long as no one knew the softy that lurked inside, which Marcelina was bound and determined to draw out if it killed her.

He picked up the fork. "You know your trial isn't for another three and a half weeks, right?"

"I'm nervous."

A quick laugh. "You act like it."

He thought she was joking. But Marcelina had been nursing a crippling sense of anxiety ever since she found herself facing hard time.

"You've been charged with felony conspiracy and possession," he reminded through a mouthful of food. "The feds only have to prove you knew about the drugs being delivered to your apartment, which will be hard to *dis*prove since your boyfriend, Jonah, left you with a classic case of holding the bag."

"That's *ex*-boyfriend."

"And let's not forget the possible five-year prison sentence. You *should* be nervous, but hounding me won't solve your problems. I'm ready for your hearing. With what we have, you may get off with some fines and a few years' probation, but there are no guarantees. Unless, of course, you have information that could change the dynamics of your case."

She paused, considering her choices over the rim of her steaming mug. "No. There's nothing."

He ate in thoughtful silence, his dogged gaze boring a hole into hers. "You see, there's that look."

"What look?"

"You're keeping something from me. I could sense it from the get-go."

She rolled her eyes. "Honey, you don't know me well enough to read my soul."

Another laugh as he took up the knife and commenced to buttering toast. "I've known you for eight months, and in that time I've learned the lengths you'll go to in order to get your way. Which now includes breaking and entering, I might add. I've learned you're restless. Stubborn. A general pain in the ass."

Marcelina sent him a droll look across the table. "In other words, your typical client."

"Exactly. These eggs are fantastic, by the way," he added through another bite. "But I'm a busy man who's trying to keep you from doing time, so when I detect a hesitance in your answer it frustrates the hell out of me."

Her spine stiffened a little. "I'm sorry, but I don't have anything more to tell you."

"So you still have no idea where Jonah King is hiding?"

Again with that? Why couldn't he just believe that her coward ex had disappeared without a trace? Was it so hard to believe she wouldn't protect him? "If I did, I'd turn the son-of-a-bitch in," she said through her teeth.

Walker's cool expression remained. "Then what are you doing here, Marcelina?"

Their stare-off ended with Marcelina on the losing end. She looked away. "I couldn't sleep."

The air between them changed, losing some of its crackle. "So you decided to take a jog over to my place, break into it, and lurk in my bedroom?"

"I don't take radio silence well. Besides, I was curious to see how a lawyer lives outside his office." Her voice teased once again. "Frankly, it's worse than I imagined."

He sat back, incredulous. "Now you're making fun of my home."

"If you can call it that."

"I don't need a big place."

"I wasn't talking about the size. This house looks like a model home. You haven't really nested at all."

He crunched toast. "And that's a bad thing?"

Her attempt to sip coffee ended with a laugh. "You live on the dark side of the duplex, Walker. No decor or Christmas lights or personality to make it yours. I'm beginning to wonder if you live at all."

"I live to *win*. Something you could benefit from if you'd cooperate with me."

The man was hopeless. She'd give anything to make *him* fidget once in a while. "And what exactly am I supposed to do for the next three and a half weeks? I don't have a job, or a car, or a home, or… Wow. When did I become so pathetic?"

He stood, took his empty plate to the sink. "I thought you were living with your friend again."

A flash of sadness broke through the distraction that was her sexy lawyer. Kendall wasn't just a friend, she'd been a sister—until police stormed their shared apartment and ruined everything. "She still hasn't forgiven me for what happened," Marcelina replied. "Our living arrangement is only temporary, and without a job I can't afford a place of my own."

He hesitated in the process of donning a maroon silk necktie. "I may be able to get you a job."

She lifted her face from the palm of her hand. "What, like helping you file papers or something?"

As he stopped at the bar, his mouth thinned out again, signaling a *no-can-do*. "Not with me. I should be out of court by three o'clock." He abandoned his Windsor-knot-in-progress and took a business card from his wallet. "Meet me at this address and I'll see what I can do." The loose tie dangled when he extended the card in her direction.

Marcelina took it, studied it while he packed his laptop and briefcase. "Isn't this near Golden Gate?"

"Yes, get there early."

"Um…no car, remember?"

"You're an incredibly capable woman." With briefcase and keys in hand, he took one last gulp of coffee. "Find a way."

When Walker headed toward his garage, the only thing missing was a kiss goodbye. His step faltered when he noticed the coffee table and its altered rendition of the scales of justice. "Is that your idea of decor?" he asked with a look of wonder. "A kid's-meal knickknack?"

A smile tugged at the corners of her mouth. "I like him. He's a burglar who steals hamburgers. And he's adorable, just like you."

Walker rolled his eyes again before continuing on. "Nice to see how much faith you have in the system," he said over his shoulder. "And no more visits to my house. It's off limits."

The door closed behind him, leaving nothing but a hint of aftershave and a stunned silence. Her smile widening, Marcelina sat back and sipped coffee. Waited. Seconds later, the garage entrance opened. When she looked back, there stood her formidable attorney, fully loaded with briefcase, car keys, and a look of chagrin.

She sighed, lowered her feet to the floor and rose from her chair. "I'm beginning to think you had no idea your front door was unlocked this morning."

"Just come on. I'm running late."

****

I almost left her there, for God's sake. Walker cracked the window to let in some much-needed fresh air. It was good she'd refused a ride home or he'd be offering up his car next. Dammit if that woman didn't throw him off balance. And since when did he ever care about the employment situation of his court-appointed clients? The growing number of pro-bono cases he'd agreed to take off the OPD's hands—thanks to his inability to make a clean break from the government—had produced some real winners. Their job was to screw up and his was to find loopholes that would keep them out of jail. Marcelina Page was no different.

Walker shifted in his seat. He hated driving with an erection, something he'd been battling off-and-on since finding her in his bedroom.

As he turned out of his neighborhood, his headlights slashed across a row of manicured circle drives, illuminating Anna Faulk's auburn hair and cleavage as she bent to get her newspaper. The woman straightened, waved when he passed. He waved back, wondering how it was he always managed to catch her at that particular time, bent over and flashing skin. Even when running late.

Okay, he got it. They were the same age. Both single. Both too busy for relationships. And, apparently, she'd been wanting another round of sex for a while now. At least she wasn't lurking in his bedroom, he supposed.

Lurking in a purple and yellow jogging outfit that showed every, remarkable, hourglass curve. It wasn't fair to him, being ambushed by sex in spandex when he hadn't had a woman since…well, since Marcelina had become a client. And what was he thinking allowing her to stay in his home after her break-in, when he should have thrown her out on her curvaceous rear end?

Another round, that's what he needed. He'd stop by Anna's later. The tenacious widow was easy on the eyes, knew the value of a one-night-stand, and she was safe. Because one sneak-peek from Marcelina Page had awakened the beast—an erection from hell that would take way more than five minutes of closet meditation to get rid of.

He wasn't the only one who needed a distraction. Marcelina needed one too, anything to shift her focus since this attraction between them had come out into the open. Never mind that it was his fault for getting caught in la-la land while she'd fiddled with her hair, or something along those lines. He couldn't remember what made him start slobbering, but she'd caught him doing it. And he'd run from the heat like a man already on fire. He jabbed a button on the steering wheel. "Call Tony Lathrop."

After a slight pause, his sedan came alive with a feminine voice. "Calling Tony Lathrop." Several rings later, the voice coming through the speakers belonged to a groggy male.

"Hullo?"

Walker rolled up the window to keep things private. "Tony, good. I need to ask you a favor."

A rustling of sheets. "What the hell, Walker, it's six-thirty."

Wasn't everyone up at six-thirty? "Are you still looking for someone to show cars at the auction house?"

"Yeah, why?"

"I have the perfect woman for you."

"Is she pretty?"

Pretty wasn't the right word. How to describe

Marcelina Page… There was something about her that went beyond the full smile and sexy eyes. Something visceral that thoroughly stripped him of his armor. "Yeah, she's pretty," he grumbled, thoroughly pissed off at his growing weakness for her. "I told her to meet me over there this afternoon."

"We have an auction this afternoon."

"Perfect."

"Or not. Your buddy, Rivera, is selling off his repos."

Walker's hands tensed on the wheel. Armando Rivera, Miami's friendly neighborhood cartel leader, had escaped Walker's reach when he'd been a government prosecutor there. It was an unpleasant coincidence that Rivera recently showed up in Naples, and had remained somewhat of a project for Walker even though he was now a defense attorney. Rivera's photo still littered police stations and DEA offices around the state, gracing the upper portion of hand-drawn pyramids diagramming cartel hierarchy. And still, Walker was closer than anyone to getting much needed testimony against the guy.

Should he risk running into him? Was he even on Rivera's radar anymore? The drug lord rarely showed his face in public, sending his lackeys out to act on his behalf. Chances were he wouldn't even be at Tony's. "Look, Marcelina needs a job." And Walker needed to keep her out of his house before he took her to bed. "Maybe a car if you have one you can loan her."

"Wait a minute…she isn't one of your clients, is she?"

Another line beeped in, lighting up the display on his console. "Captain Ross is calling, I have to go."

"But—"

"I'll see you this afternoon. And don't worry about Rivera. If he's even there we'll steer clear." Walker disconnected the call, which immediately connected him to the next one. "Bishop."

"You need to stop by the medical examiner's office on your way in," the police captain said, his grim tone effective in dissolving the last of Walker's lingering, sexual funk.

"Why?"

"We have a floater you need to identify. Just washed up near Clam Pass."

"Why do *I* need to identify it?"

"Because we believe it's one of your clients."

With Armando Rivera still fresh on the brain, one particular client came to mind—a dealer he'd finally convinced to turn against the cartel man. Their meeting with the DEA was in just a few hours. And wouldn't that be absolutely grand if his client ended up dead beforehand? "Which one?" Walker asked.

"We call him Chum. At least until you can officially identify him."

Funny. But Captain Ross knew Walker would drop everything and race over there. They'd become well-acquainted since the sheer volume of his court-appointed clients demanded many visits to the precinct, and Leonard knew all about his crusade against Rivera.

"I'll be there in twenty."

Chapter 2

The sun was just peeking through the palm-dappled yards across the street when Marcelina returned to Kendall's apartment complex. With the temperatures climbing, her jog back had been more labored, but she welcomed the distraction from her troubles and was in no hurry to face her friend's censuring attitude. Despite the hardships Marcelina had caused Kendall, at least the woman hadn't lost her job—one that she was very happy with. Great boss, nice co-workers, big paycheck… But the paycheck hadn't been big enough to keep the nice two-bedroom apartment they'd shared, so Kendall was forced to downsize to a single-bedroom in an older building. Something Marcelina caught flack over every time the faucet leaked or the air conditioner made a funny noise.

Ignoring the elevator, she used the stairs as a means to catch her breath. Gather her composure. Guilt was an awful burden, one that sometimes forced her into a flippant attitude she didn't want. Kendall was like family to her. They shared years of friendship, lots of laughs, and plenty of tears. But they could fight, too. And they'd had a few awful rounds of it since Marcelina's legal troubles started. But this morning, to show how grateful she was for the temporary shelter, she would make Kendall breakfast. Then she'd shower and try to forget all the poor choices she'd made in life.

On the second floor, as she walked the length of the open corridor, she lifted her chin up. Took the salt air deep into her lungs. Looked out at the blazing, cloud-speckled skyline. Positive attitude restored, she stopped at the door with the weather-cracked numbers *218* on it and knocked loudly. A series of deadbolts and chains came undone. Then the door opened a crack and was abandoned just as quickly. Marcelina glimpsed a blonde, tousled head through the opening. It was moving back to the bedroom.

"Kendall?" No answer. Cold shoulder. "Okay, I'll let myself in," she murmured, entering Kendall's pink, frilly domain and restoring all the locks and bolts to their Fort Knox positions. She flung her jacket on the couch where her suitcase and belongings were neatly arranged. With a sentimental regard for the small, unlit Christmas tree shedding needles by the window, Marcelina banked left toward Kendall's single bedroom. As the air conditioning cooled her damp skin, she found her temporary roommate back under the covers and with a pillow over her head.

"Don't you need to get ready for work?" she asked.

"I'm not going in today," came the muffled reply.

Marcelina frowned. "Why not? Are you sick?"

"Yes." A sniff.

"Want me to go get you some medicine?"

Kendall finally removed the pillow and turned to reveal red swollen eyes. An angry flush stained her alabaster skin. "Only if it's red and served in a wine glass."

Then Marcelina noticed the tissues, the phone on the floor within reach of Kendall's hand, and the jeweled necklace her boyfriend had given her for Christmas. It was broken and hanging over the edge of the wastebasket. The woman's cold shoulder had found a new target.

Marcelina's heart flip-flopped from fear to sheer sympathy. "Want me to go kick Richard's ass for you?"

Kendall's mouth turned down in a dramatic pout. "Yes."

Entering the clutter of Kendall's room, Marcelina lowered herself to the other side of a white, lace-covered bed. Clothes, books, and boxes were stacked everywhere on top of too-small furniture Kendall had outgrown long ago. In the old days they would have cuddled in the wake of such heartbreak, but Marcelina didn't want to push her luck. The two of them laid there, staring at the ceiling in mutual anguish. "What happened?" Marcelina asked.

"He said we were too different. That we wanted different things."

If she and Kendall had been talking like old times, Marcelina would have told her that very thing. Richard was a handsome, clean-cut pilot from New Zealand looking for a wife to take back to his homeland. Kendall—the perpetual dreamer—thought he was in Florida to stay. Though Marcelina could see their troubles like an approaching freight train, Kendall had been stuck on the tracks, blinded by the big, pretty light. Hormones may have also played a role, something Marcelina had been guilty of as well. "Three days after Christmas," she murmured. "What an asshole."

Kendall's tousled head moved with a nod. "Do you know how much I spent on that watch I gave him?"

"Probably more than what he spent on that necklace."

"Yeah. Cheap bastard."

It was a diamond and silver thing from a high-end jeweler on Fifth Avenue. Certainly not cheap as far as consolation prizes went. "So where did you disappear to this morning?" Kendall asked.

Marcelina smiled a bit. "I went to my lawyer's house."

"Really?" The subject of Richard officially shot toward the back burner. "And how did that go?"

"I saw him naked." *I saw him naked?* Not "we discussed my case" or "he may get me a job today"?

Kendall's eyes flared with interest. "Did you sleep with him?"

"No." The word came out rushed and with a scowl. "In fact, I think I left him more irritated with me than usual."

"Bummer. What does he look like naked?"

For a thirty-five year-old man, Walker wore his skin so...*so* well. A flash of his bare posterior warmed Marcelina's brain with fond remembrance. "Like a god." When her focus returned, Kendall was watching her closely. "One I'm not *allowed* to sleep with," she added.

After a reflective silence, Kendall turned toward her and tucked both hands beneath her cheek. Light poured in from the clouded louvered windows as they stared at each other for a quiet moment. "I miss you," Kendall said in a gravelly whisper. "I miss this. Being able to talk to someone who always takes my side. Makes me feel better. Distracts me from sucky break-ups."

Fighting back a wave of emotion, Marcelina pursed her lips. God only knew how much she missed her friend, too—wished she could take back what had happened. She struggled to remember a name Kendall had mentioned recently, a co-worker she was friends with. "I thought Beth did that for you."

A sound of disgust shot out, accompanied by a good eye roll. "Beth met someone at the Christmas party."

Enough said. Beth was happy, therefore unqualified to properly handle Kendall's misery. Marcelina, however, would gladly baby her broken heart, especially if it meant earning back the friendship they once shared. "Ah yes, the Christmas party." It was a big corporate affair that had taken place a week before Christmas. Kendall had been looking forward to it so she could show off her handsome pilot. "How did that go, anyway?"

Last year she hadn't had to ask. Last year the entire play-by-play had been given freely the morning after, complete with jammies, hangover cure, and dramatic enthusiasm.

Kendall hesitated before answering. "It was fun. A lot of drunk people making fools of themselves."

"Including you?"

"Of course. I accidentally felt up my boss in the conference room."

Marcelina snickered. "Only you would manage that."

"It was dark," Kendall said, throwing an arm over her eyes. "But I knew where the mini-fridge was and I ran right into him while trying to get to it. Hand on crotch and everything."

"I thought your boss was cute."

"Mr. Metcalf? He is. Looks just like a young Elvis, but he's married to a woman I happen to adore."

Ah, the wife. "Audrey, right?"

"Yep."

"What was Mr. Metcalf doing in a dark conference room?"

"I think I interrupted a phone call." The arm came down and Kendall shrugged it off. "I don't know. I was too embarrassed to linger."

"Well," Marcelina said, "he totally shouldn't have put his dick in your path."

The first tickle of amusement hit the air. A laugh escaped, which was a huge accomplishment in the face of such dire times. Then Kendall's smile waned. "It wasn't as fun as our old Christmas parties."

"Because of Richard, or the dick incident?"

Kendall shook her head, her hair rustling against the pillows. "Neither of those. I don't know, things have been strange at work lately. Mr. Metcalf hasn't been himself and there was tension between him and Audrey at the party. The word is they could be splitting up."

Though Marcelina didn't know the couple, something about that made her very sad. Possibly because Kendall had always referred to them as the "super-couple." Had used them as a model for her own relationship goals. If the super-couple couldn't make it, what hope was there in the world? It was all fucking falling apart.

What next? Armageddon?

Marcelina blinked, shook her head. The last thing she needed was more doom and gloom. It was time to right some wrongs, make up for almost saddling Kendall with the same drug charges since it had been *her* address on those packages, too. The desire to turn back time trickled through her psyche like a continual, leaky faucet. How she wished she had never met Jonah King. Fallen into bed with him. Let the man con her into accepting those packages without knowing for certain what was in them. Her naivety had reached new bounds it seemed, even though she thought she'd learned a thing or two long before that.

The room dimmed as Marcelina's thoughts slipped further into a past that kept haunting her—something that had happened long before the conspiracy charges, when she was nineteen years old and truly naïve. That past had not come to light yet, though with her current legal problems, she wondered how long it would be before it did. The smart thing would be to confide in her lawyer, but she just couldn't bring herself to do it.

After all, what were the chances she would be connected to a murder that was still unsolved after six long years?

Not that Marcelina had killed anyone, of course. But oh, how she wished she'd had the guts to come forward when Nari Puccini's body was found so they could rule her out as a suspect from the get-go. Her hair samples had been pulled from his clothing, which had prompted an active search for a Latina "person of interest."

But the reality of it was, Puccini had been a powerful and highly respected member of the Italian mafia. It wasn't prison Marcelina feared as much as being "iced" by his many allies—people who persecuted without judge and jury with the very weapons he had provided them.

Of course, she didn't know he was *the* arms dealer of the East Coast mob when they met or she would have never befriended him. Then again, if he'd known she would be sucked into his death investigation, he probably wouldn't have befriended her, either. He was too fond of her for that. They'd shared some laughs in the face of dark times, especially when she'd mispronounced his name. "No-no, it's 'Poochini,'" he'd corrected with amusement. "No 's' sound. And you must say it with the correct hand gesture like any good Italian." They'd practiced until she mastered that hand gesture complete with accent and a handful of lines from famous mob movies.

Marcelina caught herself smiling, as she usually did when reflecting on old memories of her time with Nari. It was still hard to believe his reputation had been that of a formidable mob boss with a notorious sexual appetite. She just knew him as a sweet old man with regrets.

She blinked away the old fears that had once again crept up to haunt her. Her time was limited, she knew. It was by luck alone the police hadn't taken her DNA sample when she was arrested, though she had sweated bullets in anticipation of it. If she were actually convicted in that dreaded hearing coming up, however, somehow, some way, a connection would be made to the old murder.

Since her impending doom was the result of her interactions with dangerous men, she addressed the serious need to avoid them from now on. If only they would walk around with signs on their foreheads…

"Anyway," Kendall said, bringing the present back with a heavy sigh, "since you nearly got me fired for that little trip to jail, I haven't told anyone you're staying with me again. I don't want to add to Mr. Metcalf's problems."

Damn, Marcelina thought. Since when did *she* become the dangerous one? "I'll leave if you want me to," she said with a brave face. "I don't want our living arrangement to jeopardize anything for you."

Kendall rolled over and stared at the ceiling. "No. I need you to help me forget about Richard. In fact, we need each other to remind ourselves how badly we suck at choosing men."

A mixture of gratitude and immense relief flooded her body. Marcelina sat up, looked down at her friend with an encouraging smile. "How about I make breakfast. You go to work. Tonight, we'll cook up a frozen pizza, rent a horror movie with lots of gory knife scenes, and kill a bottle of Chianti."

The pout came back. "Do I have to go to work?"

"Yes." She gave Kendall a poke. "Don't let some loser pilot rob you of a day's pay. Our sucky choices end right now."

After some thoughtful contemplation, Kendall sighed. "You're right. I'll take some oatmeal."

"With brown sugar?"

"Lots."

Later, when Kendall emerged from the bedroom showered and dressed, Marcelina placed the steaming bowl of oatmeal on the bar. There was no table. All of the tiny space was reserved for the hundreds of dolls Kendall had been collecting since childhood, something she had no problem fitting in their old apartment. They never bothered Marcelina, though many of their visitors found Kendall's obsession with dolls to be a bit juvenile. They didn't know that some of the old ones were worth thousands, still in the box complete with dated fashions and accessories.

"You look better," Marcelina observed as she washed dishes, facing a blonde who'd mastered petite and perky in less than thirty minutes.

Kendall waved away the notion as she blew on her first bite. "Nothing three layers of make-up can't fix."

"I'll drink to that." They clinked their glasses of cold

OJ, a gesture of unity that meant more to Marcelina than any amount of money in the world. She emptied her glass and added it to the soapy water. "I'm making a grocery list. Anything else besides pizza, wine, and a movie?"

"Maybe some salad and bread. And popsicles. Here, let me give you some money."

As Kendall went for her purse, Marcelina wrote down the items on her list. "I'll get the wine and the movie."

"You can't afford it."

No, she couldn't, but if Walker came through with that job, she could start contributing more. "I have enough to throw in my fair share for now."

Kendall ate a few more bites of oatmeal. Marcelina could feel her gaze on her. Could sense the questions about to come.

"How, when all your money was seized by the feds?"

It hadn't *all* been seized by the feds, just the cash they'd found in her room. And, contrary to popular belief, that had been *her* cash, not Jonah's…even though she was offering him a legit service in order to help him out. "Mail forwarding service" to be exact, for those who didn't have a permanent Naples address, therefore couldn't obtain a P.O. box. A friend of hers had made it a lucrative business and Marcelina thought she was solving Jonah's problems. Not falling into a trap. His name had been on the first few packages, but when hers began to appear on them she should have opened them. Turned him in. Not her proudest moment, but as much as she'd like to defend herself, Walker's advice ticked through her brain. "I can't talk about it."

"Yes, you can," Kendall argued. "It's just me."

Marcelina looked up through her thick lashes with a silent plea to drop the subject.

Kendall met it without mercy. "I just want you to be honest with me. Forget your lawyer, forget the drug charges, forget everything else for just one moment. I'd like my friend back, but I need to know why you risked your future like that. How you could risk *my* future like that."

"Because I'm a stupid bitch, okay?" she snapped with a defensive bite to her words. She had already pleaded her case plenty of times to Kendall, explanations that had only been met with doubt and mistrust. Marcelina let out the water. It sucked down the drain as they continued to glare at each other. "Now do I still have the couch or should I find another place to stay?"

"If we're going to live together again," Kendall replied carefully, "I need answers. You hurt me. Every time someone knocks on the door, I think the cops are here to slap me in handcuffs."

"I was hurt, too!" It came out before she could stop it. Marcelina dried her hands, fighting back the encroaching tears. There was little she could say at this point without going against her lawyer's advice. "I told you before I didn't know what kind of person Jonah was. I know it's hard for you to believe, but remember *I'm* the one who was used. *I'm* the one who could be facing five years in prison for trusting that prick, so cut me some damned slack."

The tension level eased down a notch. Kendall set her teeth as a glimmer of sympathy surfaced. "You know what? I think I actually believe you." She got down from her stool, crossed over to her display case in the far corner and turned off the lights, throwing her favorite dolls in shadow. "But as long as you're here, there will be no drug dealers allowed in this apartment. Okay?"

Leaving thirty dollars on the counter, Kendall picked up her purse and keys and walked to the door in her pink skirt and heels. Work clothes—something Marcelina hadn't needed since her last employer discovered her trafficking charges. "Works for me," she threw out as the door closed. Though their morning had been wrought with conflict, Marcelina also noted a change in the air around her. More words had been spoken between them than usual, and an argument meant the lines of communication had been officially opened.

Hope turned her frown into a smile.

****

The sheet was thrown back to reveal a bloated corpse. Walker's eyes instantly filmed over from the combined stench of rotted meat and stagnant bay water. "You said he was beaten before he was shot?"

"With a blunt weapon of some kind," the coroner answered. "Probably a tire iron."

Captain Ross stood on the other side of the table holding a surgical mask over his face. "Somewhere in all that, he took a nine-millimeter round to the groin, four in the chest and one between the eyes. The fish did the rest."

Holy shit. Walker cocked his head for a better look at the ink covering the body's right arm.

"You recognize the tattoos?" Leonard asked.

He nodded grimly. "It's Miguel Garcia." Who, coincidentally, would *not* be turning over evidence against Armando Rivera at his morning meeting with the DEA.

Disappointment hung heavily between them as Walker and the captain moved to the trashcan and removed their latex gloves and paper gowns. There were three bodies in that room of stainless steel slabs, the other two belonging to known cocaine addicts who'd been found in the Everglades. The numbers were growing by the day it seemed.

They entered the hallway, took in the fresher air with deep breaths as they walked. "Do you have any leads?" Walker asked.

"Just the usual suspects." Leonard pinched the bridge of his nose. "God, I still smell it."

"He came to me, dammit." Walker swore loudly, earning a few raised brows from passersby. "He was getting antsy and I'd convinced him to make a deal. How the hell did Rivera find out?"

When they entered the lobby, Captain Ross looked from left to right in that paranoid manner of a cop. "Someone must have caught wind. You know Rivera, all it takes is a possibility."

"But his own *nephew?*"

"A rat is a rat. Makes an impact, especially to anyone else thinking of blowing whistles."

Walker set his teeth, only more determined to rid Southwest Florida of the Colombian cartel. Rivera had moved in fast, expanding his operation from Miami to the Gulf like a turf-hungry crocodile. Naples wasn't the place, its pristine beauty meant to be largely reserved for tourism and the retirement community; not the addicts who were beginning to swarm the area for an easy buy. The truth was, Walker could care less what happened to the 87% of his clients who were guilty of the crimes they'd been charged with, but this one hurt. The only reason he'd agreed to counsel Miguel Garcia on the sly was to convince him to turn against Rivera, a feat that had taken weeks to accomplish.

"This sucks," he murmured.

Leonard headed for the vending machines. "I'm sure that's what Garcia thought when he took a nine to the balls."

"Garcia was a tool." When they reached the machines, Walker paid for two coffees. "What chaps my ass is that no one with a set of testicles is going to come forward against Rivera in the foreseeable future."

Leonard thought about that as he reached for the first cup. "Maybe we need a set of tits instead." When Walker only frowned at him, he shrugged. "Boobs are a distraction, and Rivera happens to like them. If we can get a *woman* on the inside, she may have better luck."

Walker smirked while he reached for his own cup. "If I run into him at Tony's Auction House this afternoon I'll ask him his preference. 'Hey, Rivera, you prefer blondes or brunettes? Tall or petite? Oh, and where would you *not* check for listening devices?' "

With a shake of the head, Leonard sipped coffee. "Joke all you want, but it worked with Nari Puccini six years ago. Women were his weakness, so his enemies used one to assassinate him. You should know all about that."

The sting of those words hit Walker right where they were supposed to. In the ass. It was no secret his father had been tight with the deceased mobster. As Puccini's lawyer, friend, and confidant, Conrad Bishop had saddled his family name with a black mark that would never go away. "Fuck you, Leonard," Walker muttered. "And we aren't talking about a dried up eighty-year-old man. Rivera just had his *nephew* taken out. He won't get careless."

They moved toward the front doors. "I take it that means you won't be carrying on the family tradition and befriending our local crime lord," Leonard jabbed with a smirk.

"That was my father's forte, not mine." Walker's scowl deepened as he followed the police captain outside. "I actually *want* to run for office someday."

Chapter 3

That afternoon, Walker left the courtroom, his nerves on edge after sitting through a painful testimony during which his client slipped on a lie within the first few minutes in the hot box. Many tissues later, the court had adjourned to decide Mrs. Rosenberg's fate over her private "experiment" with a high school chemistry student. It wouldn't be pretty. Statutory rape in her case would carry a max of fifteen years. At that point, Walker was ready to wash his hands of the whole thing. He didn't like being lied to, and nothing pissed him off more than learning about it in front of a judge and jury.

"So much for the he-said-she-said defense."

Walker looked back to find the prosecuting attorney shadowing him down the crowded hallway toward the elevators. "It's the smile that gets me, Bill," he threw over his shoulder.

The shorter man had to jog to catch up. "Come again?"

"That zit-faced pecker you represent smiled every time he mentioned the sex."

"Three orgasms will do that to a seventeen-year-old."

"So will bragging rights. It's why I believed my client when she said he was lying."

The man shrugged. "Looks like he was telling the truth."

"And he's still bragging." Yes, Walker hated being lied to. But there was something about that kid that reeked of evil, and he figured it would take less than a year before Mrs. Rosenberg's accuser would end up in court again.

They reached the elevators and Walker dove in with a dozen or so people, forcing the prosecutor to wait for the next one. "When his family takes this to civil and he gets that nice settlement, Ms. Rosenberg will end up his first paying gig." He saluted over the small mob of heads. "I see a bright, shiny stripper pole in his near future."

"Ha-ha." Bill's dry response was cut off by the closing elevator doors.

Walker checked his watch as he descended to the first floor. Thoughts of Mrs. Rosenberg and her unfortunate sex life slipped clean away as thoughts of Marcelina Page took over. It was almost four o'clock, much later than he'd anticipated. She would be waiting for him at the auction house, tapping her pretty fingertips while Tony sized her up as his next model—a gorgeous woman to sit behind the wheel of a high-end vehicle and toss her hair as the bids climbed higher.

Would she be pissed? Could he handle her pissed? It was hard enough keeping his pheromones in check every time she appeared out of nowhere, but the thought of those dark eyes flashing with fire…

"You look pleased for a man whose about to lose," came a voice below him.

With a jolt, Walker realized he *was* smiling. Going grim, he nodded down at the colorful journalist he remembered loitering in the back of the courtroom. "We'll see."

Three miles and four phone messages later, he

reached his humble little law office on the north side of town. Situated on the corner of a small office building, it was nothing fancy, but it was clean and crisp with the appropriate dressings of a successful practice. A work in progress, he liked to call it.

He pulled at the glass door and entered a modest-sized lobby containing a black leather couch, matching chairs, and a well-stocked coffee station. His decorative choice of photography depicting the local flora added a positive vibe that, he was sure, his clients largely ignored. His paralegal, Judith, stood up behind the counter with a bright smile and a fistful of pink papers. "How did Mrs. Rosenberg's deposition go?"

"I'll answer that tomorrow, after I've had time to lick my wounds."

"Uh-oh."

Walker accepted the papers, wondering how long it would take for Judith's optimism to wane. "Leslie Moore," he read from the top message. "Man or woman?"

"Man."

The thought of taking on a new partner became more painful with each failed interview. He rolled the name change around a bit. " 'Bishop and Moore.' Not sure how that would look on the sign."

Judith tucked a wisp of thin brown hair behind her ear and snickered as she sat back down in her rolling chair. "Sounds like a Catholic discount store."

"Set up a meeting, anyway. If he's worth his salt, the Virgin Mary could be our new logo." While her overzealous laughter filled the lobby, Walker thumbed through the other messages. "Anything from Marcelina Page?"

"Actually, yes."

Leaving the papers on the counter, he picked up his briefcase and headed down the hall. "Call her back. Tell her I'm on my way."

"But—"

He slipped through his office door…and stopped dead. There she was again, Marcelina Page, sitting behind his desk with long legs crossed over a corner. She wore a summery, peach-colored dress that enhanced the natural bronze of her skin, the layered skirt pulled up enough to showcase those incredible legs of hers. Hair loose and fanning over her shoulders, she was beautifully surrounded by his backdrop of framed honors and diplomas. Her sparkling gaze moved down the length of him. "Hello, handsome."

Walker gave himself a mental nudge, set his briefcase down on the couch and began to unbutton his suit jacket. "I thought we were going to meet at the auction house."

She watched his every move from where she sat. "I told you I don't have a car. And you said to find a way, so here I am."

"And Judith just let you wait in my office?"

"She thinks I'm in the bathroom." Marcelina smiled. "She's delightful, by the way. And grossly unperceptive."

Jacket removed, Walker threw it next to the briefcase and approached her. Held out his hand. "I'd call it overworked." She took it, allowing him to pull her out of his throne of plush leather. "You aren't allowed in here without supervision."

His strict tone only broadened her smile. "Don't worry, I didn't touch anything on this slush pile you call a desk."

Walker turned her by the shoulders and ushered her to the client-side of the desk. "First you make fun of how I keep my house. Now you're insulting my office."

She indicated the cluttered bookshelves and the stacks of thick ledgers blocking a portion of the window. "The contrast is amazing. I don't remember it being so messy the last time I was here."

"My caseload has grown considerably since then." He woke up his computer screen and logged in.

"Is your reputation preceding you?"

"Court-appointed cases. One of our public defenders was hit by a bus last Tuesday."

She paused by the window with a look of genuine dismay. "Oh, right. I heard about that on the news."

"The driver was a client of his. Now he's a client of mine."

A choked laugh. "Does that mean you may be next?"

"Could be."

While he absently scanned his schedule, she leaned in close, giving off a faint hint of flora and spice. "I would be very sad if you were hit by a bus," she purred.

Walker found himself staring at that tantalizing mouth, wanting more than ever to dive in and have a taste. At this rate, a splash of cold water would be next. Marcelina's bold flirtations of late weren't the problem, it was his mindless reaction to them. He straightened and gathered random files, noting how her gaze once again travelled down his torso. "If you want a ride, Miss Page, keep those eyes up here." He pointed to his own eyes, knowing full well where her thoughts were going.

She laughed as he crossed over to his briefcase with

files in hand. "Sorry. It's so much easier picturing you naked now that I've—"

"That's enough."

As he packed his homework—or what he *hoped* was his homework—she pushed his private door closed with a small click and leaned against it. Her eyes fairly smoldered. "We could even the score, you know."

"No."

"You showed me yours. It's only fair that I show you mine."

His briefcase closed with a *thwack* and he rounded on her with a look that scolded. "Jesus, Marcelina, what don't you get? We aren't five-year-olds and this isn't a game of show and tell. One day you'll have to start taking this seriously again." Even though the idea of her gloriously naked—preferably draped across his desk— was one he'd entertained often. And now that he'd allowed her to see it, she was relentless.

Disgusted with himself, Walker reached behind her, opened the door, turned off the light, and waved her on through. She sauntered down the hall in front of him, her heels softly tapping against the carpet.

And dammit if he wasn't watching the feminine sway of her hips.

"I can always tell, counselor," she tossed over her shoulder.

Feeling caught once again, Walker grumbled out a farewell to Judith as they left.

As usual, traffic was a beast during Monday rush hour, on Airport Road in particular. Despite the air conditioning, it was getting warmer in that car with every passing mile. As he drove, Walker loosened his tie. Rolled up his sleeves. Then he popped the top button of his shirt and loosened the collar.

"Want me to help you with that?" Marcelina asked beside him, amusement clear in her voice.

Instead of dignifying that with a response, he clamped his mouth shut and fought the urge to turn up the fan.

"This is a very nice car. Luxury at its finest." She reached out, pushed a button. "What does this do?" After a moment, she looked down, shifted in her seat. "What's going on?" When it registered, her teeth gleamed with a half-smile.

Walker couldn't help his own smile. "You like that, huh?"

"Cooled seats." Marcelina wiggled into a comfier position. "For a moment I thought my skirt was gone."

Oh, hell. He drummed up an image of his great-aunt Camilla in her prim dress and lacey head covering during Holy Mass—God rest her soul. The car flooded with a series of rings. One glance at the display told him to ignore the incoming call.

"I don't remember my calls ever being ignored by you," Marcelina said.

She had a point there. "Another client," he informed with a dry smile. "Unless you want to get out at the next light, I can't discuss much with him right now."

"I don't think he'd care. Several of them came to your office while I was waiting for you. It's amazing how loose-lipped people get when they're upset."

Right again. "It can be the most frustrating part of the job, trying and failing to muzzle your clients." He repeated something his father used to say. "Words are like quicksand for the guilty. Keep quiet and you never will be." A small, bitter laugh. "Can't believe there was a time when that didn't make sense."

"I'm not sure it does." Marcelina watched him through her thick, winged lashes. "Judith said you're looking to expand. As nice as your office is, there isn't much room in there for another lawyer."

"I like having a team." He draped a wrist over the wheel and crawled through another intersection. "It's what I miss most from my years as a prosecutor."

"She also said you were looking for a house. A *real* one."

Walker nodded. "Something fairly new. With some landscaping and room for maybe three more offices."

"*Offices?*" Marcelina tsked in disgust. "You really are hopeless."

He turned into the crowded lot of Tony's auction house. The building had undergone a facelift recently, and now boasted bigger showrooms with lots of glass. Street lamps littered the parking lot, replacing the waning brilliance of day with artificial light. A loudspeaker was heard, emanating a steady spew of words from an auctioneer. People milled around a variety of cars from classic to new, ranging in all colors. Toward the back of the lot was a roped-off area where most of the action was.

Knowing this was Armando Rivera's auction only heightened the angst, making Walker want to rush through what was swiftly becoming a bad idea. He scanned the crowd for familiar faces in case the drug lord had decided to attend after all. "It looks busy. Let's come back later."

"No, let's go now." Marcelina unbuckled her seatbelt.

They exited the car and began to weave through

bodies. The heat was slowly fading with the sun, but Walker still wished he could raid his gym bag for shorts and a tank top.

While Marcelina looked around with fascination—her hair and flowy dress catching the soft breeze—his thoughts wandered. She frustrated him in all ways, not just sexually. It was mostly her unwillingness to give him full disclosure. To trust him enough to protect her when she needed him most. And he desperately *wanted* full disclosure, especially after that disastrous episode with Mrs. Rosenberg. Defending a teacher who admitted to statutory rape wouldn't look good for him if he were to run for office someday. Putting Rivera behind bars would certainly help on that front.

In regard to Marcelina, though, Walker felt the desire to win a case for someone other than himself.

Her hand brushed against his. "Why the frown?" she asked.

He stopped walking. They were beneath the building's awning and completely alone. When she looked up at him with a question in her eyes, Walker realized what that feeling was. Desperation. "Why won't you be straight with me?"

Shoulders drooping, she halfway turned from him. "Not again."

He pulled her back around, forcing her to face him. "I'll keep hounding you until I get the truth."

The allure was completely gone from her countenance. "Walker, I'm not hiding anything."

That was the funny thing about truth and lies. Normally, he was quite good at telling them apart, until Mrs. Rosenberg of course. Now he was rattled, sensing more than ever that Marcelina was hiding something.

And hell if he would let her cause a repeat of what had happened to him earlier that day.

No one was within earshot; still, he shielded her with his body for a more private conversation. "Good people make mistakes all the time. We're working on yours, but in order for me to effectively do my job, I need *full disclosure*."

Walker took a step closer, holding her gaze with his signature determination. "I watched a woman crumble on the stand today," he said. "The hidden truth has a tendency to come out when one least expects it, and in her case it was in front of a jury. At that point I was powerless to help her, and truthfully…I didn't want to anymore. I don't like to lose, Marcelina."

"So you said."

It was a snarky comment that had him cursing under his breath. "I don't want that for you, either, especially if Jonah King were to make a sudden reappearance in your life. Let me *help* you. Let me do my job."

Her eyes swirled with something akin to fear. Her lips parted. As Walker waited for her to confess whatever she'd been hiding, her expression went blank once again. "You're standing awfully close, Mr. Bishop," she murmured.

Indeed, he had her flush against the wall with no room to flee. Walker backed up a step, ran a hand through his hair. They began to walk again, slowly progressing toward the entrance of the building. "I don't get you," he grumbled.

"Don't get what?" She was watching him out of the corner of her eye.

"You're nervous about your trial one moment and blasé about it the next. Did something happen since we parted ways this morning?"

Her head dipped slightly. "Kendall and I sort of had it out. But she also forgave me."

"That's…good."

"I don't know. It reminded me of how much trauma I put her through."

Walker could feel her sadness as if it were his own. "You came through for her when it counted. Quit punishing yourself."

She gave a helpless shrug. "I can't help it. I feel so stupid for letting this happen. I should have seen Jonah coming from a mile away. I thought I was smarter than that."

They stopped walking again and faced each other. "We both know you aren't stupid," he murmured. "But it would be irresponsible of me not to remind you how important it is to keep quiet, even with Kendall. The prosecution will put her on the stand and they'll suck out anything and everything you ever discussed with her. So until she agrees to come on board with your defense, no heart-to-hearts or emotional confessions that could damage your chances in court. Unless it's with me, of course."

Her eyes grew heavy with a look that instantly set his blood on fire. She came closer and reached up to fiddle with one of his shirt buttons. "In that case, I'd like to have a little heart-to-heart right now."

In an attempt to keep things grounded, he grasped her wrist and held it away, but the contact did dangerous things to his system. Before he could reply, her lips were skimming across his in soft, seductive strokes. Then her arms were around his neck and she was leaning into him with the force of a steaming tidal wave. Her voluptuous breasts flattened against his torso, filling him with an insane need to feel more of her against him. More than drugging lips that tantalized and tasted of longing.

She drew back just enough to whisper against his mouth, "You're kissing me back, Walker."

The reminder delivered a punch of reality that left him stunned. It was as if he'd been taken over by someone else, letting her toy with him in a bid to change the subject. After a deep, meditative breath, he broke out of her hold and stepped back. "Don't do that again," he ordered, feeling more dangerous than ever. "This is a very fine line you're walking, Marcelina, and it's about to get wobbly for both of us. The last thing you want is for me to lose my balance."

There was a new kind of allure in her eyes, as if she'd just discovered something wonderful. "And you've never lost your balance, have you?" she asked softly.

It was something he took pride in. Something he just might abandon if she kept looking at him like that. "No," he answered with firm resolve.

"Not even a small time-out?"

"I'm not allowed any time-outs. No. Time. Outs." If he said it enough, maybe it would sink in for both of them.

She must have sensed his personal struggle because she smiled a bit. "Okay, Walker."

He turned away from that smile, ran a hand over his jaw in abject frustration. The woman was her own worst enemy, and it was becoming more and more clear he would need a miracle in order to save her from herself.

"There's a man staring at us," she said beside him in a low voice.

Walker followed her gaze and spotted a tall, well-dressed Columbian who was indeed watching them with bold curiosity. It was Armando Rivera in the flesh, the sight of him causing an avalanche of foreboding inside Walker's gut. A thug-like bodyguard hovered close by him. "His name is Armando Rivera. This is one of his auctions."

"Is he a car dealer?"

Walker returned the man's attention with hooded disdain. "On paper he's a financier."

"So he loans people money," she deduced.

"And then he taketh away."

A light came on in her eyes. Marcelina also looked around, soaking in the crowd, the notable diversity of the people scoping out possible bargains. "So these are all repossessed cars?" At his nod, she asked, "What does this Rivera guy do *off* paper?"

The woman was quick. She took his suggestive morsels and processed the truth out of them with pinpoint accuracy. "He's a high-ranking member of the cartel."

"He's a *drug lord?*" she said with an incredulous laugh.

The irony of it wasn't so amusing to him. Walker shot her a glance. "Don't get any ideas."

Instead of taking offense, she cocked her head. "Actually, I think he's staring at *you*."

"Walker!"

They turned to find a beanpole of a man walking their way with a lit cigar between his teeth, puffing smoke beneath a worn leather fedora. Tony was showing his lack of professionalism as usual in shorts and short sleeves. When he reached Walker's side, they shook hands, though the man's attention was all on Marcelina.

"Whoa." The cigar came out. "You weren't kidding, were you?" Tony extended a hand. Marcelina took it.

Keenly aware they still held Rivera's attention, Walker made a distracted introduction. "Tony, this is Marcelina Page. Marcelina, Tony Lathrop."

"You're hired," Tony said with comical speed.

Marcelina's return smile was warm. "To do what, exactly?"

A brow was aimed in Walker's direction. "You didn't tell her?"

"I figured I'd leave that up to you." Walker let Tony have the floor, glad for the chance to keep his senses honed on Rivera. The mean looking bag of muscles behind him was probably the one who'd put the bullets in Miguel Garcia the previous night.

"We have what we call block models," Tony droned on beside him. "They showcase the cars and make everything brighter on the auction block. It helps drive up the bids." Walker listened to the spiel with half-hearted interest. Something about different types of auctions, how much skin to show, and that she'd have a choice whether or not to show it. More skin more money… His attention began to shift, not liking the thought of Marcelina showing skin.

"Mr. Rivera prefers a classier look for his auctions," Tony said to her. "Sort of like what you're wearing now."

Walker realized he was still in the throws of a stare-off with the aforementioned cartel man. "How long has Rivera been a client of yours, Tony?" he asked.

Tony turned toward him puffing smoke. "A couple months I think." Back to Marcelina. "Why don't we sit and watch for a while. You can decide if this is a good fit for you."

Or was Rivera looking at Marcelina? Walker wondered. She knew how to draw attention, which wouldn't be so bothersome to him if Captain Ross's words weren't still rolling through his mind. *Maybe we need a set of tits...*

His phone buzzed in his pocket. He took it out, checked the screen. It was his neighbor, Anna Faulk, returning his call from earlier. With Marcelina's kiss still warm on his mouth, Walker needed this opportunity to bury himself in a woman other than his client. He excused himself and stepped back a few paces before answering.

"Hello, Walker," came a smoky voice over the phone. "I was wondering how many morning papers I'd have to get before I heard from you."

Her bold honesty made him chuckle. "How are you, Anna?"

"You said something about dinner tonight. I know it's late, but I'd prefer to eat at my place, anyway. Interested?"

He glanced at Marcelina. "I have a few things to finish up first, but I can be there in less than an hour."

"Good. I hope you like barbeque."

He hated barbeque. "Can't wait."

Chapter 4

While Tony continued the rundown of what was required of a block model, Marcelina watched as more and more money was pledged with the single wave of an orange slip of paper. Though she tried to observe the activities of the beautiful woman showcasing the cars, she couldn't help but absorb the other activities going on around her. Dusk turned to dark, giving the cars rolling on and off the auction block a special shine beneath the lights. Everything was moving so fast, but not too fast to keep up: the buyers, the numbers, the drug lord who continually undressed her with his eyes behind thick, dark glasses…

Yes, she could always tell. But no one left her with the heebie-jeebies quite like that guy.

A car rolled out of the roped-off area and a new one took its place. As the block model walked the parameters with her shimmering dress and new sign, an older man in a business suit walked up to Tony and fished an orange paper out of his back pocket. "There she is, Tony," the man purred. "I've always wanted a Benz. Looks new, great condition."

Tony agreed as a gleaming, silver luxury car was pushed onto the block by two men wearing black uniform shirts.

"Looks pricey," Marcelina added.

"You're at a repo auction, Ms. Page," Tony

reminded her.

The stranger chuckled under his breath, waving his orange paper as the auctioneer began to rattle off numbers. "No one wants to pay much for a car as-is, with no maintenance record to go with it."

Since there had been no introduction, Marcelina ignored the man and kept her words for Tony. "I was wondering why some of the high-end ones were going for such low prices."

With his eyes glued to the random waves of orange, Tony spoke through his cigar. "By the way, Walker said you'd need a car to get to work and back. I can help you with that."

Her heart sank a little, accustomed to men making big offers—for something in return, of course. "I don't have any money," she said a little tightly.

"It'll be a loaner until you get on your feet."

Or on my back. "Thank you, that's very generous. I'll think about it."

Walker's voice came over her head. "She'll take it."

And then there was Walker, the only man in her life who *didn't* want something extra from her. She turned around to pin him with a look. "Excuse me?"

He shrugged. "You need a car."

And he had no clue how much she'd have to pay for it. Where had he come from, anyway? "Did you get your phone call taken care of?" she asked him.

Though his short nod was impassive, she'd heard enough to know the call hadn't been from a client. A shaft of jealousy pierced through her playful side, making her want to quit the games and just take him already. Because the thought of him in bed with whomever the hell *Anna* was didn't sit well. At all.

"Damn, who is this guy, anyway?" Tony's suit-wearing friend frowned in the direction of a man toward the left of the crowd. By that time, his was the only other orange paper waving. "Am I missing something, here? Is this car lined with gold?" The bid was up to twenty-eight five. "Thirty and I'm done."

When thirty thousand came and went, the man let out a juicy curse and took it up to thirty-two.

"Do I have thirty-four…" said the auctioneer.

"Shit! Really?" After thinking about it, he gave the signal he was out and stormed off. The silver Mercedes went to a bidder who, Marcelina guessed, had just settled on a ridiculous price for that particular repo. She craned her neck to see the new owner. A man moved toward the tent where money exchanged hands. He was tall, dark headed, and carried a strong resemblance to Elvis. "Hey, I think the King just won your friend's Benz," she quipped.

Tony jerked his chin. "Graham Metcalf. He's been dropping some pretty serious green at these auctions for a few months now."

Kendall's boss? Marcelina watched Mr. Metcalf hand over an envelope, sign some papers, and then re-take his seat. It wasn't long before she realized she was alone. A quick check revealed Walker and Tony still walking and talking, unaware that she had stopped.

"You look most interested in what's going on up there."

She whirled around to find a tall, square-faced man with curly hair and tanned skin loitering behind her. It was a shock to her system, not having detected Armando Rivera's larger-than-life presence sooner. "It's fascinating," she responded with a quick, dismissive smile.

Rattled, she turned to walk away, but he stopped her with a touch to the elbow. "It seems we've both been taken by something fascinating tonight." He offered his hand. "Armando."

"I know who you are, Mr. Rivera." Her tone was flat as she ignored the hand. "And I'm *only* interested in the auction. I hope it's a successful one for you."

She left the man standing there with a bland smile on his face that told her they weren't finished yet. A shiver racked her shoulders, one she hoped Mr. Rivera didn't notice as she walked away.

"There you are," Walker said when they found each other. "I have to go. Come on, I'll give you a ride home."

"Or the lady could stay a little longer," came Rivera's voice once again. Marcelina jerked around to find him still at close range, his eyes solely on her. "I have many cars yet to hit the auction block. Afterward, you and I could have dinner."

"I told you I'm not—"

"She has plans with me," Walker interrupted before she could finish. They headed toward his car, the slight push to her lower back forcing her to hurry. "You don't want to get mixed up with that guy," he murmured low as they walked.

"If you would have let me finish, I was about to tell him for the second time I wasn't interested."

"Mr. Bishop!"

They both turned to find Rivera watching them, without the dark glasses this time. His bulked-up bodyguard—who was never far from his side—also watched.

"I heard about your unfortunate trip to the morgue

this morning," Rivera said above the noise. "Perhaps you should keep a closer eye on your clients."

Marcelina felt Walker's alarm, thick and palpable behind the slight pressure of his hand—as if he hadn't expected such attention from a known drug lord. Without answering, they continued their walk with Rivera's low laugh following them the rest of the way.

"What was that all about?" she asked.

"Just another message," Walker returned with a grim look.

"Huh?"

"Never mind, I'll explain later."

He escorted her to the passenger side of his car and opened her door. As soon as they were both settled behind the dash and out of hearing range, she faced him. "*I'm* one of your clients. I want to know now."

Walker started the car, hit reverse, and threw an arm across the back of her seat as the rear tires spun. "One of the high-level dealers I'd convinced to turn against Rivera was found floating in Clam Pass this morning."

"Dead?"

With a glance in her direction, he threw it in drive and pulled out of the lot. "You know, you're pretty good at this. Ever think of becoming a private investigator?"

She replayed Rivera's parting words in her mind. "So I guess what he said was some sort of challenge?"

"You didn't answer my question."

"About becoming a private investigator? I thought you were being a smart ass."

After a tense, prolonged silence he ran a hand across the whiskery shadow of his lower jaw. "Before now, I didn't know I was back on Rivera's radar."

"*Back* on his radar?"

"We had history when I was AUSA. He was sort of a mission for me. Still is, I guess."

Marcelina had scoured Walker's website bio when he'd first been assigned her case. Though she'd spent more time studying his picture, she remembered reading that AUSA meant Assistant US Attorney. A *prosecuting* attorney. "But aren't you supposed to be defending people like him now?"

A curious amount of anger sparked his gaze. "I defend who I choose and it will never be a man like Rivera. In fact if I can find a way to put him behind bars from the other side of the aisle, I'll do it."

"By turning your clients against him," she surmised with a frown.

He glanced at her. "As a prosecutor, I got tired of trying to fight a corrupt system. Sometimes there *is* no fighting it, unless an opportunity like Miguel Garcia comes along. I won't turn it away."

Assuming Miguel Garcia was the deceased high-level dealer he'd spoken of, she guessed Walker was also in some sort of danger. And his troubled tone worried her more than his words. "Rivera wouldn't try to hurt you too, would he?"

Walker took his time before answering. Too much time. "Garcia was his nephew. I suppose if he sees me as enough of a threat, he might try."

The man killed his own *nephew?* A bath of shivers washed down her arms. "He never tried to before when you were attempting to prosecute him?"

His chest jumped with a laugh. "He would have had the entire judicial system on his back."

But not anymore. Marcelina wondered if switching to his own private practice would ultimately cost Walker his life. The thought didn't settle well, especially since he'd become sort of a symbol of hope for her. Or was he more than that? This new sick feeling in her gut told her yes, he was more than that. And to brace herself…

Because she was pretty sure her world was about to get a whole lot bumpier.

****

When Marcelina entered Kendall's apartment, the place already smelled like cheese and sausage. Her roommate was waiting, curled on the floor in her fuzzy slippers, picking at the tray of pizza on the coffee table. "You're late," she accused with a glare.

Marcelina set her purse on the couch and swept a hand downward to indicate her skirt. "I was applying for a job."

Kendall perked up a little. "You're totally forgiven. What kind of job?"

They both headed to the kitchen where the wine bottle was open and breathing. "You know that auction house on Tropicana?" Marcelina took down two glasses from the cabinet.

"By Golden Gate?"

"Mm-hmm. Walker set up an interview with the owner."

Kendall took a full glass. "Are you hired?"

She hesitated while pouring her own. "I'm not sure I want it."

They clinked glasses to being single and sipped, enjoying that first flood of smoky Cabernet on the tongue. "Forgive me for pointing this out," Kendall said, "but you don't have many options."

As if she needed the reminder. Marcelina grabbed a couple of napkins and headed back to the pizza with stomach rumbling. "Let me put it this way. There was an unexpected kink in the plan."

"What kind of kink? Did the owner hit on you?"

"Not the owner." She'd already deduced Tony's offer had been extended without strings. "Tony's eccentric but very nice. It's his clientele I'm worried about." Marcelina explained what happened between her, Walker, and Armando Rivera upon leaving the auction house. "Rivera wasn't exactly subtle in getting his point across. He scared me. And I think he scared Walker, too."

They were both on the floor, eating from the tray with gusto. "Then you'd be wise to turn down that job," Kendall agreed.

Marcelina took up a napkin, wiped her mouth. "By the way, I think I saw your boss at the auction tonight."

Kendall stopped chewing for a moment. "Really? How do you know it was him when you've never met him before?"

"I *don't* know it was him," Marcelina laughed, retrieving a rogue sausage from her lap. "In fact, I'm pretty sure it was Elvis, but his last name was Metcalf."

"Did he talk to you?"

The accusatory nature of the question had Marcelina looking up. "No, Kendall. I only saw him from a distance. Why?"

Now that the spotlight was shining in *her* eyes, Kendall began chewing again. "Just making sure he didn't hit on you or anything."

Marcelina had just picked up her wineglass, but she set it down again with a touch of disbelief. "Why would you think he'd hit on me?" When Kendall's look turned droll, she dismissed it with a look of her own. "I thought you said he and his wife are some kind of super-couple."

A sniff was her answer.

Marcelina's look narrowed. "*No.* Has he been stepping out?" Not that it was any of her business, but Kendall was fairly bursting at the seams.

"Shauna from accounting said some things today," came the emotive reply. "But it's probably just gossip, and I shouldn't be gossiping because that shit always comes back at me somehow. Besides I love Audrey too much to cater to it." Her look turned sour. "Pretend I didn't say anything."

Smart. If the boss was cheating, Audrey the wife would figure it out on her own eventually. And if it were the old days, Marcelina would have been forced to suffer through a detailed account of who said what and why. So, counting her blessings where she could, she indicated the TV with her half-eaten pizza slice. "Good part's coming up."

Yes, a change of subject was in order. With a determined set to her mouth, Kendall retrieved the remote and turned up the volume. An ax-wielding maniac's unrelenting search for victims ensued. Bloody screams filled the apartment. And as the comfort level slowly returned, the two women picked up their wineglasses, extended them across the coffee table, and once again toasted to being single.

****

Walker navigated his way through the busy diner located just ten minutes from his office. The place buzzed with an active lunch crowd, most of the folks spilling in from the courthouse close by. Steak burgers hissed somewhere behind a square opening littered with ticket orders, their glorious smell having greeted him all the way out in the parking lot. As hungry as he was, it surprised him that he was there at all since he had phone messages out the ass, a closing argument to rehearse, four client meetings, and case files spilling over his desk.

But this was about Marcelina's case, which was a priority he couldn't seem to put in its rightful place. It made him edgy, and the fact he'd passed up a chance to release his sexual frustrations with Anna Faulk didn't help. But Rivera's threat had worked on him, and instead forced him back to his office where he had spent the night with another file he couldn't put down—one that detailed the rise in power of an untouchable drug lord.

A hand waved in the far corner. Walker recognized Kendall from the time they'd spoken before. The tone had been much different then, the woman brimming with anger over having just been falsely arrested for possession.

When he reached her corner booth, he skipped the formalities and sat down. "Thank you for agreeing to meet me here," he said. "Since you're the one who reached out to me, I should have come to you, but my afternoon is booked."

Bracelets rattled as the petite blonde shoved aside a half-eaten Panini. "This works out since I'm on my lunch break. I would have been happy to meet you at your office, though."

"I have another meeting here in a few minutes. You said you wanted to discuss Marcelina's case?"

She leaned in, spoke low. "Yes. And I'm willing to help any way I can."

Quick, to the point, and music to his ears. Walker nodded, not entirely surprised but thoroughly pleased. A waitress came by and he waved away the offer of a menu.

When she was gone, he said, "I assumed you two had been talking again. I'm glad it's working out, but I must stress the importance of—"

"I know." Kendall threw him a dry smile. "Don't worry, Marcelina's been a good girl. She hasn't discussed anything with me about her case. But I believe her when she says she didn't know that Jonah was running drugs."

Sounded promising. He could certainly use Kendall as more than just a character witness. "Do you think she knows where Jonah is?"

A quick shrug. "I think she'd turn him in if she did."

It would be the logical thing to do, but logic rarely played a factor in these types of cases. Jonah King could be anywhere, using threats or blackmail to keep Marcelina quiet. Kendall seemed ready to help. But would she lie if Marcelina asked her to? "Has she been in contact with him that you know of?" he asked. "Gotten any upsetting calls or texts?"

"Not since she moved back in."

"No suspicious cash laying around?"

Toast crunched as Kendall took another bite and laid her sandwich down. Shook her head. "You see that's why I changed my mind," she said with a hand covering her mouth. "She had a good job before all this happened. She never needed Jonah's money, which makes me believe the cash they found in her room really was hers and that she was just doing a favor for a boyfriend. And now that she *does* need the money, she won't take or borrow one red cent from me."

"You've offered?"

"Sort of. I had this expensive necklace my boyfriend gave me for Christmas. When we broke up, I ripped it off my neck and threw it in the trashcan. Now if you know women at all, you'll know we tend to run on the stubborn side."

He suppressed a smile.

"I told her she should sell it," Kendall continued, "but she refused. That necklace was going in the dumpster because it was tainted *and* a symbol of my suffering."

He nodded in a show of appreciative understanding.

"I half-expected her to fish it out of the trash before it was too late, but the thought never crossed her mind. In fact, before I threw the trash bag out, I checked and it was still in there. I mean who would pass up a seven-hundred-dollar necklace?"

"Did *you*?"

"No! I fished that sucker out and took it to the nearest pawn shop this morning."

Walker was beginning to like this chick. An honest woman who could do some great things for Marcelina's case. "That's the reason you decided to help her? Because of a necklace?"

Kendall swallowed and put a napkin to her lips. "It proved to me that she has more integrity than I gave her credit for. I truly don't believe she knew about the drugs, Mr. Bishop, and I'm willing to say that in court."

He handed her another business card, knowing the first had probably ended up in the wastebasket. "Call my office and Judith will schedule an appointment for you. We'll talk more in depth about the events leading up to Marcelina's arrest."

Kendall took the card and put it in her purse. "Okay. I suppose you know I was subpoenaed by the federal prosecutors."

As long as she was batting for the right team, Walker knew it would work in their favor. And now he had time to prepare her for her testimony. He gave her a kind smile. "You're doing the right thing by coming to me. And by letting Marcelina back into your life."

"So do *you* think she's innocent?"

If he had a nickel for every time someone asked him that… "Honestly, I always thought so," he replied. Well, aside from protecting her ex-boyfriend, of course. "She just never fit the profile."

Kendall stuck out a hand in wholehearted agreement. "And you would know because you represent the guilty."

"I also represent the innocent. Not as often, but it makes a difference." He checked his watch and saw that it was past time for his next meeting. Walker took out his wallet. "I have to go. You'll be in contact soon?"

Kendall nodded, frowned when he laid some bills on the table. "I can get my own lunch, Mr. Bishop."

"This one's on me," he said as he stood up and tucked the wallet back in his pocket. "You've made my day, Kendall. Marcelina is lucky to have you on her side."

They parted ways and Walker followed the signs toward the restrooms. Once he entered the hall, he pulled on the "Employees Only" door and was immediately blasted with thick, greasy air from the kitchen. Burgers hissed beneath columns of rising steam, drowning out his first bid for attention. There were several folks at the grill wearing stained white uniforms and hairnets. Walker guessed the burly guy in the apron and sweaty ball cap was the head honcho who'd arranged this meeting, but when he caught his eye, the man pointed his dripping spatula toward the back. Walker followed directions, careful to avoid dropped food and oily puddles as he made his way out of the food prep area and into a cluttered hallway. There was an office back there, it's only giveaway a small window with crooked blinds. He knocked on the door. When it opened, a familiar face greeted him.

"You're late, Bishop."

Chapter 5

It took Walker a moment to absorb the fact he'd just been lured here by none other than Captain Ross. And it probably wasn't to talk about OSHA, or the building owner's obvious disregard for sanitation laws.

Then Walker spotted a pair of long, shapely legs just visible from the other side of the desk. The sinking feeling in his chest grew. Only one woman owned a pair of legs like that…

With a fair amount of caution, he stepped through the door and Marcelina's full form came into view. When she saw him, her expression brightened somewhat, but he caught enough to know she was uncomfortable. "I smell a clear disregard of my client's rights," he grumbled as he set his briefcase down on the floor since there was no room on the desk.

Leonard closed the door and leaned against it, arms folded. "We haven't discussed anything you wouldn't approve of…besides our mutual love for circus peanuts, that is." He winked in her direction.

Walker knew the game. The captain had spent this time alone with Marcelina to find some common ground. Put her at ease. And circus peanuts—assuming he meant the squishy orange kind—were disgusting. But Marcelina's nod of confirmation offered some reassurance that nothing untoward had taken place. Yet.

Her thick hair was up in a sexy, messy jumble that

revealed the slim column of her neck—a neck his lips desperately longed to explore. He tore his gaze away and hoped a glass of iced water would appear out of thin air. "Why are we here, Captain Ross?" he asked. "And why did you summon my client without my knowledge?"

Leonard held up a hand. "Relax, Mr. Bishop, we're all on the same side."

Not likely. Walker sensed a deal coming on, one that most likely involved Marcelina getting close with Armando Rivera. Leonard must have had an undercover cop at the auction who witnessed her interaction with him.

"Now that your attorney is present," Leonard continued to Marcelina, "I called you here because I have a proposal for you. One I think you'd like to consider."

"Guessing by the cloak-and-dagger arrangement of this meeting," Walker cut in with eyes narrowed, "he wants to make a deal with you, Marcelina. But you are in no way obligated to take it."

She looked between them from her place in the corner. "A deal? I scratch your back, you scratch mine kind of thing?" When Walker nodded, she asked, "Is that legal?"

"Depends on what's required of you."

Leonard ignored his dirty look. "You're up against some pretty serious charges, Ms. Page. The DEA and I spoke with federal prosecutors this morning. It's all set. If you help us gather intel on a separate investigation, you will never see the inside of a prison cell for your own crimes."

Walker felt her go still all over. As the words sank in, Marcelina's gaze grew hopeful. "You mean…"

"No jail. No community service. No probation."

The man was good. Not everyone feared the idea of going to prison, especially those of the three-hots-and-a-cot mentality. But for Marcelina it was comparable to getting the chair.

"What does the Drug Enforcement Agency have to do with this?" she asked.

Walker watched her carefully. "They want you to be their informant."

"A source," Leonard corrected. "Last night we intercepted several phone calls from Armando Rivera. One was to his advisor requesting a background check on you. Seems you've…piqued his interest."

Though the news was grim it came as no surprise to Walker. Now that he'd been caught stirring up trouble for Rivera again, the games would officially begin. Did the man mean to start picking off his clients one by one? "More than just 'piqued his interest' if you believe she's even a viable candidate for this," he said.

Leonard nodded. "There were other conversations that indicated she could be an Achilles heel for him. She's already making him careless. Slip up. We got some leads we'd like for her to follow, and that's from last night's wire taps alone."

Achilles heel. The words settled into Walker's head with the weight of a cinder block. Whether Rivera knew he was being listened to or not, the man had just guaranteed himself a place in Marcelina's life.

"Since your arrest was months ago," Leonard continued to Marcelina, "we couldn't exactly erase your record, but we were able to fudge it a little. Not much, just enough to let Rivera think you've been uncooperative with police." He held up a hand to halt her protests. "Your lawyer is present, Ms. Page. We all know you claimed to have been cooperative, but if you agree to our proposition this will only work in your favor. Rivera needs to know you were not only loyal to your boyfriend but that you're anti-police."

"I'm not loyal—"

Walker cut her off and gave the captain a dull smile. "She isn't interested."

To her credit, Marcelina kept silent, watching him out of the corner of her eye. But she was thinking about it. Weighing her options, wondering if it would be worth the risk of getting into bed with the cartel. When her lips parted with what he feared were more questions, Walker spoke first. "Before this conversation goes any further I'd like a chance to speak with my client alone."

But Captain Ross was still blocking the exit. He extended a card. On it was the DEA logo and some contact info. "We need her, Walker. If Rivera wants her as bad as we think he does, she's as good as in."

Marcelina got up, took the card, flipped it over. "Would I be working with the DEA or with you?"

"I have some background with the DEA, so I've agreed to act as liaison in this case." Leonard flicked a look in Walker's direction. "If you should accept it, that is."

"I *should* have been present when you decided to make deals with federal prosecutors, Captain Ross," Walker injected, sensing he'd been kept out of the loop on purpose. He knew his friendship with Leonard would bite him in the ass one day. "This was a bullshit move, especially for you."

When he picked up his briefcase, Marcelina put a hand on his sleeve. "Walker, please…I'd like to hear him out before we go."

"Thank you, Ms. Page." The captain's look warmed on her. "Though I appreciate Walker's concern, time is of the essence here. This city needs you to give back, and like I said you will be highly compensated."

"My client can't be bought with pretty words or a mutual love for circus peanuts," Walker growled. "If she agrees to this deal of yours, she'll know exactly what she's getting into, and I can guarantee she'll take her chances with the judicial system rather than whore herself out for the DEA."

When Marcelina blanched at the implication, Leonard sent her a placating look. "We wouldn't ask you to do anything you don't want to do. As long as you know that the evidence you bring us needs to be the kind that can put Rivera away in order to get complete immunity."

"I...I don't want to sleep with him," she said, her voice laden with a kind of disappointment that made Walker want to punch Leonard in the face.

"We know he asked you to dinner last night," Captain Ross said. "Just accept the offer. Talk to him. See where it leads."

Walker kept his stone-cold gaze on the captain, though his words were for his client. "Marcelina, the only way you'll get that kind of evidence is if Rivera trusts you. You'll have to prove your loyalty, which means you'll not only have to sleep with him, you'll have to break some laws. Maybe snort a little coke. That's what it always comes to no matter how innocent Captain Ross tries to paint it." He leaned toward the captain. "Nothing is too unethical as long as the end justifies the means, right Leonard? But if she even *survives* Rivera, she'll have to live with herself afterward while your

DEA buddies pat themselves on the back for a job well done."

A flash of annoyance crossed the captain's face, though he regarded Marcelina with an apology in his eyes. "Again, Ms. Page, however you choose to get that information is entirely up to you."

Marcelina stared at him, clear doubt in her countenance. "And if I break some laws in the process, I wouldn't be prosecuted for it?"

Leonard's answering nod came quickly enough. "As long as you continue to help us, we won't file charges against you." A crooked smile. "Just try not to kill anyone."

She cocked her head and returned his smile. "If I come up with something useful, how do I know you'll honor your end of the deal?"

"We would honor it."

"Maybe your idea of 'useful' will never jive with mine. I've seen the TV shows. I've seen how easily that get-out-of-jail free card is taken away."

"It's a legitimate deal, Ms. Page, not some street-level negotiation." Leonard extended a hand with the patience of a cat waiting for his mouse. "Walker here will make sure your cooperation is fully documented."

"Walker doesn't want me to do it," she returned with a raised brow.

And it sounded as if she wouldn't. A sense of warmth entered Walker's blood, accompanied by a new respect for her and a profound wave of relief. He could barely contain his own smile when Leonard finally looked at him with a silent plea for help. "You heard her," Walker said. "Her answer is no, and Leonard…stick with the street snitches."

It would be less of a tragedy to find them floating face down in Clam Pass. Walker helped Marcelina out the door and they both left the kitchen, then the café and its gaggling lunch crowd.

But when they got in Walker's car, he barely had time to turn the key when Marcelina buckled her seatbelt and turned to him with thoughtful contemplation. "Why shouldn't I take the deal?"

That sense of dread came back and, with a heavy sigh, he cranked the AC. "Whatever came through on that wiretap last night, I don't think it was about some love-struck fascination Rivera has for you."

"What do you think it was?"

She hadn't even looked offended by his remark. She was all business and ready for rational conversation—a refreshing change from their brief stint with Captain Ross. "Rivera isn't careless," he began, feeling like quite the authority on a man he'd spent years investigating. "If anything, he's playing the DEA." He looked at her then. "And probably gunning for *me*. I think he blames me for turning his nephew. He's a master at games, and if he saw that kiss yesterday he'll think we're a couple."

She sank back into her seat as loose wisps of her hair fluttered against the airflow from the vents. "Oh yeah. The kiss."

"It's just a theory, of course, but he hasn't avoided prison this long by being stupid. He won't give you anything unless he *knows* he's turned you." Walker shifted into reverse and threw her a brief, poignant look. "Which is why you need to stay far away from this."

Her eyes were hidden behind the large sunglasses she'd just donned. "Ever since meeting Jonah, I've been involved in the drug trade, something I never thought would touch me. It's getting bad out here, Walker. My instinct *is* to stay far away from it, but…" She turned to look out the window, "I have to wonder if prison would be any better."

"Assuming I can't keep you from doing hard time." Something he would move heaven and earth to achieve if she'd let him. But she was scared and he got that. "Kendall is on board, you know. She agreed to testify on your behalf."

Marcelina didn't seem surprised to hear it, but she smiled a bit. It was a smile that said she doubted Kendall's testimony would make the difference she needed for a guaranteed acquittal.

Nothing could do that…except for the DEA, of course. "The decision is ultimately yours," he told her. "As your attorney, it's my job to lay out your options. Yes, informants with defense counsel tend to get better, determinate deals. I wouldn't let them burn you." He glanced at her, noting the tense set of her shoulders. "But I'll be powerless to defend you against Rivera once you're inside his organization. And if this is what I think it is, the DEA won't get to you fast enough when it matters most. You'll be very much alone. Think about that."

****

A chill hit Marcelina's bare arms as soon as she stepped out of the cab, though the temperature had already reached the eighties—meaning the chill was more reactionary to the sight of Armando Rivera in the distance. It was auction day again, only this time it was a lovely, cloudless Saturday afternoon. And this time she was at Tony's only to observe, preferably without being noticed.

New Year's Eve had come and gone. She'd spent it alone with little more to do than mull over Captain Ross's proposed deal. Walker didn't want her to take it, of course, but there was a small voice inside her head that needed to be silenced. One that demanded assurance that she was making the right choice.

Feeling well hidden in her sunhat and oversized shades, Marcelina tucked her clutch beneath an arm and skirted around the crowd toward the front entrance of Tony's establishment. Her low ponytail and dashiki-style dress kept things plain, the loose fabric flowing freely around her elbows and knees without lending any shape to her figure. It was about as unassuming as she could get without appearing too obvious. With any luck, no one would notice her at all.

"Marcelina!"

Or she'd be spotted before hitting the sidewalk. She looked ahead to find Tony sitting on a bench, watching his auction from beneath the shaded portico. He'd all but yelled her name from twenty feet away. So much for inconspicuous.

When Marcelina reached him, she put on a friendly smile. "I see the weekend doesn't affect your turnout."

Showing some manners, Tony stood up for the greeting then offered her the seat next to him. "It's not the day so much as the reputation. Our auctions are top notch."

"It's a popular place."

"You would fit well here," Tony said. "I could certainly use you. Pay is good."

Marcelina watched Armando Rivera through her sunglasses while he spoke to one of the block models. He was dressed more casually that afternoon in a button-down shirt that was open enough to show a furry chest and lots of gold. "Can I have more time to think about it?" she asked.

"I'd want an answer today. Save you some cab fare."

A small laugh. "I take it that means the Jetta is still on the table."

"As a loaner. You should be able to afford something of your own within the first month."

"Really?" She peered at him from the corner of her eye. "And I wouldn't have to sleep with you?"

Tony's head fell back with laughter. "I knew Walker had his hands full with you."

An orange 2022 Challenger rolled off the block. The new owner stood up and headed for the tent.

Elvis. Marcelina frowned as recognition set in. What was Graham Metcalf doing here again? "Hey, Tony…that man over there. Does he come to many of Rivera's auctions?"

Tony thought about it for a moment. "Actually, he *only* comes to Rivera's auctions."

Marcelina knew the Metcalfs were wealthy, but even she couldn't imagine unloading so much money in one day. "How many cars does he buy at each auction?"

"I don't know…three? Four? He has some kind of online dealership. Buys 'em cheap, turns a profit."

"Unless that car is lined with gold?" she asked, repeating those scathing words from a bidder the other night.

Tony laughed again, crossed his arms as he watched Graham Metcalf retake his seat. "Yeah, he must have really wanted that Benz."

When one of the models summoned Tony, he left Marcelina to observe the activities on her own. It was a good spot under the shade, one that muted the purple pattern of her dress. If Kendall weren't six inches shorter, Marcelina would have raided her closet for something a little less conspicuous.

A new presence loomed beside her. "You're back." The hairs at the base of her neck tingled as if they'd been freshly plucked out. "No doubt to continue your observation of something that…*interests* you."

Armando Rivera had not only noticed her, but had sought her out with obvious intent. Perhaps even conspired with the block model to get Tony out of the picture? To do what, exactly? Ask her out again? Harass her? It was hard to tell knowing that Walker was on his radar, too. What exactly had the police overheard in that wiretap to get them so excited? The curiosity of it all had burned a hole in her brain, but at the moment—with the man breathing down her neck—it was a bit frightening.

She swallowed back the lump of apprehension in her throat and played along. "Men who flatter themselves are destined for disappointment," she returned with stiff censure. "In other words, Mr. Rivera, you aren't my type."

His answering smirk lacked humor. "I take it Walker Bishop is your…*type?*"

"He's a *friend*."

"He's your lawyer—with benefits, according to that kiss I saw you two exchange the other day."

Her eyes closed behind the sunglasses. "You know an awful lot about me for a man I've barely spoken with."

Rivera shrugged that off as he watched the bidding activity before him. "I won't deny I've been fascinated since the first moment I saw you."

"As much as you've been fascinated with Walker?" she bit back.

Annoyance touched his eyes. "Touché." He refocused on the crowd. "He's a man of many talents. First a formidable prosecutor, now a successful defense attorney. I have no doubt he'll soon be deeply embedded in the pockets of organized crime just like his father was."

Marcelina didn't know anything about Walker's father, but sensing Armando was going for a rise, she absorbed the information tight-lipped and with a grain of salt. Walker's ethics were too solid to bend rules for anyone, despite what his father may or may not have done. Or was it in spite of it?

"Tell me, Miss Page." Armando sat down next to her and got comfortable. "How is it you're able to afford him when you can't even scrape together enough money for a car?"

If he'd had her background checked, he would already know Walker was helping out the OPD. His words were designed to rattle her, and they did. Rivera knew way too much for comfort, and the fire emanating from him was too dangerous to play with, something she could recognize and summon the common sense to avoid. The decision was made. She'd take her chances with the judicial system and trust that Walker could work his magic.

Marcelina got to her feet. "You know so much already, Mr. Rivera. Any answers from me at this point would be, well…redundant. Don't you think?"

She made her escape, bidding a silent adieu to Tony, her one job opportunity, and Captain Ross's proposal.

"I want you to have dinner with me tonight," Rivera

said behind her.

Unbelievable. He was actually following her down the sidewalk. "Thanks, but no thanks."

"If transportation is a problem, I can solve that for you."

How was she supposed to wait for a cab with him breathing down her neck? "I wouldn't get in a Rolls Royce if you sent one for me."

"Who said anything about *sending* a car?"

A gust of wind threatened to take her hat, so she held it in place and turned with a disgusted look. "What?"

They were stopped by the line of cars that were waiting to be auctioned off. Armando extended a hand toward the one they stood next to—a sleek Porsche 911. "Take this one."

Marcelina stared at it, too shocked to speak. Porsches of any kind were simply sex on wheels. This one's red polished paint gleamed in the sun, tantalizing her with the idea of hopping in and claiming it for her own.

"She isn't interested."

The gruff voice coming from nowhere shook her back to reality. Her lawyer had arrived just in time to see her consider something so stupid as taking a gift from a known leader of the Colombian cartel. A peek out of the corner of her eye showed a pissed-off Walker wearing jeans and a piercing glare.

"Mr. Bishop." Rivera appeared to be only mildly annoyed. "Your timing is impeccable."

Walker kept his steely gaze on her. "Lawyers are good at that. It's how we keep our clients out of trouble."

"Your client is in no trouble with me. I only wish to look out for her."

Walker cupped her elbow and all but shoved her away from the man. "She isn't and never will be yours to look out for."

Chapter 6

If Marcelina didn't know better, she would have sworn there was a possessive twang to his words, but Walker was too pissed for her to mull it over for long. "I wasn't going to take it," she mumbled beneath the shade of her hat as they marched over to his parked car.

"That's not what I got from the stars in your eyes."

"Those weren't stars, they were…" Her breath came out in a whoosh. "Okay, they were stars, but you didn't give me time to recover from the shock."

Once again, he put her in his car before circling around to the driver's side. Marcelina was already turned, ready to plead her case when he slipped behind the wheel and shut the door. "I know what it looks like, but I only wanted to watch him for a while before I made my decision."

The engine started with the rattle of keys and a sound of ridicule. "If you keep putting yourself in his path, he'll make the decision for you."

God, he was right. So *painfully* right. Marcelina removed her hat and sank into her seat, which was still cool from his ride over.

Walker entered traffic swearing under his breath. "I should have never brought you here to begin with. What the hell was I thinking?"

"You wanted Tony to give me a job. It was very noble of you."

"That changed when you caught Rivera's attention the first time." He barked out a laugh. "Those parting words he yelled across the parking lot the other day? Those were *threats*."

"I get that." Marcelina let the silence simmer between them for a moment. "How did you know where I was?"

"Tony called me when he saw you get out of that cab. At least *someone* was thinking clearly."

Tony. The Judas with the Jetta. "Just so you know, he was still trying to sell me that job."

When they reached the stoplight, she glanced at his rigid profile. "We've been spending a lot of time in your car lately. Have you noticed that?"

Walker's lips curled with a sneer that vanished just as quickly. He rubbed at the whiskers he'd failed to shave that morning. "I'm beginning to understand you more every day," he said, his voice deceptively calm, his eyes on the road. "When you feel restless or cornered, you bring up sex in order to derail me."

Her mouth fell open. "I didn't say anything about sex."

"You were about to."

He was right. She held back her comment about trying out the back seat sometime and crossed her arms with an affronted look. It seemed the man was getting to know her better than anyone, even Kendall. It was…disturbing.

Walker must have read her thoughts because he gave a disgusted laugh. "If you want to change the subject so bad, you can tell me what you're hiding about Jonah King."

As always, the request sounded more like an

accusation. Her heart sank a little bit more every time. Marcelina looked out the window. "I understand why the cops think I'm protecting him, but you're my lawyer."

"Yes, I am. And you've got to learn to trust me sometime."

"Did it ever occur to you to trust *me?*" When she realized her hands were balled into fists, she relaxed them. Took a breath. "I guess since I slept with him, that automatically makes me his puppet."

"If you don't want me to think it, quit lying to me."

But she wasn't lying about Jonah. And she *wanted* to tell Walker her secret about Nari Puccini despite her inner voice that told her not to open that can of worms. It would be so, *so* liberating, not only because her lawyer was a genuinely good man, but because she liked him and wanted him to understand her. She wanted him to throw away his damned ethics and take her to bed. She wanted to see more of his human side, to watch the pulse at his jaw go wild, to watch him lose control. As her mind wandered completely off course, Marcelina fidgeted in her seat. Struggled to remember why they were fighting. Oh yeah…

"Okay, Walker." She sighed, lifting a hand in defeat. "I'm hiding Jonah. Kendall doesn't know this, but he's been camped in her utility closet for the last few days eating peanut butter and reading books by candlelight."

"Don't make light of this—"

"The truth is I'm keeping him for the sex because he was just that good in bed. Worth every bit of five years in prison, because hey. What *wouldn't* I sacrifice for a guy who can tie cherry stems with his tongue?"

"You can stop talking now."

Indeed, it looked as if he were choking on the image

she'd presented. "What's wrong? Is the truth too painful to hear?" When he remained tight lipped, she cocked her head and wiped the teasing quality from her voice. "I'm beginning to wonder…are you afraid that I'm hiding something? Or that I'm *not* hiding something?"

"What the hell is that supposed to mean?"

"I don't know. Maybe you need to believe I'm tainted."

A look of derision accompanied his answer. "That's absurd."

She nodded as if seeing the light for the first time. "It's the only thing keeping you from taking me to bed. I can sympathize with that, I just hate that you're wasting our time trying to demonize me."

"Quit turning this into my problem, Marcelina," he snapped. "My *job* is to detect the truth when I hear it. I know you're keeping secrets, but I also believe you're a victim in all this. You're human. You let your ex-boyfriend snow you. That's as far as your mistakes need to go, so learn from it and listen to your lawyer." He counted her offenses with his fingers. "No secrets between us. No deals with the DEA. And, most importantly, *no contact with Armando Rivera.* Can you do that for me?"

With both hands back on the wheel, his knuckles were white against a fierce grip. The air practically sizzled with a heightened frustration she'd never felt from him before. "I can walk if you want me to," she suggested.

"You'll stop traffic in that dress," he returned with bite.

She looked down at the pile of fabric bunched beneath her seatbelt. "I was going for inconspicuous."

His roll of the eyes indicated a monumental failure on that front. "Guess that means you're still in no mood to talk. I'm getting tired of hitting brick walls with you."

Giving way to his dangerous mood, Marcelina kept quiet for the duration of the ride, her nose to the glass and her shoulders drawn up again. After eighteen more agonizing minutes, they finally pulled into Kendall's apartment complex and stopped at the front entrance.

Walker slowed her exit with a stiff warning. "Do not undermine me again, Marcelina. I may have elected to help the OPD, but that doesn't mean I won't turn your case over to someone else."

The finality in his voice scared her. She hesitated, her fingers curled around the handle. "I get it."

"I won't sit back and watch you self-destruct."

The underlying sentiment of his words took some of the sting out of his threat. She looked up to find that his eyes had lost their chill. The man was afraid of more than just losing. She swallowed again, this time against the emotions swelling in her throat. "Do you always care this much about the fate of your clients?"

His brow furrowed. "No."

It wasn't just the honesty of his answer that stunned her, it was his lack of denial. The "Walker" way of telling her she'd been right. That he cared a little too much.

And couldn't do a damned thing about it.

A genuine sigh of regret passed through her lips. "Okay, Walker. I won't so much as leave Kendall's apartment without telling you first."

A quick nod. "That's a start."

She considered him further, sensing a bit more behind his demands than just her interests. "It's more personal with Rivera than you're letting on, isn't it?"

When he didn't deny it, she asked, "Is it because your father was in the pocket of organized crime?"

The question apparently took him by surprise. "Who told you that?"

"Rivera. I think he believes you're still a legitimate threat to him."

Walker's head jerked back with a bit of startled amusement. "He really has been doing his homework."

Was he flattered? Excited? Lord knew he loved a challenge. "So it's true?" she asked.

After an uncomfortable silence, he looked away. "I lost respect for my father a long time ago."

Though expected, his confirmation still came as somewhat of a surprise. "And it makes you want to fight against what he fought to defend," Marcelina concluded.

"I tried that already. Like I said, you can't fight corruption, but at least now I have the freedom to choose my battles."

When his gaze found hers again, her heart belonged to him a little more. "I'm beginning to understand you more every day, too, Walker," she said softly. "And it is…*really* a shame I admire your ethics so damn much."

With a sigh of regret, she pushed the door open and exited the car. A blast of warmth hit her air-chilled skin, sending her body into climate shock. He waited until she disappeared inside the elevator. When she exited onto the second floor balcony, it was to see his shiny black Infinity turn out of the parking lot. As she walked to Kendall's apartment, she thought about their car ride over. The argument. The extra something in Walker's look that told her she was getting to him. Maybe that was why he threatened to drop her case. If so, she would back off for now. Quit pushing his buttons before she lost him completely.

One hour into her "prison term" in cellblock 218, Marcelina was entertaining the thought of breaking out, therefore breaking her promise to Walker. The apartment was empty and things were just too quiet in her world for a Saturday afternoon. Though she'd filled up that time with the TV on, taking down Kendall's dying Christmas tree, packing away the ornaments and vacuuming the mess it left, there was this restless feeling she couldn't abide, as if someone were holding a big shoe over her head. Aiming. Waiting for her to keep still so they could drop it on her. So, with a small amount of guilt, she walked to the bookstore that was located just three blocks from Kendall's neighborhood. It was a safe enough place, one she'd found solace in plenty of times before. A place where men like Jonah King and Armando Rivera would never linger.

Once she entered through the glass doors, the smell of boutique coffee and leather bindings infused her system with goodness. She removed her floppy hat and sunglasses, looked around as if she'd found Nirvana. There were nice, cozy places to sit in here, and with Kendall's borrowed laptop in hand, Marcelina picked an isolated corner to camp out for a while.

As she skimmed through the classifieds, a keen sense that she was being watched had her looking up. A man stood there, his attention on her from above the latest issue of *Women's Magazine*. Below it, a potbelly accompanied the football jersey and spandex shorts combo she'd seen in countless 80s comedies. As soon as their eyes met, his darted back down again.

Subtle. Marcelina was accustomed to men ogling her, but there was something about this guy that stood out—his failure to hide. Bushy black eyebrows moved as he looked up for another peek. She cleared her throat and went back to what she was doing, giving off a clear signal to leave her alone.

And that must have given him the nerve to approach her. "Excuse me, Miss?"

She looked up with annoyance. "Yes?"

"You probably don't remember me, but I'm a friend of…" He hesitated, his nervous gaze darting around the store before he leaned forward and mouthed the word "Jonah."

Her ex-boyfriend's name never failed to incite that all-too-familiar feeling of loathing, even when formed by silent lips. It wasn't the first time she'd encountered someone from Jonah's circle, but this was *her* bookstore. *Her* safe place. "No, I don't remember you," she snapped.

He tucked the magazine under a sweaty armpit. "That's okay, I'm just supposed to give you this. It's important."

She stared at the yellow piece of paper he held out to her. Her first instinct was to tell him to shove it wherever the spandex would allow. The hell if she was going to take anything from Jonah. But then a tiny voice of logic told her it might be something that would aid the police in their search for him. So she reached up and snatched it out of the man's hand.

"That's just half the message," he said, swiping an arm across his forehead. "I'm also supposed to tell you he'll be in touch."

Jonah, in touch? Didn't he know the police were looking for him? Wasn't her arrest the reason he'd skipped town? As the confusion moved in, the man backed away, his gaze bolder now and laden with meaning. He turned, shoved the magazine back in the rack and disappeared among the staggered bookshelves. Shell shocked, Marcelina looked down at the note in her hand. It was grungy from being palmed for however long in a sweaty fist. Careful to avoid the wet corners, she unfolded it, hoping beyond hope that Jonah was having a change of heart. Maybe he was finally willing to turn himself in and let her off the hook. All he needed to do was tell the police she had no knowledge of what was in those packages and she would be a free woman.

But when her gaze settled on the four words he'd left her, it delivered an entirely different kind of blow to her system.

—I know your secret.—

Very slowly her lungs collapsed inside her chest. Was he for real? Did he really know her secret or was he playing games?

No. The second half of his message said he was going to be in touch. If so, it would be a bold move that could get him caught, but not if he blackmailed his girlfriend.

Ex-girlfriend.

Gasping for breath, Marcelina shut the laptop, grabbed her stuff, and rose on shaky legs. Jonah knew her secret. But how? She'd never told a soul…unless she talked in her sleep, which was possible. All he would need was one mention of it, and then he'd have the motivation to research *her* background. Figure out stuff like timing and proximity. Make connections that would provide him with just enough leverage to control her.

As she left the bookstore, it was with the fear of God that her problems would only compile from there…and that there was no longer a safe place on earth for her to hide.

****

Sweat, willpower, and body odor. Walker absorbed all three coming off the overweight guy next to him who seemed determined to fulfill his new year's resolution in one evening. It was a quest that would probably end in failure, especially if he wasn't willing to push it past three point five miles per hour. But Walker could appreciate the effort. At least that guy was willing to *entertain* the thought of saving himself from an unpleasant fate.

Unlike Marcelina, who continuously headed for disaster like a speeding car without brakes—who also kept popping into his head despite his best efforts to exercise her out of his system, if only for a few hours.

As Walker upped his own speed to a steady nine point five, the phone at his side went off, cutting into the music flowing through the headphones.

Ignore it. Let it ring. Just two miles to go…

But, as always, his internal lecture failed to overcome the importance of his job. Walker reached down and plucked his phone from its holster. Looked at the screen. With an oath loud enough to gain some attention, he stepped off of the belt and let the treadmill whiz beneath him on its own. "Bishop," he panted.

"This is Kendall. I'm worried about Marcelina."

He wiped the sweat from his eyes with a towel, ignoring that instant hit to his solar plexus. "I can't help you right now, Kendall."

"When I came home I could tell she'd been crying. She wouldn't tell me what was wrong, but it must have been big because she went for a walk without her purse or her phone."

Despite Marcelina's promise to stay put, the act hardly warranted a red flag. "Well, she *is* dealing with a lot right now."

"Yes, I know, but my gut tells me something happened today that really upset her."

The worry in Kendall's voice began to sink through his layers of armor, the ones that kept him from fucking up. He'd slipped earlier when he'd given Marcelina an inch of himself and admitted he cared. But her actions had scared the hell out of him, prompting him to say things he shouldn't. "She's probably upset with me. We didn't exactly part on the best of terms."

"You didn't quit on her, did you?"

The accusatory tone put him on instant defense. "No, of course not." But he'd threatened to. Would that send her into a fit of tears, though? "Do you know if she went out earlier?"

"I think so. My laptop case was warm like she'd just come home from a walk. I asked her if anything happened but she wouldn't say. Now I may not be the brightest crayon in the box, but that usually means yes."

Pinching the bridge of his nose, Walker headed toward the wall of windows and looked out at the heavy evening traffic beyond them. His recuperative breaths fogged the glass as he absorbed and processed. "Do you have any idea where she went?"

"Are you going to talk to her?"

"If I can find her, yes." For the second time that day.

"It could be a number of places," Kendall said. "She's on foot, so it's somewhere close. The beach is a three-mile walk from here. She likes to go to the pier sometimes. Then there's a bookstore a few blocks down.

Or I guess she could have gone to that old apartment complex on 28th and Banyan. A guy she used to date lives in 16-A. Santiago is his name."

"Is she still acquainted with this Santiago person?" And was that the lawyer asking or the hot-blooded man who wanted to put his fist in the wall?

"I don't know." Kendall sniffed. "She mentioned him the other day, so they may have reconnected over the last eight months. Regardless, I'm sure if a booty-call were in order, he'd be up for it."

Precisely twelve minutes later, Walker stood in front of 16-A in his wet gym clothes, jaw pulsing, and with the fires of hell raging through his veins. He pushed the buzzer three times. Then three times more.

A thick Colombian accent came through the door. "What do you want?"

"Are you Santiago?"

"Maybe."

That far into the conversation and Walker decided the guy was an asshole. "I'm looking for Marcelina Page."

As he stood on the ground level amid a string of front doors, bicycles, and failing Hibiscus shrubs, a few quiet seconds passed before the door opened as far as the chain would allow. A strong element of sex instantly hit Walker between the eyes...making them haze over with red. The waning sunlight revealed a brown-skinned man lounging in nothing but his skivvies, flip-flops, and a scowl. Music played somewhere in the background and the smell of strawberries wafted past the threshold.

The man gave Walker a complete once-over through the gap. "What do you want with Marcelina?"

Ignoring the flaccid, satin-covered outline of the

man's junk, Walker set his teeth. "Is she here or not?"

"That depends on your answer, Tank Top."

None of your goddamned business, Banana Hammock. "It's a legal matter," Walker said instead.

"What are you, a cop or sunthing?" Santiago's impassive gaze swept down to his gym shorts. "Don't you fellas yooshually come with badges?"

The urge to bust through the door Hollywood-style was tempered when a pair of slender, blue-tipped fingers snaked around Santiago's shoulders. "Who is it, Boo?" came a high-pitched, bimbo-quality voice.

Definitely not Marcelina. Walker narrowed his gaze. "I take it she *isn't* here, then."

A splendid set of white teeth showed through the gap. "No."

"And you haven't seen her?"

"Not since the *bruja* ditched me at mini-golf last year."

The fires of hell slowly ebbed, giving rational thought some room to breathe. "So the twenty-questions routine was just you being nosy," Walker asked.

"Pretty much."

He supposed he should be pissed about that. Instead, his shoulders lost their starch and he gave the man a good-natured salute. "You two have fun."

"You tell her I found a woman who don't mind losing to me," Santiago shouted as he walked away. "A good, sexy woman!"

"Come on, Boo, you promised me that massage."

Along with the slamming door came the tremendous relief that Marcelina had *not* gone to Rico Suave for that booty call. His troublesome, curvaceous client was getting too far under his skin, something he'd need a lot more than a good workout to fix. As he walked back to his car, the worry began to set in. Where was she? What state of mind was she in? Kendall seemed to think there was something to worry about, and the woman knew Marcelina better than he did. Obviously.

After a quick check of the bookstore, Walker headed to the last place on Kendall's list. If Marcelina walked to the beach, she probably would have ended up close to the pier. So, with the windows down, he drove a half-mile north of it, which seemed like a good place to start.

Since the sun had just set, most people were either leaving or already gone. Parking wasn't a problem and Walker found a spot close to the entrance. He got out. Nodded at a couple who walked past him hand-in-hand. At the end of the sand-coated boardwalk, he stopped and scanned the length of the beach for signs of Marcelina. He looked past the post-sunset stragglers who randomly stopped along the darker, ribbon-like strandline to pick through gulf debris. And the gulls that swarmed the surf in search of a turned-up meal. He looked for that one person in the flowing knee-length dress Kendall said she was still wearing. The same one from the auction that had showcased her long, silky legs below the hem.

Nothing.

Dammit, where was she? Should he go left? Right? He asked another couple if they'd seen a woman fitting Marcelina's description and came up empty, so he chose to go left toward the pier. When his athletic shoes began to fill with sand, Walker took them off along with his socks and carried them. The cool granules actually felt good beneath his feet, almost like a massage. They needed it after the punishment they'd endured at the gym.

Gentle waves swooshed to his right. A slight breeze scented with a mixture of salt and surf ruffled his clothing, caressed his bare arms. It would be dark soon and he had to face the possibility she wasn't here.

So was he wasting his time?

Something told him no. As he neared the pier—the giant structure spanning a good thousand feet into the Gulf of Mexico—the lights came on, reflecting off the clear, rippling waters.

When he passed by the last, barnacle-crusted pylon, he decided Marcelina had not come that direction. So he walked back. When he reached the boardwalk he'd entered from, instead of heading to his car, he continued north. By then it was twilight and getting harder to see, but he forged on…until he spotted a slender form in the distance, far out from the beach and silhouetted against a sapphire sky. Long hair billowed around drooping shoulders as the woman headed out further into the gulf. It was as if she was calling for someone or something to come sweep her away. Testing the limits of the tide. Offering herself up to the sea gods, whoever they were.

And she was still walking.

It was Marcelina. What the hell? Was she trying to drown herself? He broke into a jog, his progress slowed as the sugary sand swallowed every step. Walker called out to her, but she either didn't hear him or she ignored him. He stopped, dropped his shoes and tucked his phone and keys inside of them. Then he was off, his feet slapping against wet surf until he was knee-deep in cool waters. It was there he slowed, caught his breath. From that point it was clear she wasn't progressing into the depths, which had been more of an illusion caused by the ever-moving waves.

No, she was just standing there, waist-deep in the middle of complete solitude, her dress catching each movement of the water. Walker couldn't look away. He watched her for a while until his breathing slowed to a more normal rhythm. His heart, however, seemed to have stopped altogether.

As he waded to her side, he sucked in air and waited for the water to warm against his skin. They stood there, side-by-side, looking out at the dark horizon.

Finally, he took in a deep breath, let it out. "Okay, what are we doing? Counting waves? Looking for boats? What?"

She sighed, too. "Look down, Walker."

When he did, it was to encounter another illusion, this one in the form of a faint, green glow surrounding her hands. It was magical. Something out of a movie, and he touched the surface of the water with a sense of wonder, as if there were aliens living under there.

"Move your hands beneath the surface," she instructed. "It gets brighter. Leaves a trail."

Sure enough, when he swished a hand from left to right, a trail of sparkly light followed. "Well, I'll be damned," he murmured.

"You've never seen the algae lights before?"

He looked at her, noted how her thick hair appeared even softer when it caught the breeze. "I don't like the water."

"You live in a tropical paradise and you don't like the water?"

Why did he suddenly *want* to explain himself? "I had an unpleasant encounter with a jellyfish when I was ten. Never been back."

Her gaze was on him. He felt it as he continued to

stroke the water.

"So this is quite a moment for you," she said softly.

"I'm saving you from drowning yourself."

A small laugh. "Heroic."

Despite his efforts not to, he looked over and locked eyes with her, knowing now he'd never be able to look away again. Not since realizing just how deeply she'd burrowed under his skin.

Marcelina swallowed. "I take it Kendall called you again."

"I wish *you* would have."

"You've already rescued me once today. I'm still trying to figure out how you found me."

"She gave me some leads. The first one took me straight to the doorstep of one Rico Suave."

Her play with the water halted for a moment. "Huh?"

"Santiago."

Then she did laugh, the sound carrying over the gulf. "I haven't seen him in a long time."

"Yes, I heard. Since you ditched him at mini golf."

"Santiago cheats. He had it coming."

Okay, enough about Santiago. As much as Walker loved their easy banter, the lawyer in him needed to make an appearance before he completely lost his mind. Which was coming. "Do you want to tell me why you need rescuing again?"

More splashes as she returned her attention to the water. "Not really." She swallowed. "But I suppose I should."

Something told him this was about the secrets she'd been hiding. Someone must have pushed her into the right corner. "I take it something happened after I dropped you off this morning."

A sadness descended unlike anything he'd ever sensed from her before. "I went to the bookstore a few blocks down from the apartment," she said. "I thought it was the safest place to be invisible for a while."

"Was it Rivera? Did he harass you?" Walker didn't often entertain the thought of killing a man, but he was now.

She shook her head. "No. It was someone Jonah had sent to find me."

As he processed that particular nugget, he blinked. "You see, those are the things you need to tell me right away."

"Walker..." She made an exasperated sound. "Haven't you ever been scared a day in your life?"

"Of course."

"Then you'll understand that I had to get my bearings. He had this guy deliver a message that...I don't know, that completely changed the game for me." She looked up at him. "Jonah isn't done with me yet. He expects me to continue to help him."

This was the kind of surprise Walker expected. "Why does he think you would?"

"Be—because he has leverage against me."

Chapter 7

Her breaths were growing ragged and her lips began to tremble. Walker raised a dripping hand to touch her hair, but stopped himself. Lowered it back down again. "Talk to me, Marcelina." He could tell her words were on the cusp of spilling out, though she remained silent. "Everyone thinks their problems are unique," he pressed. "The truth is they're typically more common than you realize and there *are* answers to them. You need to get them out so we can face them together. It's what I'm here for."

There was a heavy pause, much like the quiet before the storm. "You won't like it."

Probably not, but if it was finally the truth, he was ready. "Try me."

She stood there in more silence, weighing her options behind those exotic eyes of hers. "Ha—have you ever heard the name Nari Puccini?"

Often. But hearing it from her lips was a shock he wasn't quite prepared for. "Yes."

"What do you know about him?"

More than she ever would. His father had thrown a rose over the Sicilian arms dealer's casket, after all. But he would keep that connection to himself for now. "He was one of the top crime lords on Florida's east coast. Moved weapons and money until he was taken out in a hit about six years ago."

Her shoulders notably stiffened. "What do you know about that hit?"

"It's a cold case now," he answered, watching her closely. "But investigators believe his mistress did it."

"A woman his wife said he'd been meeting with on the sly."

Why did it sound like she was correcting him? "It wasn't an unfair accusation," he said. "The man had a known appetite for beautiful young women, which is why his enemies used one to kill him."

As she fidgeted with the water for a while, Walker braced himself, sensing what was about to come.

"I was that woman, Walker," she murmured with head hung low.

He closed his eyes as the dread descended upon him. "You killed Nari Puccini?"

Marcelina shook her head. "No, I didn't. But those were my hair samples found on his clothes and in his car."

It was a case he knew intimately for reasons he didn't feel like disclosing at the moment. "Along with the blood and the gunpowder residue."

"I don't know anything about that. Whoever killed him must have gotten in the car right after I left it."

The woman was certainly calm enough to indicate she spoke the truth, not that it made him feel any better about it. "What were you doing with a man like that, Marcelina?"

"I wasn't sleeping with him." Spoken with conviction. "We were…friends."

Puccini? *Friends* with a woman who looked…who smelled…who emanated raw sex appeal like Marcelina? "You're right about one thing," Walker grumbled. "No one will believe you."

"But it's the truth. I was nineteen. I was into young beach bums with muscles and attitude and he was like my grandpa. The thought of sleeping with him would have turned my stomach if he'd suggested it, which he didn't."

The man's age had never deterred young women before, but for some reason Walker believed her. "Tell me about your relationship with him."

She sighed, a soft, tired sound. "It was brief. I was volunteering at a petting zoo east of Fort Meyers. He started coming around, just an old man in a windbreaker, big plastic shades, and ball cap. It wasn't until later I realized he was in disguise."

"Why was he there?"

Her cheeks ripened with a smile. "He liked to watch the potbelly pigs."

Walker made a sound of disbelief. "Are we talking about the same man?"

"You see that's just it. I knew him as a completely different person. I saw an old, lonely man who'd dreamed of living on a farm when he was a youngster." She quoted the last word with her fingers. "We talked a lot that first day. We even discussed our problems and unanimously decided mine were the biggest." When he didn't ask, she glanced over at him. "My favorite chocolates had been discontinued. Couldn't find them anywhere."

Walker smiled.

"Two days later, a box arrived at the petting zoo with my name on it. Inside was a year supply of the discontinued candy I thought was impossible to get. It came with a note that said, 'Nothing is impossible.'

"The next day I spotted him watching the pigs again. I thanked him for the chocolates but he would never say how he'd gotten them. He said only to use it as a reminder when things looked grim. That same night, infamous mob boss, Nari Puccini, hit the papers as a missing person. They had a black and white surveillance photo taken of him exiting a limousine. I immediately recognized him as the same man I'd been talking to every day for nearly a week. But instead of fearing him, Walker, I *hurt* for him. He'd been so troubled and I thought I knew why. To my surprise he was at the zoo the next morning, but he stayed on a far bench close to the woods. Waiting for me, almost to see if I would come. I felt his misery even from there, so I walked up to him, sat down, and told him I knew who he was." Her smile appeared. "I mispronounced his name and he gave me a lesson in how to speak godfather. We talked as if nothing had changed. He admitted committing some terrible crimes throughout his lifetime and that all he wanted was to know a little peace. But peace was unachievable for a man like him, and his regrets were many." She swallowed, the smile gone. "So I dug through my purse, found a piece of my favorite chocolate and placed it on the bench between us. He laughed it off as a menial thing. I said, 'this is your proof to me that nothing is impossible. If you don't take it I'll know everything you said was bullshit.' Or something along those lines."

"Did he?"

Marcelina faced the empty horizon that had dimmed to nothing more than streaks above black waters. "Yes. I took another one out of my purse and we unwrapped them together. I'll never forget the look on his face when he took a bite. It was like he was surprised it was actually good." Her next laugh came from a fond, faraway place. "I imagine he was accustomed to the finer things, and it was the first time he realized that simple wasn't so bad."

Walker thought about that, his mind warring with the image she painted. "Wasn't that why he was there? Wishing for a simpler existence?"

"Exactly. That's when he told me he believed there was an assassination plot brewing against him. He didn't know who to trust, who to fear… In his world, everyone could be bought. And every time he closed his eyes at night he wondered if he'd wake up to see another sunrise."

Ah, the wonderful world of organized crime. The cake itself was fantastic, but too hot to hold any icing. Puccini thrived on hot, and was revered for handling it well. That's why it was so hard to picture him going into hiding. Other people hid from *him*.

"Nari told me something that I thought would never apply to me." Marcelina turned to him with a frown. " 'Don't ever get involved in organized crime' he said. 'Resist no matter who tries to suck you in, because the romance of it is a lie that can only end in horrible tragedy.' "

Her voice adopted a suspicious, nasally tone. "It was strange, this bond between us. It was almost as if fate put us together. He even gave me one of his charms—a *Coccinella* he called it." She shrugged. "It looked like a cheap little ladybug to me, although I *did* value it as a small reminder of him."

Walker's body tingled with a sudden charge. That small piece of jewelry was more important than she thought. It had belonged to Puccini's mother, and was one of the most sentimental possessions he'd owned. When it was discovered missing among the rest of his jewelry—which hadn't been touched—the charm became a key piece of evidence in his murder investigation. Evidence that was kept from the public eye in order to weed out the false leads.

"A few days later his death made national news," Marcelina continued. "I cried for him, Walker. Despite all the lives he may have taken, in my mind his life was the horrible tragedy. When the assassination plot surfaced, his wife told police she suspected he'd been with a new mistress. Sure enough, they found hair samples belonging to a woman they believed was his killer. Without more to go on, they had nothing to point the way to me, so I kept my mouth shut. No one at the petting zoo had recognized him. I thought I was safe."

Which wouldn't bode well in the courtroom, especially six years after the fact. "So you let police continue to look in the wrong direction."

She looked up at him, the panic now coming off of her in waves. "Yes. Nari had enemies, but he also had friends. He told me if he were killed it would start a war. And it did."

It was a "turf" war of sorts that had ended with seventeen casualties. As soon as Puccini's wife was cleared as a suspect, she had put out a substantial reward for his killer. The news trickled outside the tight circle of the mob until fake leads poured in from common folk who'd hoped for some quick cash. The excitement had faded over time, but could spark again with new information. Assuming this was the leverage Jonah King had on Marcelina, he could be anywhere, ready to spill. "What were you doing in Puccini's car?"

Marcelina's shoulders went up. "He gave me a ride home when I needed it. Simple as that. No limousine, no driver. Just an old man in a brown, midsized sedan."

One they found out he'd borrowed from an auto repair shop in Fort Myers. All leads had grown cold: the hair samples, the slug found in the ground near Puccini's shattered skull, even the missing amulet.

"Do you have the charm he gave you?" he asked, almost fearing her answer.

She shook her head. "I don't know what happened to it. I've moved an awful lot since then."

Her answer wasn't exactly comforting, but then again this whole conversation was like some sick nightmare. "Puccini was killed between 11:00 and 11:30 PM on a Friday night," Walker said, ticking off the details from memory. "And he had dropped you off at home by then?"

"Yes. I was staying with the owner of the petting zoo. Her house was in the country and she was out on the town that night. That's why I needed a ride."

"So no one could vouch for you," he concluded on his own. Before he could pose the next question, he realized she'd been staring at him with a fair amount of suspicion.

"How do you know so much about Nari's murder?" she asked him.

Should he tell her about his father's connection to Puccini? That this was the kind of information Conrad Bishop had been looking for to aid him in his quest for justice? Until Walker knew Marcelina wouldn't run, and that his father wouldn't chase her, he decided to keep it all to himself. Just for now. There was enough to process for one night. "I watched a documentary," he answered truthfully. "It was a big deal at the time."

And it would be a big deal again. Without more to go on, Marcelina had no defense. If she spoke the truth, her relationship with Puccini had been so brief, so innocent, and so far removed from the mob it was no wonder she hadn't been connected to those hair samples. He could understand her desire to hide. But now that Jonah King was involved, it was no longer a viable option.

"You need to come out," he said. "And not just because Jonah knows your secret. If you're prosecuted in this trafficking case your DNA will eventually end up in the CODIS database and the feds will make the connection."

"I thought if they were going to take my DNA it would have been when I was arrested."

"It was their prerogative at the time, but your crime didn't warrant it as much as a suspected killer would have. If you leave that courtroom in cuffs, though, it *will* happen. We need to be prepared. We'll question possible witnesses starting with your petting zoo friend. Who knows, maybe she'll remember something you don't."

Her head shook vigorously. "I can't come out, Walker."

"You can't hide anymore, Marcelina. And we can't wait for a verdict, not with Jonah holding this over you."

"Assuming that's the secret he knows."

"Are there others?"

She went boneless, as if disappointed in her lack of alternatives. "No."

"He's using your fear of getting caught like a fist in your hair. But confiding in me is the first step in breaking that hold. It was the right thing to do." Even though the last thing she needed was a ruthless Conrad Bishop breathing down her neck, outing her as a suspect and throwing his experience at her from the prosecution side of the courtroom. It would be a father-son battle unlike any the Florida judicial system had ever seen. Something he needed a lot of time to prepare for.

Lordy, he knew she'd been hiding something, but this was not what he expected. Protecting Jonah would have been a breeze in comparison. Walker was oddly comforted by the knowledge she wasn't.

Marcelina hugged her arms against the still-warm breeze. "If I'm not iced by the mob first, I'll go to prison for life." Her breath hitched. "I'll be gang raped by hairy women with broomsticks and forced to eat urine-soaked sandwiches. I've heard the horror stories—"

He turned her by the shoulders. "Stop." When she went silent, he looked down into her moonlit eyes, falling a bit further into their bewitching depths. "Do you think I would let that happen to you?" The doubt in her countenance tore him apart. She was so scared. Unwilling to trust that there may be a way out. "Marcelina, you can try and deny it, but you were involved in organized crime way before Jonah came along. Your association with Nari Puccini alone achieved that. You have to break free of it now."

"I can't break free of it," she choked.

Walker reached up and moved hair from her cheek. It was damp with the tears she'd been wiping away on the sly. "Nothing is impossible," he reminded gently. "Though I really hate quoting Puccini, the man was at least right about that."

Her eyes then welled with a vengeance, spilling tears that were left to drip into the briny water below.

"Oh, God," she whispered. "This is the end for me, isn't it? You're going to make me do this."

Ignoring all the reasons he shouldn't, Walker pulled her into his arms, muffling the terrified lilt of her voice against his shoulder. As his whiskers grabbed her hair, his arms tightened with a fierce need to protect. "You aren't alone in this anymore," he whispered. "I'm with you all the way. We'll fight it together and we'll beat it."

Without the protective layers of his suit, he could feel her heart pounding against his own. Their combined body heat burned away the last remaining scruples he had. His dick was already hard beneath the loose fabric of his gym shorts. Instead of backing away, however, he let it throb between them as Marcelina's emotional breakdown came to a shuddering end.

After a few recuperative breaths, her head came up. Her eyes shimmered. Her lips were swollen, inviting him to take a taste. Her belly tightened in response to the erection pressed against it. "You don't feel like my lawyer right now."

Her voice…it was a combination of sweet and smoky that drove him even closer to insanity. Holding her in his arms, feeling her curves flush against his body, watching the same desire darken her eyes, Walker knew he didn't stand a chance.

"Damn." It came out a breath, just before he crushed his mouth to hers. It was a desperate kiss from the start, one that surprised him as well as opened him up to the sinful pleasures he'd been denying himself since first laying eyes on Marcelina Page.

****

Was she dreaming or was her tough-as-nails lawyer suddenly consuming her like a raging inferno? All

Marcelina could do was be swept away, as she had been since he appeared in her peripheral vision moments ago. He was a younger, more carefree Walker in his gym clothes and playful bravado, but that wasn't all. Her building lust for him had turned into deep feelings somewhere along the way. It wasn't because he was good looking or that he had a physique that would turn any woman's knees to jelly. It wasn't because she was sex-starved. It was because, despite his arms-length stance toward their professional relationship, he was all she had. He was the only one she could trust to be there for her. And he had been, never letting her down when she needed him most.

"Walker," she whispered, unwilling to become a regret for him should he lose his way. "You're kissing me again."

But instead of pushing her away like before, he continued to kiss, his hands roaming downward to catch the hem of her dress. Bunching the fabric around her waist, he began to walk her backward, closer to shore, his fervent kisses keeping her lost in the undertow of his clear need for her. The demand of his lips turned frantic, his attempts to reach dry ground faltering under the rising heat until they stopped altogether. With her lower half now out of the water, he reached down, moving his hands beneath the wet lace of her panties to cup her bare buttocks.

"You haunt me, Marcelina," he rasped before claiming her mouth once again in a series of short, devouring kisses. "My thoughts. My dreams. Every damned breath I take."

And she was ready to take him. More than ready as his touch moved into dangerous territory, finding and delving into the evidence of her desire. "Does this mean you're finally going to make love to me?" Marcelina gasped, throwing her head back as the oxygen left her lungs.

"Oh, yes," came his rough reply.

The promise filled her with breathless anticipation. Sure enough, her panties made a clean descent down the length of her legs. She stepped out of them, sending them on their way as he reached down and freed his massive erection. He lifted her. She wrapped her legs around him. In one swift move, he was inside her, filling her so completely her mind, body, and soul soared with the force of their connection. It was amazing, better than she'd ever imagined. Ever dreamed.

For a second or two, he simply held her, suspended in that moment as he touched his forehead to hers and caught his breath. Then he walked them out of the surf and back onto wet sand where they fell together. With solid earth beneath them, he boxed her between his powerful arms, withdrew and thrust inside her again. Marcelina cried out, taking all of him, absorbing every blessed sensation. His pace began to quicken. With each thrust, he was dominating her in a way she'd never experienced before. Tearing out her heart and claiming it—along with her body—for his own.

Her need to touch drove her to claw at his shirt, delve beneath his shorts, exposing as much skin as possible. He groaned, lowering his warm mouth to her breasts, teasing through the fabric of her dress and sheer bra, making her want to tear them off so that there were no more barriers between them. "Please, Walker," she gasped, not knowing exactly what she was begging of him. *Please make me yours. Please hold me forever.*

Help me live again.

Because she knew, at that moment, he would be all she ever wanted.

Chapter 8

When Walker awoke the next morning, it was to find himself alone in his bed. No Marcelina, though the evidence of their carnal activities remained. When he brought her home, it was with the promise that there would be no regrets—that for one night they could escape reality and just lose themselves in each other as deeply and as often as possible. He'd woken her twice throughout the night, his hunger for her insatiable. It was as if he were staking his claim on something he couldn't have. Proving to her that she wanted him enough to resist whatever Armando Rivera was about to throw her way. She didn't seem to mind, always ready for him when he needed another taste. Now the sun was rising.

And their time was over.

But his interest peaked at the sound of life coming from the kitchen. At the same time, his nose picked up the heavenly aroma of fresh-brewed coffee and breakfast.

Don't get used to it.

It was becoming a chant, one he'd been repeating since their first round of lovemaking on the beach. Now she was cooking again, adding a certain comfort to his home that had never been there before. One that made him *want* to stay in lieu of heading to the office. It scared the hell out of him.

Buck naked, he rolled out of bed and headed toward

the bathroom. A quick shower later, he emerged with a fresh shave and a sense of renewed strength. He retrieved his bathrobe from the floor, donning it one arm at a time as he left the room.

In the hall, he passed by the humming dryer and the accompanying scent of fabric softener. He found Marcelina in the kitchen, reading the Sunday paper with a cup of coffee, hunkered over the counter in one of his dress shirts and a messy up-do that begged him to make love to her again.

Well, hell.

"Good morning," she said without looking up. "Sleep good?"

He grumbled in response as he opened the cabinet and took out a mug.

"I'll take that as a no."

He poured coffee. "We need to talk about last night."

She peered at him over the rim of her mug. "I thought you said no regrets."

"I don't mean the sex. I mean the talk we had before that."

"Oh." Her face fell, giving away the underlying dread that always hovered near the surface. "Can't it wait?"

"No," he pressed on, feeling a bit ruthless in his quest to staunch the blood flow to a penis that didn't want to quit. "I won't lie to you, Marcelina. It'll be a long road, but with the right strategy we can maybe get by with some character witnesses and a no-contest plea."

Ignoring his intense scrutiny of her profile, she flipped a page. "How about a not-guilty plea?"

"You hid the truth for years." Walker swiped the

paper she'd obviously retrieved from his front stoop and headed toward the table. "And if Jonah knows your secret, you can't exactly plead ignorance. We need to play on the jury's sympathy, make them understand how young and scared you were." He sat down, drank coffee, wincing against the burn.

"Have you even thought this through?" she asked from her place by the counter.

He sent a dry look over the bar. "It wouldn't exactly be my first murder trial."

A hint of vulnerability showed itself as she hugged her arms and approached him. "This won't be a court appointed case. Like you said, it'll be a long road, much longer than any conspiracy lawsuit."

"So?"

She shifted from foot to foot. "Walker, I can't pay you."

Oh, that. He scanned the headlines. "We'll work something out."

"More sex?"

God, yes. "No!" To soften the gruff nature of his response, he took a breath, looked up at her. "As long as I represent you, that can never happen again. We talked about this."

Her lips softened into a smile that forgave. "Yes, I know. Don't worry, it won't come up again."

A flash of regret pierced his chest. It was her untold reward, though he fought to keep the stern countenance. The stove timer buzzed.

Marcelina sighed, walked back into the kitchen, and grabbed a potholder. "Casserole?"

Walker paused, his mug suspended halfway to his mouth. "Seriously? A whole casserole?"

A nervous laugh came from behind the bar as she fished a dish from the oven. "I'm like the MacGyver of all things edible."

How could he possibly think of food when her disappointment seeped beneath his skin like that? Seconds later, she set a small plate in front of him. "I'm going to check on the dryer while you eat."

He looked down at the steaming pile of something with orange and green specs in it. "Marcelina…you aren't running scared, are you?" he said to her retreating backside.

In the hallway, the dryer door opened and closed. "No, I just have a lot to do today."

He took a small, reluctant bite. "Like what?"

"Well, for one I'm sure Kendall hasn't slept a wink. I need to get back to her apartment. Make sure all is well over there and that I still have a couch to sleep on."

The casserole was a fluffy concoction with the combined flavors of cheese and spinach. Walker frowned down at his plate. "How in hell did this come from my kitchen?"

She re-emerged wearing the purple dress, struggling to put his shirt back on a hanger. "Good?"

He mumbled an answer through the next mouthful.

"I figured it was safe to use the spinach since it wasn't quite a frozen brick yet."

"Mm-hmm." Suddenly he was starving, even after the last bite. While she went to put the shirt away, he got up to spoon out another helping. Apparently he'd worked up quite an appetite satisfying his sexual needs with the MacGyver of all things edible. The sound of his closing closet door was followed by rapid footsteps. "I'm sure you still have a couch," he assured when she appeared from the hallway. "In fact I think Kendall has come around full circle. She was really worried about what happened to you. Speaking of which, I'll need to go over what was said between you and Jonah's friend word-for-word." When he looked up from the casserole dish, Marcelina was headed toward the door in her dress and high-heeled sandals. "Where are you going?"

"I figured I'd walk. It's only a couple of miles."

Panic made him drop the spoon. "Dammit, not so fast." He followed, leaving his half-loaded plate on the counter.

"Don't worry," she said breezily, "it's a nice morning. I'll be fine."

Reaching her just in time, Walker grabbed hold of her hand before she could make contact with the front door handle. Ignoring the urge to pull her into his arms, he kept his voice low. "You weren't so eager to leave before I brought up the no sex thing."

Her composure slipped a little, revealing the vulnerability he'd sensed from the get-go. "Sorry." A wobbly smile. "I guess I'm just feeling a bit uncomfortable."

He frowned. "Uncomfortable about what?"

Marcelina removed her hand from his slackened hold, turned her attention toward the sheer curtains and their filtered view of his immaculate front lawn. "Talking about…well, my secret." Her slender throat moved with a swallow. "I've kept it locked inside for so long. And I still don't know how Jonah could have found out."

Sympathy welled in his chest. It was something he'd learned to check with ease, but that infamous Bishop resolve was repeatedly failing him where Marcelina was concerned. He channeled it now, taking her chin in his hand. When her gaze returned to his, he was all business. "I get that you aren't comfortable. Deal with it, because it's about to get a lot *more* uncomfortable." She nodded, her eyes clear with understanding. "We may need to put you in protective custody. You may lose contact with everyone you know. But you won't lose me, Marcelina." He gave her chin a little shake. "As your attorney, I'm going to fight for you. You just need to quit making it so damned hard."

When he thought she'd argue, Marcelina's gaze instead turned glassy. Her mouth quirked just before she darted up to deliver a quick peck on the lips.

Walker reared back, but not fast enough. The brief contact left his lips burning for more. "Ah-ah. None of that," he scolded.

Her smile widened. "Yes, counselor."

****

Later that morning, they pulled up to Kendall's apartment complex. Marcelina stared up at the second floor of her last safe place on earth. Or was it? Would there be any surprises waiting for her there, too? The second half of Jonah's message rolled through her head. *He'll be in touch...*

Walker also scoped out the second floor. "See any familiar cars in the parking lot?"

She scanned the colorful array of them to her right. "No."

"Good." He turned toward her. "Now, remember what we talked about."

Looking good enough to eat in his T-shirt and faded jeans, Marcelina had to refocus fast. *No touching, no touching.* "Yes. I won't mention anything to Kendall about what we did last night. As far as the other thing, I will sew up all my loose ends in preparation for doomsday."

Which it very well could be, though he refused to view it as such. He truly believed she still had a chance…as slim as it was.

"I'll be at the office today working on your defense so we can get this in motion." He threw her a grim smile. "Wish me luck."

"Good luck." It only seemed natural to lean over and give him a quick kiss on the lips. Realizing what she'd just done, Marcelina covered her mouth with a hand, her eyes wide with genuine shock. "Oh! Sorry!"

But she hadn't exactly acted alone. Having met her halfway, Walker bobbed his head with a "damn" and averted his gaze out the window while she exited the car. When he drove off, a smile curved her lips. All thoughts of doomsday dimmed against the sudden onslaught of a positive attitude. How could it not when the sun shined brighter? When the breeze felt cooler and the birds around her sounded sweeter than ever?

As her light step topped the second floor, Marcelina was somewhat surprised when she didn't find Kendall tapping her foot on the outside welcome mat. The door didn't open for her, either, meaning the woman hadn't been watching for her through the window. She raised her knuckles to give the door a soft tap before entry. Voices sounded from inside, instantly putting her on edge. Since one of the voices belonged to a man, her thoughts raced backward to the bookstore encounter with Jonah's "friend" and his message. So help her, if he was back to harass—

The door opened. "Thank God!" Kendall gushed,

throwing her arms around Marcelina's neck. "I was so worried about you."

"Who's here?" Marcelina asked with a cautious mien.

"Someone looking for you." Kendall pulled her inside. "He says you know each other through Walker."

A dark, dangerous gaze met hers from the direction of Kendall's recliner. Marcelina's feet froze, forcing Kendall to push her aside in order to close the door. Jonah would have been a blessing compared to the challenge she now faced in her friend's living room. "Mr. Rivera." Her throat closed with a nervous swallow.

Kendall's smile dissolved as she addressed the man rising from the chair. "Wait a minute. You said you were Juan from risk management."

"What are you doing here?" Marcelina demanded, unsuccessfully hiding her angst.

Armando spread his ring-studded hands in a gesture that lacked guilt. "I was curious. I wanted to see how you lived. Meet your lovely roommate," he said, though his eyes were all on Marcelina as they skimmed her length. "Isn't that the same dress you wore yesterday?"

"Um…" She looked down as if realizing it for the first time. "I suppose, yes."

A wooden smile. "What are you still doing in it?"

None of your damned business. Before she could verbalize the scathing reply, Kendall stepped in.

"She, uh…went for a walk this morning," Kendall said. "It was the closest thing within reach."

Marcelina sent her a look.

"You were worried over her whereabouts when she came home," Armando replied, his smile softening. "As if you hadn't seen her all night. Yet she's here and sporting a rather…*healthy*…glow."

Some would call it *after*glow, but Marcelina guessed he was just being couth about it. Overcome with a fierce need to protect, she stepped between Armando's dangerous vibes and a bumbling Kendall. "I'm sorry, but this really isn't a good time."

After a tense-filled moment, he nodded his assent. "I see that. Please accept my apology."

The man was such an imposing figure, sullying Kendall's cheerful, innocent dwelling with the sheer threat of his presence. As he passed her, Armando took Kendall's petite, alabaster hand in his large tanned one and raised it to his lips. "It was a pleasure, my dear. Perhaps we'll run into each other again one day."

All Kendall could produce was a dumb nod, her green eyes wide with curiosity. Marcelina made a mental note to never let the man near her again.

He stopped beside Marcelina next, even though she'd given him a wide path to the door. "May I speak with you outside?" he asked ever so politely.

Everything within her revolted against the idea, but if it would get him out of the apartment any faster… She turned to Kendall. "I'll be back in two minutes."

In other words, alert the police, the media, and the National Guard if she didn't return by then. Kendall's lips pursed with understanding.

When the door closed behind them, Armando touched her arm and asked her to walk. "Just to the stairwell. I don't like open spaces."

I'll bet you don't, Marcelina thought, noticing how he'd put her on the outside—to catch whatever flying bullets may come his way, no doubt. As soon as they reached the safety of the stairwell, he stopped, straightened his jacket, and looked around. "Thank you for indulging me, Miss Page."

Since a girl could never be too safe while in the company of a murdering drug pusher, Marcelina chose to linger in the open. A quick glance found his human bulldozer of a bodyguard hanging out in the breezeway close to the elevator.

"I couldn't leave without explaining why I came in the first place," Armando said.

Folding her arms, Marcelina scowled. Out of the direct sun, his image remained dark against the brilliant morning light shining in her eyes. "You have less than two minutes."

Annoyance tightened his tone. "I don't like the way we left things at the auction house yesterday."

"How *we* left things?" she challenged. "Or how *Walker* left things?"

The man pushed out a sound of ridicule. "Whatever he told you about me, I would like the chance to make my own impression."

"Does it really matter? Because I remember telling you I wasn't interested *before* Walker showed up."

"All I want is one dinner," he continued as if she hadn't spoken. "You'll see there is no reason to fear me."

"Frankly, Mr. Rivera," she returned without missing a beat, "you scare the *hell* out of me."

His head fell back with a laugh. "I love an honest woman."

At a loss, Marcelina threw her hands up.

"A public place, then." Armando gripped the handrail in a show of patience. "You can leave whenever you want, you have my word. I'll send a car for you at four."

The audacity of the man put her back up all over again. "I didn't agree to have dinner with you, and I am *most certainly* not getting in any car you send for me."

"Fine." His nod of assent came easily enough. "You pick the place and meet me there on your own." The shock must have shown in her eyes because he smiled. "Marcelina, I am not an inflexible man. All I ask is that you come alone."

"The answer is still no," she ground out.

Armando cocked his head in consideration then stabbed the air with a finger. "Let's make it *Le Marée*, then. Five o'clock. Oh, and wear something…" His gaze made another pass over her dress. "Different."

Hands on hips, Marcelina watched him begin his descent down the stairs. "You don't get turned down much, do you?"

He threw her a charming smile over his shoulder. "No, Miss Page. I don't."

"Excuse me," a deep voice rumbled as the human bulldozer passed by without even a command to follow.

"I won't be there!" she yelled after him, the words echoing off the stucco walls. "I have other plans!"

"You'll want to change them," came his echoing response, calm as a stagnant pond.

"And if I don't?"

"I'll simply have to find another dinner companion. Your lovely roommate, perhaps…"

The veiled threat hung out there like the reverb of an ominous gong. Marcelina went to the balcony and watched in utter bemusement as an olive-green Humvee slowed over the thin carpet of pine needles blanketing the pavement below. A rear door popped open from the inside and Armando got in, followed closely by his bodyguard. The thing had barely come to a stop before it was banking left and out of the parking lot.

"Un. Fucking. Believable." What the hell was she going to do now? The first thing that came to mind was to call Walker. The second was to pack Kendall up and send her to Maryland for a nice long visit with her folks. Marcelina needed no verbal clues to understand what Armando's intentions were by showing up here and she'd be damned if she'd let Kendall get caught in the crossfire.

With fear and anger as her driving force, she stormed into the apartment and headed straight for the kitchen. "What happened to the no-drug-dealers rule?" she grumbled to a stunned Kendall on the way.

"What did he say?" Kendall asked, replacing the chain and turning locks.

Marcelina produced a bottle of tequila from beneath the sink. "Not much. It's what he *implied* that worries me." She poured a shot into a glass and downed it without so much as a wince. The liquid burned a path straight down to the large hole in her stomach.

"Wow." Kendall leaned against the bar, glancing from the bottle to the empty glass in her hand. "You're really scared."

Marcelina poured another round. "You should be, too." After another dose of liquid courage, she considered her friend beneath thick lashes. "How do you feel about a trip to Maryland?"

****

It was a Sunday morning, yet Walker sat in his office ignoring the fact he'd rather be somewhere else for a change. *Doing* something else, like maybe enjoying the beach or giving the gulf waters another try. Wrestling with this quandary always took his thoughts to a certain Latina and her continuous string of surprises.

Her magical lightshow of green algae; her decision to open up to him; her exquisite face; the sensuous mouth that produced the most delicious sounds while in the throes of passion...

Walker squeezed his eyes shut, cleared his head. Her growing case file came back into focus. With a curse, he reached over and woke his laptop up again.

It was quiet, that was his problem. No chaos, no people, no phones or overzealous paralegal to answer them. It wasn't unusual for him to spend his weekend like this, but something told him Ms. Page had shifted his focus for a lot longer than one night.

No, it wasn't allowed. He was a professional who'd sworn to give a client the best representation possible. And now that Marcelina had fessed up about her past, he had his work cut out for him.

Having finally found his motivation, Walker buried himself in his laptop. By the time the coffee pot went dry, he'd already tweaked his list of trial questions for Kendall now that she would be testifying on Marcelina's behalf, and he'd also developed a plan of action for Marcelina's impending murder trial. Hopefully there wouldn't be one if his investigation turned up anything new. The car Puccini had driven was old and untrack-able, proving the seasoned gangster knew how to steer clear of Big Brother. No one knew where he'd been or could trace his whereabouts for the eight days he'd been missing before his death. The leads were few and had dried up quickly. But Walker now knew more than the police did, which was a good advantage to have but not for long. Sitting on information like that could get him into some serious trouble.

His cellphone buzzed yet again. This time Marcelina's face lit up the screen. Instead of letting it go to voicemail like usual, he answered with an unsuccessful attempt to hide his smile. "Bishop."

Her voice came through the speaker. "It's me. I figured you'd want to know I'm meeting Armando Rivera for dinner tonight."

Smile officially killed, Walker sat up in his chair. "Come again?"

"He was inside Kendall's apartment this morning when I got there. I think it was meant as some sort of threat."

Violent rage sliced through his gut. Hands fisting on the surface of his desk, he slowly rose to his feet. "This guy doesn't do 'sort of,' Marcelina. You aren't meeting him tonight or ever."

"It'll be at a public place. He said I could leave whenever I want."

And she actually believed that? "He's harassing you, dammit. Do *not* go."

A deep sigh. "I just need to get it over with. Humor him through this dinner so I can hear what he has to say and then get my own point across."

Since his commands only seemed to work during sex, Walker went for an air of calm, hovering over his phone with a careful check on his temper. "If he wants you bad enough, you won't be leaving."

"He won't want me when I'm through with him."

Didn't she know a thing about men? "You'll just present more of a challenge."

"I'll let you know how it goes."

"Marcelina, don't you—"

But the line was already dead. She'd hung up on him. Of all the…

Walker dialed her back. No answer. With a muffled curse, he dialed Kendall's number. When she answered, he told her to put Marcelina on the phone.

"She left a half hour ago," Kendall informed him through a mouthful of food.

"Do you know where she went?" Because, dammit all to hell, he was going after her again.

"No, she wouldn't say. I think she's meeting with that cartel guy tonight, though. He was here earlier."

Hot rage blanketed his vision, turning the door of his private office into a bubbling shade of red. "Yes, I heard," he ground out. "I'm going to have to start walking her to your door every time I drop her off." Or chain her to his bed, whichever came first.

In the background, a refrigerator door opened and closed. "I'm just as nervous as you are, Mr. Bishop." Paper ripped. "This is my third freaking cream-cicle. I'm really sorry, but Mr. Rivera gave me a different name and said he knew Marcelina through you."

Which was the sick truth. Now more than ever, Walker regretted his rare decision to involve himself in the personal life of a client. If he hadn't taken Marcelina to Tony's for the prospect of a job, there would have been no run-in with Rivera.

When he ended the call, it was with nothing useful except for Kendall's promise to call him when Marcelina got back. So, with briefcase in hand, he stormed out of his office and took a long drive straight to the precinct.

****

With the hot afternoon sun beating down his back, Walker pushed through the glass doors and into the lobby, his temper only slightly cooled from the twenty minutes it had taken to get there. The clock above the front desk said 12:55 PM, which meant there was plenty of time to find Marcelina and have her followed.

He approached two uniformed officers, one sitting behind the desk, the other hovering over it with a steaming paper cup in one hand. Walker jerked his head toward Captain Ross's closed office door. "Is he in?"

"Hello to you, too, Bishop," said the large one who sipped coffee, his thick neck boasting many trips to the donut shop.

Reining in his temper, Walker took a breath and acknowledged the officers he only knew on a professional level. "Officer Tillman. Sanchez." He'd managed it with a modicum of civility. "As much as I'd like to shoot the breeze, I'm in somewhat of a hurry. Is Captain Ross in?"

"It's Sunday," the shorter Hispanic cop answered without looking up from his newspaper.

So? Crime happened on Sundays, too. Deeming the officers useless, Walker gave them his back as he dug out his phone and made a call. After several rings, the captain's impatient greeting came over the line. "I got burgers on the grill and a beer in my hand, Walker."

"We need a detail on Marcelina Page if we can find her."

"Why?"

"She's meeting with Armando Rivera tonight." In the background, someone screamed *cannonball,* then a big splash was heard. Childish screams ensued and Leonard yelled for someone to get the dog out of the pool—not exactly the reaction Walker was looking for. "Leonard?"

"If she wants to meet with him," the man finally said, "there isn't much we can do about it."

Though he wouldn't mention the deal on an unsecured line, the hope in Leonard's voice was poorly masked. Hand on hip, Walker stopped pacing and leaned in. "This is *Rivera* we're talking about. He's a threat to her."

There was a tense silence, then a rush of a frustrated breath. "From my understanding, he's pretty good to the ladies."

Was he serious? "Damn it, Leonard, did it cross your mind he might be using her to get to me? I've already lost one client to him." A quick look over his shoulder showed he had the two officers' undivided attention now.

"Calm down, man, I was half-kidding," came the captain's reply. "I'll make a call. See what I can wrangle up."

"Thank you. I'll be at the precinct in case there's any news." A headache was forming. Walker disconnected the call, pinching the bridge of his nose.

Tillman spoke up from behind. "So Armando Rivera has his sights set on Miss Page?"

He gave a grim nod.

"You mean that knockout brunette that turns every uniform here into a three-legged schoolboy every time she's brought in?"

Walker turned and glared.

The two cops exchanged a look. "Sure. It's all about you."

Chapter 9

Le Marée. It was a quaint French restaurant situated on the waterfront with a clear view of Naples Bay's pelican-studded waters. Outside the floor-to-ceiling windows, folks strolled the boardwalk, some having left their boats in the marina and some just enjoying the mild day on foot. Didn't matter, they were all loaded. *That* Marcelina could tell from their manner and dress alone.

As for her, a tablecloth would be a better choice of fashion in lieu of her present attire. No shower. No makeup. Hair in a low, unflattering ponytail, and the evidence of a brisk Florida walk staining the upper portion of her paint-spattered T-shirt. She followed her tuxedo-wearing host through the restaurant, feeling every bit as out of place as she looked. Though she would love to tell Captain Ross to shove his deal up his ass, she also figured it was best to remember that she was now—what did he call it? Anti-police? Rivera would also think she was protecting the man who got her in trouble. The ruse went against everything she felt toward Jonah, but she didn't want to tip Rivera off that the cops were listening, either. When they arrived at a corner table, two familiar faces turned upward to greet her. Armando Rivera wasn't alone.

Elvis…

The sight of Graham Metcalf up close and in bad company caused her already heightened nervous system to implode. What the hell was he doing there? And why did he look angry?

Armando, who also sported a tux, simply watched her with a suppressed smile, as if his present company didn't exist. Yes, he was probably more amused by her very presence than he was by her appearance.

"You can lose the smirk," she said, gathering her composure as she lowered herself into the unoccupied side of the circular booth.

"There is no smirk." His gaze travelled downward, taking in the awful gray shirt. "I'm just glad you came."

She also looked down at her clothes and shrugged. "You said to wear something different."

The corner of his mouth turned further upward. "You make that look like an exquisite work of art." He leaned toward Graham. "Don't you agree?"

The man scanned the room, clearly annoyed by her untimely presence. "Yes, exquisite."

"Though I much prefer you in that peach dress you wore when I first saw you." Armando's eyes were flashing. "The color set off your skin like a tropical sunrise."

Marcelina made a mental note to limit her usage of peach, particularly in the presence of Armando Rivera. Ignoring the sultry vibes coming off the drug lord beside her, she cocked her head and addressed Graham. "I remember you from Tony's auction house. Did I interrupt anything important?"

"No."

"Yes—"

Having answered in unison, Graham shot Rivera a seething glance. Whatever signals passed between them were wrought with tension. Frustration. Danger. Leaving no doubt in Marcelina's mind that Kendall's boss was deeply involved in some dirty business.

"It can wait," Metcalf growled. "But not for long."

There was a threat in those words, an understanding that turned Armando's dark eyes into three shades of cold. But Metcalf didn't wait for a response, instead sliding out of the booth and storming through the maze of tables, into the marble-studded foyer, and out the double doors. Before Marcelina could process the dramatics of his exit, Armando flicked a finger. The waiter appeared with a crystal decanter of water and a basket of rolls. "We'll order now. Do you mind?" he asked her with a raised brow.

With a sigh of pleasure, she relieved the waiter of his decanter and loudly guzzled straight from it. When she came up for air, the neck of her shirt was wetter than before, having collected the ice-cold rivulets streaming down from her mouth. "You don't have to order for me." She sat back, keeping the decanter close to her chest. "Just get me the most expensive thing on the menu."

The poor waiter glanced at Armando who gave him an amused go-ahead.

Marcelina challenged his lack of concern with a cocked brow. "And put that in a to-go box."

As the amusement faded from Armando's countenance, a little bolt of fear raced down Marcelina's spine. "I don't think they have to-go boxes here," he said.

With nerves fully in check, she shrugged. "To-go box, foil swan, it's all the same to me as long as I get to leave when it comes."

If her attitude annoyed him, he showed no sign of it as he gave the waiter their order in what sounded like perfect French. When they were alone again, he sat back and regarded her with that unsettling smile. "It's clear your intention is to put me off."

A sardonic laugh followed another loud pull from the decanter. "Nothing else has worked so far."

The man folded his hands on the table, holding her gaze in a way that dared her to break it. "What if I told you my motives aren't what you think?"

"I'd say don't waste our time trying to convince me." She looked away to prove she could. "Men like you have no boundaries. You see something pretty and want a piece of it no matter what kind of carnage you leave behind."

"Men like me? What exactly is it you think I am?"

The laughter in his voice brought her attention back around. She leaned in close, lowered her tone. "We both know what you are. But I'll refrain from going into detail because I don't want to end up floating face down in Clam Pass."

He leaned forward also, clearly undaunted by her offhand accusation. "I see you *have* been getting an earful. I'm curious to know how you and Walker Bishop spend your time when you aren't talking about me."

She returned the decanter to the tabletop with a *thunk*. "What exactly are you implying?"

A humorless smile. "There are rules against lawyers fucking their clients. It would be a shame for his license to be suspended because of you."

Marcelina felt her blood congeal, no doubt the way he intended. With a poker face worthy of an Oscar, she replied, "Our relationship is a professional one. That's all."

He gave her a sideways look that called her a liar. "So he isn't the one you kissed goodbye when he dropped you off at Kendall's apartment this morning? Because my driver informed me otherwise."

Her lip curled, giving away her disgust. "Making threats already. And my seat isn't even warm yet."

Eyes, dark as Satan's heart, shifted with his mood. "No threats. But you're right, we've strayed off topic." He took a roll from the basket and broke it apart. "Despite what you've heard, I assure you all my business ventures are legal. In fact, the reason I wanted this meeting was to offer you a job."

Marcelina's crushed bravado slipped even more as she watched him butter the roll with a knife of sterling silver. "A job?"

"Yes." He held the crusty bread out to her. "Have you ever heard of collateral recovery?"

She took his offering and placed it on the little plate before her with no intention of eating it. "You mean what repo agents do," Marcelina said, crossing her arms in an attempt to hide her reaction to the sudden chill in the air.

"Yes. I loan money to a lot of people, which means I have a lot of debtors. When those debtors stop paying, my…*repo agents*…go out and recover those assets for me." She watched the second roll he buttered go on his own little plate, also to be left untouched. "It can be a difficult business," he continued. "The debtors don't always want to cooperate which can lead to a messy confrontation. So, my men prefer to use diversionary tactics. Avoid conflict altogether."

The pieces were starting to fall into place. Marcelina narrowed her gaze. "And that's where I would come in."

His smooth palms flattened on the tablecloth. "You turn heads, Marcelina. An undeniable fact."

Okay, so the man wanted to hire her, much for the

same reasons Tony did. Not that it mattered, but her curiosity was thoroughly piqued. "Wouldn't that be kind of dangerous?" she asked him. "I mean, what if the debtor caught on and got pissed? I'd be the one within reach."

Light moved across the slicked-back waves atop his head as he nodded. "I won't lie to you. There is some small risk involved, but there would always be someone close by in case you need them."

She scooted her chair back. "Thank you for the offer, but—"

His hand clapped over hers before it could leave the table. "Wait until I'm finished, please." When she glared at him, he cocked his head. "We haven't discussed the pay."

Marcelina reclaimed her hand. "I don't care how much it pays."

"There would be a trial period, of course," he continued as if she hadn't just flat out turned him down. "But this is what I'm offering for each job successfully completed." He produced a folded slip of paper from his inside pocket and slid it across the table.

She nudged it open for a better look. Her brows went up. "That's quite generous."

"I want you, Marcelina."

Her gaze met his. Their surroundings faded, along with the clink of silver on fine China as the weight of his words blocked everything else out. "As part of your repo team, you mean."

The intensity in those dark eyes meant something entirely different. "Of course."

As they stared at each other, their dinner came. The waiter set a matte-black box with fancy gold lettering before her, then a silver-rimmed plate of something small and decorative in front of Armando.

"And for the beautiful mademoiselle." When the waiter presented her with a rose, Marcelina took it without thought. It was in full bloom, its stem short and free of thorns. And it was the color peach.

"For your hair," Armando said with a smile.

She dropped it beside her to-go box as if it burned her fingers, drawing a chuckle from the man across from her. Hands in her lap, Marcelina waited while the waiter filled two wine glasses. The ritual of five-star service took longer than her patience could afford, but she waited anyway, choosing to make her last move without an audience lest she throw up. When they were alone once again, she pushed the folded paper back toward her dinner companion, swallowing the very real pain of turning down such a large sum of money. "It's tempting. But I can't." She picked up her black box and stood, leaving the rose on the table as a clear message that he could keep his flattery, his job offer, and his obvious intent to get into her pants.

"You mean you won't," he said, also rising to his feet.

Her brows furrowed as she gazed down at the elegant box in her hands. "A wise man once told me to never get sucked into the kind of life you lead. The romance of it is a lie that can only end in horrible tragedy."

When she braved a look, Armando's eyes were narrowed with suspicion. "Not that I'm admitting to anything," he said, "but who exactly was this wise man?"

The simple act of repeating Nari Puccini's words out loud was enough to square her shoulders. Marcelina—

keenly aware that many sets of eyes were scrutinizing her from all over the room—smirked. "No one you need to worry about anymore. Thanks for the meal." She aborted her first attempt to leave with a raised finger. "Oh, and I hope this wraps up any lingering confusion about my feelings toward you. Right?"

A sick sort of amusement seeped into his stony countenance. "As long as you know the offer won't last forever."

"I won't change my mind," she countered through gritted teeth. Ponytail swinging, she turned and marched through the dining room.

"I'll never be far if you do."

Asshole couldn't even give her the last word. Would she always detect a threat in everything he said? Would he forever be lingering close to her? Popping up at Kendall's apartment? Spying on her and Walker?

Maybe dinner wasn't such a good idea, after all.

As soon as she was outside and past the first row of cars, a voice stopped her in her tracks. "I'd lose the food if I were you."

She whirled around, almost dropping her to-go box. There stood Graham Metcalf, a picture of wealth himself as he leaned against a late model Maserati in his tailored slacks and carefully groomed hair. "Excuse me?" she asked.

No emotion touched his countenance. "It isn't worth it. As soon as you take the first bite, he'll own you. Think about that."

She took a tentative step closer. "Does he own you, Mr. Metcalf?"

His face registered a flash of surprise over the use of his name and Marcelina regretted her words. But her curiosity had reached its limit of unanswered questions.

Eyes narrowed, he asked, "Do we know each other?"

The thumping in her chest resumed and she shook her head. "I remember your name from the auction."

The logic of her answer seemed to appease him. He drew a set of keys from his pocket. Smiled bitterly. "Not for long."

But then a movement caught his attention and his smile faded. She followed his gaze and saw Rivera's bodyguard settle against a pillar at the restaurant's entrance. Watching them. It wasn't until Metcalf got into his car and drove away that Marcelina realized his last words were the answer to her question.

So, she was right. Graham Metcalf was not only doing business with a powerful drug lord, he was nervous about it. It smacked of a guilty conscience, and Marcelina had to wonder if he was putting his family in danger.

After one last look at the muscle-bound man loitering against the pillar with open interest, Marcelina turned her back to him and began her long journey home.

Two miles away, she still had three more to walk when the hairs on her arms tingled. Someone was following her. She quickened her pace, scanned the desolate stretch of road that would take her into the busy part of town, half expecting to see an olive-green Humvee on her tail.

What she did see was a police car, keeping pace with her steps. She turned back around, ignoring the sinking feeling that they were there because of her so-called dinner with Rivera.

The bop of a siren reclaimed her attention. With a

heavy breath, she stopped. Waited. The car pulled up beside her and a window rolled down. "Marcelina Page?"

Refusing to look, Marcelina stared straight ahead, her skin burning yet again… "Yes."

A uniformed officer stepped out and approached. "We've been instructed to bring you in."

Not that she needed to ask, but she did it anyway. "Why?"

"An APB was put out on you."

An APB? Seriously? Was this yet another stunt by Captain Ross to taint her image for Rivera's sake, or did Walker Bishop have something to do with it? The fact the two addressed each other by their first names—being such good buddies and all—meant it could have gone either way. Regardless, she cooperated without a single argument.

The cop opened the rear passenger door and waved her in. When she lowered herself to the back seat, he instructed her to watch her head, then pointed to the box in her hands.

"*Le Marée*. Nice."

****

Captain Ross blew out a breath and hung up his phone. "She went to dinner with the guy."

Walker sat across from him as the two waited for Marcelina to be brought in. "At least that's *all* she did," he answered with an air of detachment. On the inside, however, there were violent things going on that were wreaking havoc on his nerves. He didn't like it, this attachment he'd formed with his client. Not that he'd had much control over it.

"Are you sleeping with her?"

The captain's question prodded Walker out of his stupor. Any trace of emotion he may have worn was wiped clean with a deadpan stare. "You know me, Leonard. Why would you even ask that?"

Intuitive eyes narrowed against dark skin. "Your lack of a direct answer gives me pause."

Walker shifted in his chair. So much for trust. "Can we stay focused, please? My client is being harassed by a very dangerous man. The least you can do is put twenty-four-hour protection on her."

"We aren't babysitters, Walker." Leonard rolled backward and separated the blinds for a peek into the parking lot. "Hell, you're lucky you got the APB."

True enough. Fortunately, Leonard had consumed enough beer to make him pliable. Walker took in the man's plaid linen shorts and sauce-stained shirt with no small guilt. They were happy clothes that reeked of charcoal smoke and good times. "Guess you don't normally come in on Sundays."

The blinds snapped back to their original order. "Hence the intense look of annoyance on my face."

A rush of noise entered the office as the door opened behind him. They both stood, Walker turning to find Marcelina flanked by two uniformed officers. She looked hot, windblown, and tired, her long ponytail littered with fly-aways—an achingly beautiful mess with sweat-stained clothes, a defiant tilt to her chin, and a black cardboard box in her clutches.

When the officers backed out, closing the door behind them, it took all Walker had not to shake the hell out of her.

Leonard circled around his desk. "Ms. Page. Sorry about the APB but your lawyer was worried."

She shifted her load to accept his handshake. "He's afraid I'm going to take the deal." Her harried gaze darted to Walker's. "Which I'm not, by the way."

"Duly noted." Leonard pointed to the box. "*Le Marée*. Nice."

She shrugged. "So I hear."

"My wife's been begging me to take her there. What did you order?"

While Walker observed from his highly ignored stance on the sidelines, Marcelina's lips quirked with a smile. "I have no idea."

Leonard laughed. "And that's exactly why we haven't gone." He indicated her grungy attire. "I see you at least dressed for the occasion."

Visibly relaxed now, she laughed with him. "Look who's talking, Captain."

Why was everyone taking this so goddamned lightly? Annoyed, Walker stepped in, cutting off all attempts at lighthearted banter. There was no room for the good cop routine here, not with Armando Rivera as a key player. "I'll take it from here, Captain Ross, thank you."

Leonard nodded, somber now as he moved to the door. "You have ten minutes. Then I'm reclaiming my office *and* my precinct."

As soon as they were alone, Walker shoved hands in pockets and for the first time couldn't find the words. He knew what needed to be done, what he'd normally do with any nightmare client who lacked the ability to take advice from anyone. After so many warnings, those clients usually found themselves dumped on the public defender's doorstep since Walker had little time or use for them. This one, however, had him at a loss.

Marcelina peeked over at him then cleared her throat. "You kicked the captain out of his office?"

"It's private. No cameras or microphones."

"Oh." Shoulders back, she set her box of food down on the corner of the desk. "I guess I really am going to get it, then."

"What the hell were you thinking?" he asked softly.

Marcelina shrugged. "It wasn't so bad. I got a nice meal out of it."

"Come here." In no mood for lame jokes and bravado, he opened a file. Her look of apprehension deepened. "This is what happened to the last person who challenged Armando Rivera," he pointed out.

Neck bent for a better look at the gory photos, Marcelina's healthy pallor instantly paled. "Oh my God."

"Do you recognize him?"

With a hand over her mouth, she shook her head.

"Neither could anyone else. I had to identify him by his tattoos."

This time when she met his gaze, all traces of defiance were gone, leaving the raw shock he hoped would settle in permanently. "*This* is the client?" she whispered.

Walker spread out the photos, covering the captain's desk with a full-color display of violent endings. "And here are others who had a known association with Rivera. These are just the ones who've been discovered."

"I get it." It came out a choked gargle as she backed away.

"I don't want your photo in this pile, too, Marcelina." He caught her arm before she could back out of reach. He held her there, under the intensity of his gaze. "Promise me you'll avoid him at all costs from now on."

Her gaze travelled to the black box with gold lettering. "I left him at that restaurant without any doubts—"

"It doesn't matter." He gave her arm a little shake. "Promise me."

After a heavy silence, she finally nodded. "Okay, Walker."

"This means if he contacts you again, don't go all rogue. Call me or the police and we'll take care of it." Turning her to face him, he took her by the shoulders, stopping himself short of pulling her into his arms. "You were lucky this time. But remember you are *never* in control with this man."

"You're right. I'm sorry, it won't happen again."

It was the humble tone that got him. His gaze softened. "I've never wanted to turn someone over my knee before."

A smile teased the corner of her mouth. "That could get interesting."

Yes. Yes, it could. Marcelina made everything interesting. Hell, she even wore the coppery tones of sweat and heat as if it were a high-end fragrance. Walker took a deep, steadying breath and shook his head to clear it, but not before a reaction stirred down below. For once, he didn't try to hide the growing tension in his pants. "Tell me what happened with Rivera."

Her answering smile was slow and catlike. "Time for another cold shower, counselor?"

"Change of subject, Marcelina."

The desperation in his words melted the smile. She moved away, her expression going completely somber.

"His driver saw you drop me off this morning." At his look, she nodded. "And the kiss. He said they can suspend your license if we're found out."

Not likely, though it had been known to happen. "Your case would suffer worse than I would," he replied.

"How is that?"

"First of all, they'd assign you new representation. Then it could be argued that any secrets revealed to me outside our legal relationship may not be protected under attorney-client privilege."

"Like what I told you at the beach." It came out a whispered revelation. "I take it that would be considered outside our legal relationship?"

His gaze swept the length of her body, remembering how those voluptuous curves had fit so perfectly against him. "I'd say."

This was getting out of hand. Even surrounded by gory crime-scene photos and an uncertain future, they couldn't keep the sexual tension at bay. "What else happened?" he asked, clearing his throat.

As they moved further away from each other, Marcelina flattened her hands against her hair and paced. "He said everything you told me about him were lies, that he's a legitimate businessman. And then he offered me a job."

When Walker processed that last bit of information, his back instantly went up. "What kind of job?"

"I think he called it collateral recovery. I'd show a little leg and divert attention away from his repo agents while they stole stuff."

They shared a brief smile. "At least you kept things in perspective."

"Despite what you may think," she returned with

grim humor, "I do learn from my mistakes. No more being duped."

"Right." Again, Walker found himself stressing over her uncanny ability to attract the attention of dangerous men. "And I assume you turned down the job."

She gave a sigh of regret. "Yes, along with *a lot* of money. And since he got his one dinner and my final answer, he shouldn't bother me again." A hint of darkness crept into her eyes. "But I think he'll stay close for a while. Silent yet watchful. I'm still not sure who he's more interested in, you or me. But now he also has Kendall on his radar, and that worries me more than anything."

Walker leaned against the desk and crossed his arms. "I need for you to repeat those exact words to Captain Ross. Tell him everything that happened at Kendall's this morning and at the restaurant. We'll convince him to assign a squad car to her building. Make sure help is always close."

Chapter 10

When they entered Kendall's parking lot, Marcelina unbuckled and prepared for a swift exit. The threat of Jonah reappearing dimmed in comparison with the prospect of Rivera lurking in the shadows. No way would she give the man more ammo to use against her attorney. But instead of slowing at the entrance to the stairwell, Walker wheeled his car into an empty space and killed the engine. "What are you doing?" she asked.

"Parking."

"Are you sure that's a good idea with our new audience?" Marcelina looked straight ahead at the cop car going dark at the edge of the parking lot.

Walker palmed his keys and opened the driver's side door. The overhead light illuminated the determined set of his mouth. "I'm not taking any more chances. If someone's up there, I'd rather be with you just in case."

Oh. Right. Kendall's apartment *had* been on Rivera's radar lately.

They stepped out into the night, bathed not only in cloying, balmy air, but also the melodious song of tree frogs. They were everywhere, surrounding them with a guttural symphony one might appreciate under better circumstances.

By the time they reached the second-floor landing, Kendall was hanging outside her door. "You really need to start answering your phone."

Marcelina handed her the to-go box on the way inside and fished her cellphone out of her pocket. "Sorry, I forgot I turned it off."

"Ooh, *Le Marée*. Nice!"

Rolling her eyes, Marcelina turned on the phone and was immediately assaulted with a litany of texts.

Walker—Call me back!—

Kendall—Call me. Your lawyer is pissed—

Walker—Tell me where you are and I'll come get you—

Kendall—Worried. Let me know if u r dead—

Kendall—R u dead?—

Kendall—Call me!!—

In the kitchen, Kendall opened the black box and peeked inside. Curiosity finally won out and Marcelina peered over her shoulder. "What is it?"

"It looks like a frittata of some kind." Kendall nudged it with a pinky finger. "I think that's lobster under all the caviar. You didn't eat any of it?"

"I was making a statement." Marcelina's statement was now a drooping landslide of black slimy eggs. "I hope it cost him plenty."

A blonde eyebrow arched as Kendall tasted the stuff. "I'm sure it did. That's a lot of caviar."

Walker appeared on the other side of the bar, throwing the meal a look of utter distaste. "I'm heading back to the office. Remember, there's a squad car out front if you need immediate help."

"Squad car?" Kendall dropped the lid of the box. "You mean with police officers in it?"

When Walker and Marcelina reached the door, he faced her, his blue eyes going all soft and serious. "Call them first, me second. Okay?"

She could tell he wanted to kiss her goodbye. It was an irresistible pull she felt just as strongly. "Are you sure you don't want to stay for fish eggs?" she asked, smiling.

His brow flattened with a *no thanks*. "I'll grab something on the way."

But he made no further move to leave. Marcelina reached up, smoothed a hand over the front of his T-shirt, reveling in their close proximity for as long as she could. When she spoke, her words held a tender ring to them. "Always working," she murmured.

"I didn't get much done today," he murmured back. "Or yesterday, for that matter."

"I suppose that's my fault."

Walker's warm chest rose and fell beneath her hand. "I really…*really* need to go." He pulled the door open, stepped through it and turned his back to her. "Lock it behind me."

By the time all the locks were returned to their Fort Knox position, Kendall was at the window, peeking through the curtains. "I take it those cops aren't here to barge in and put us in handcuffs this time."

Marcelina joined her, peering out into the lamp-lit parking lot. Only the back half of the lot could be seen beyond the railing. The lone squad car sat dark along the outer perimeter lending a sense of security that wasn't there before. "They're here to help us enforce that no-drug-dealer rule," she replied with a sigh. "Who knows, maybe they'll even catch Jonah."

Kendall also sighed, dropping the curtains with a pout before moving back to the kitchen. "They still make me nervous." She opened the silverware drawer with a clank. "So, this is pretty serious, huh? You really think Mr. Rivera will try something?"

"Walker thinks so, and I didn't exactly leave the restaurant with a good feeling." Wondering how much she should divulge about her encounter with Graham, Marcelina reached over the bar, retrieved a clean glass from the drain board, and filled it from the tap. "Remember when I told you I saw your boss at one of the auctions?"

"Yeah."

Kendall's attempt at a casual answer was contradicted by a sly peek in her direction. Marcelina noticed and was instantly sorry she'd brought it up. But Graham Metcalf was the one who'd approached her, not the other way around. "He was at *Le Marée* this evening. With Armando Rivera."

That earned her the full, wide-eyed look of disbelief. "Are you sure?"

She nodded, knowing her misgivings were showing but unable to hide them. "Same table and everything. Kendall…he didn't look happy."

The woman blinked, stared straight ahead as her wheels turned. "Maybe he just had a problem with one of the cars he bought."

But Marcelina knew better. Graham's warning was wrought with too much tension for his relationship with Rivera to begin and end with a bad sale. There was something going on with all those repos he bought, especially the ones "lined with gold." However, since she was unwilling to drag Kendall down with her suspicions, she accepted the suggestion with a nod. "Probably."

Grateful for the out, she happily dropped the subject. She couldn't—*wouldn't*—get involved in someone else's problems, especially someone she didn't know.

Kendall, on the other hand… "I really wish you would go stay with your parents for a while," Marcelina said absently, her mind rolling through all the worst-case scenarios as she brought her glass to her lips.

Kendall poked at the food. "If Mr. Rivera wants to find me, that'll be the first place he looks. Don't you watch TV?" Her initial bite produced a pained grimace.

Marcelina lowered the glass. "You aren't really going to eat that, are you?"

"A free meal from *Le Marée?*" Kendall glanced up before the second bite went in. "If it kills me."

****

Walker stepped out of his cold shower having somewhat rid himself of the discomfort that had been plaguing him since leaving Marcelina. It was getting worse, this need for her, to the point where he'd do anything to find her loitering in his bedroom again. This time he wouldn't force her out. This time he would lose the towel, undress her slowly, and drive into her with the same desperation as the night before. The woman was like a drug, an addiction that only became more powerful with each hit.

And with her connection to Puccini about to come out, he was committed to her case for possibly years. But he just couldn't trust her defense to anyone else. Somewhere along the way she'd become so much more than just another client. How in the hell had he let that happen?

By the time he donned a pair of boxers, the alarm clock said 12:45 AM. He'd worked like a fiend just to keep his active thoughts from drifting. A good night's sleep, that's what he needed. Tomorrow would be the start of another crazy week with no time for play. No time for memories. No time for stubborn women with too much time on their hands.

Moments after he turned out the light, his cellphone rang, vibrating on the nightstand and bringing him out of what could have been the start of something wonderful and recuperative. He picked it up, checked the screen. It was an unfamiliar number. The third ring. Fourth.

With a curse, he answered. "Bishop."

"You really should keep a closer eye on your clients," came a memorable voice over the line.

Every hair on Walker's arms came to attention. "Rivera." It wasn't a question, more of a verbal shit-yourself kind of observation. "To what do I owe this pleasure at one in the damn morning?" And how in hell did he get his number?

"The pleasure is all mine. Or will be, once I get Marcelina in my bed."

As his suspicions were confirmed in the most in-your-face way possible, Walker sat up on the edge of the bed, his blood charged and ready. "She knows better than to tangle with a psychopath like you."

"Psychopath?" came the reply. "I'm just a guy who appreciates loyalty from my people. You went after my nephew. My *family.* Granted, Miguel was a weak, cock-sucking fool, and I didn't exactly shed tears over his loss. But I must, at the very least, return the favor."

Walker was used to the posturing. Had heard it before and never so much as twitched in response, but hell if he wasn't twitching now. "Can't we just let bygones be bygones?" he said in a bored tone.

"That's where you should have left things." Rivera's tone was equally devoid of emotion. "Don't get me wrong, I understand your frustration. It must have been hard watching me walk time and again after all your efforts to put me away."

"You don't need to take it so personally."

He chuckled. "Believe it or not, I always admired your persistence. Until recently, that is." A deep, exaggerated yawn was heard. "As much as I'd like to keep the banter going, I must get some rest now. Try and do the same, Bishop. You'll need it more than I will."

The line went dead. Walker stared at the blackened screen of his phone, wanting more than anything to launch it straight at the wall. Since there was no chance in hell of him getting any sleep now, he got up, went into the kitchen, and attacked his long-ignored supply of single-malt whiskey.

****

The alarm blared at five-thirty. Having caught forty-five minutes of restless sleep, Walker rolled out of bed with no chance of producing a clear thought except for those that derived from Rivera's phone call. Having somehow changed into a crisp suit and tie, he entered his garage with briefcase in hand. His cellphone rang. It was a scramble to unload everything into his car in order to answer it in time, just in case…

But it was only Captain Ross. "Better get to the precinct quick," he said. "We're bringing in Ms. Page for questioning."

Dread exploded in his gut. "What for?"

"I have another homicide she may have information about."

Another line beeped in. Walker checked the screen. "I'll be there in twenty." He switched over without saying good-bye. "Marcelina?"

"The police are in Kendall's living room," she said

with a suspicious wobble to her voice. "They want to bring me in for questioning."

Wide-awake now, Walker climbed into the driver's seat with a sudden need to mash the gas. "I know. Don't let them interrogate you without me. I'll meet you at the precinct."

"They won't tell me why."

The engine roared to life as the garage door slowly lifted. "Try not to worry," Walker soothed, wishing now more than ever he didn't have to leave her every night. "You did good by calling me."

When Walker entered the police station's glass doors, Captain Ross was there to meet him. "She isn't here yet," the man said with a hand raised.

He allowed himself to be redirected toward the private offices that were fronted with glass. "Who died, Leonard?"

"See that woman in Kyle's office?"

When he looked, he saw a thin, pretty blonde in her early thirties, sitting across from the detective, answering questions with the look of a terrified woman. "Yes."

"Her name is Audrey Metcalf. She's being informed that her husband's car was just found burning at an abandoned hotel in the Everglades. There was a body inside it."

Walker could feel the woman's fear from there. "His?"

"Yet to be determined."

He tore his gaze away from what would likely unfold as the worst day of Mrs. Metcalf's life. "What does this have to do with Marcelina?"

Hands on hips, Leonard's service weapon jutted out from his open jacket. "Graham Metcalf was at *Le Marée* with Armando Rivera last night, same time as Ms. Page. We know Mr. Metcalf exchanged words with her in the parking lot as she was leaving."

Walker hid his rising anxiety behind his practiced mask. "How do we know that when the police were actively searching for her at that time? Or did you always know where she was and didn't bother bringing her in until *after* that dinner?" When the captain didn't answer right away, Walker released a juicy curse. "Damn it, Leonard!"

"We had eyes on her the whole time. And it *was* her choice."

"Let me question her first," he said through his teeth, watching through the glass as Audrey Metcalf swiped a tissue from the box that was extended to her.

"Mrs. Metcalf wants answers." Leonard glanced at him. "If her husband is our vic, we'll want them, too."

Walker nodded. "If Marcelina knows anything, she'll want to help." The question was why didn't she say anything about her encounter with Graham Metcalf last night?

Officer Tillman passed by, jerking his double chin toward the rear entrance. "Heads up." They all looked over and saw the woman in question being escorted down the hallway by two other officers. Kendall was behind them, clutching a pink handbag in her fist.

Marcelina looked tired. No makeup. Frazzled. Worried as hell. And yet she still made that hallway look like the red carpet. "Can I have an interrogation room?" Walker asked. "No cameras or microphones?"

The captain answered without hesitation. "Room 2."

Walker met the entourage halfway. "I need a few minutes with my client," he informed the officers.

"These policemen won't tell us what this is about," Kendall fumed, directing all her anger toward the gym-rat-in-uniform Walker remembered from her parking lot.

Officer Sorrick, was it? A good looking, Hardy Boy type through and through, but the man looked a tad stressed at the moment. "We've already explained no one is under arrest," the officer said, his light freckles standing out against the flush he was clearly attempting to keep at bay. "We're just following orders."

Marcelina stopped just short of the interrogation room's doorway, her hair curling in damp waves down her back, its clean watery scent accompanying her. "Rand, can you take Kendall to the lobby, please? She just needs some coffee."

Walker noted her casual use of the officer's name, felt the bite of jealousy and immediately shoved it into the dregs of his mind for safekeeping. When Kendall and the cops moved on, he ushered Marcelina into the small, box-like room and closed the door. "Those officers didn't ask you any questions on the way here, did they?" he managed with an air of calm as he indicated a chair beside a small desk.

Hands in lap, Marcelina sat down and shook her head. "No."

"But you're on a first name basis with Officer Sorrick." He took his own seat in the interrogator's chair.

Her thick gaze lifted to scour his face. "He's the one who handcuffed Kendall and me the day we were arrested. He came up and talked with us a little, but I think he just wanted to clear the air." She must have detected something in his iron composure. "Is that a problem?"

"Only if you get too chatty. He's a cop first.

Remember that."

A small, knowing smile teased her lips. "Walker, are you jealous?"

Yes! And it sucks! He scrubbed his face with his hands. "I'm not allowed to be jealous, Marcelina." But it was grossly apparent he needed more coffee too, and with Rivera's threat fresh on the brain, he may as well punch out for the day. "We need to talk about why you're here."

Her gaze darted around the tiny room. "Are we on camera?"

"No." At least he hoped not. "They're going to ask you questions about Graham Metcalf." The subtle shift in her eyes told him all he needed to know. "You know who he is, don't you?"

She tucked hair behind her ear, fidgeting as he watched her. "He's Kendall's boss. I figured it out after I saw him at Tony's. And I…*may*…have run into him at *Le Marée*."

Kendall's boss? That was new to him. "Did you exchange words?"

A small shrug. "Maybe a few." When he continued to stare, she sagged over the tabletop. "I know. I should have told you, but after my multiple encounters with Armando yesterday, I had enough to process."

"His car was just found burning in the Everglades. There was a body inside it." Walker watched as Marcelina went still. "They'll want details about your conversation. Why you chose not to disclose that information yesterday."

What color she had left in her cheeks instantly vanished. "Because I didn't think it was relevant."

"Maybe not to them, but it was relevant to *me*."

Worry darkened her eyes, and Walker knew they were now on the same page. "They're working to identify the body."

Marcelina stood up, walked to the corner of the small room, and put a hand over her mouth. "He's going to end up in your pile of photos, isn't he?"

"Probably." Walker stood, too. "What exactly did he say to you?"

"Not much. He told me not to eat the food in my to-go box." When she turned back around to face him, her dark, alluring eyes were glazed over with fear. "He said that Rivera would own me after the first bite. I asked if Rivera owned *him*, but that big bodyguard guy had come outside and was watching us."

"Rivera's bodyguard heard your conversation?"

"Yes. It looked like he was hovering on purpose. Mr. Metcalf muttered something that made me think Rivera *did* own him. Then he got in his car and left."

Her confession ended on a note of guilt. Yes, she not only knew who Graham was, she knew he was involved with Rivera. And didn't say anything. However, if he was Kendall's boss, Walker could understand Marcelina's desire to stay out of his way. "Aside from not telling me about it, you haven't done anything wrong."

She bit her lower lip. Kept her gaze down. He didn't like this side of her. She looked…defeated. "The best thing you can do for Mr. Metcalf's family right now is to be honest with the police," he said. "Give them something to go on. I'll be with you throughout the questioning."

****

Afterward, Walker was able to escort Marcelina out

of the interrogation room having suffered minimal damage. The detective assigned to the case had been courteous and Captain Ross's presence had offered her a familiar, friendly face. Now Walker wondered if he could get her through the lobby without running into more trouble or if he'd have to take her out the back way.

When they rounded the corner, Walker saw that Kendall was seated with a paper cup in her clutches, talking to a distraught Audrey Metcalf. "I'm going to take you right through the front door," he murmured to Marcelina. "Don't say anything to Mrs. Metcalf, okay?"

"Okay."

When they passed by, he gave a respectful nod to the women while Marcelina stole a quick, worried glance their way. Just then a detective came back onto the scene to speak with Mrs. Metcalf. Kendall gave the woman a hug and some parting words of encouragement and followed Marcelina out the door.

"What happened?" Kendall asked.

"How is she doing?" Marcelina asked in unison.

Kendall's worried look deepened as her heels made a rapid advance across the asphalt. "She's confused and scared as hell. We both are."

"Did you tell her that Marcelina saw her husband at *Le Marée*?" Walker asked.

"Yes, of course I did."

His mind did an instant replay of what that entailed and decided no harm could come from it. In fact he was glad Mrs. Metcalf had Kendall with her during such a difficult time. A police car intercepted their progress through the parking lot. The window rolled down. Officer Sorrick was behind the wheel. "We're supposed to escort you back to your place."

As much as Walker wanted to take Marcelina home, he was already late for his first meeting that day. "I'll stop by after work," he told her. "My last hearing is at three. Shouldn't take too long."

"What if the body is identified before then?" she asked, her voice tinged with panic.

He placed a chaste, comforting hand on her shoulder. "I doubt it will be. And when it is, I'll hear about it before you do. Don't leave the apartment and don't worry."

She moved closer, forcing him to drop his hand and back further away from their audience. Then she whispered, "What if Rivera is watching? He'll know I was here answering questions."

Walker also whispered. "He already thinks you're corruptible. I reviewed the changes they made to your record, and well…you'd only look good to a guy like him. Too good in fact."

Her eyes rolled with dismay. "Great."

"I wouldn't worry about him suspecting you as much as I would another surprise visit. He's determined to sink his hooks into you, Marcelina. More than I realized."

Her breath caught. "What do you mean? Did something happen?"

Walker looked away. "Not exactly."

"Did he *threaten* you?"

"No," he answered quickly. He backed away yet another step and ran a hand over his jaw. Her line of questioning—as well as the attitude behind it—was leading down a road he hadn't thought of before. Rivera *wanted* him to tell her about the phone call. Was probably banking on the likelihood that she would make some rash decisions as a result. If she had so much as an itch to protect him, Walker didn't want to risk nurturing it.

It still stuck him in the craw how authorities had "fudged" her record, and he had no doubt Leonard would continue to fudge it as long as there was a possibility Marcelina could change her mind. "Just keep assuring me you won't go to him," he said finally. "As long as I know that, everything will be fine."

Before she could answer, Kendall came up from behind. "I better get to work." She sniffed, giving Marcelina a hug. "Audrey wants me to update everyone."

When they parted, Marcelina took her face in her hands. "It'll be all right. I promise. Maybe when you get home we can do our thing. Wine and a comedy?"

The blonde shifted her attention with a shaky smile. "Yes to the wine. No to the comedy."

"Call me if you need me." As Marcelina got into the back seat of the squad car, Kendall bent, bracelets rattling as she pointed to the driver. "You take care of her, Sorrick."

The officer donned a pair of mirrored shades. "Will do, ma'am."

When they drove off, Walker caught Marcelina's lingering stare through the window and returned it. Kendall's yellow Volkswagen Bug soon followed the squad car out of the parking lot, leaving him alone to contemplate things as lush palm fronds rushed with the breeze overhead. For the first time, guilt pervaded his system over having other priorities, other clients to defend with equal care. This was what happened to lawyers who got in too deep. And he hated it, the sick feeling in his gut that indicated another major slip-up coming on.

"That's one hell of a woman," said a voice from a few rows down.

Walker craned his neck to find Captain Ross smoking by an unmarked sedan. "What?"

Leonard doused the cigarette under his shoe and walked toward him. When they were close enough for some private words, he said, "Marcelina Page is looking more and more like our ticket to a major conviction."

Walker felt his whole body tense up like a drawn bow. "Her answer was no."

"We need her."

"*No*, Leonard," he hissed. "I'm not losing another client to him." *Especially that one*.

"She's already a lot closer than the others. Hell, Rivera's practically courting her."

There was a reason for that, and it wasn't because of his ticking, biological clock. Walker pointed a stern finger as he wrestled his briefcase through the open driver's side door. "That's partly your fault," he reminded. "And I'm going to pretend we didn't have this conversation." He got in, jammed the key in the ignition and started the engine. A knock sounded on his window. With a curse, he rolled it down.

Captain Ross's shadow blocked the rising sun, his voice a hushed tone as he bent close. "When that body is identified as Graham Metcalf, she'll figure out it's the right thing to do. With or without your advice."

Ignoring the man, Walker threw the car in reverse and backed out.

"Have a good day, Walker!"

****

Later that morning, court adjourned wrapping up a round of testimony that had taken his present case into its second week. Walker felt good about it, having firmly established that his client had not been a threat to the public when he'd been released from prison eighteen months prior. The string of witnesses he'd called to the stand had confirmed the man's medication had a history of causing blackouts, and that it was plausible he was unconscious when his car plowed into a street corner killing one person and seriously injuring another. His closing statement, set for Thursday, was sure to score him another win.

One that would normally put a smile on his face. Instead, he had a much more pressing matter to attend to. He leaned over, spoke a few words of encouragement to his client, and left him to go chase down the judge.

With papers hanging out of his briefcase, Walker squeezed through the rear exit and dodged security in order to intercept the judge on her way to her chambers. "Your Honor, I'd like a word."

Judge Ursula Dickens tromped down the narrow hallway in her size-four manila loafers. "Just one? That I can do."

The woman looked no more than a child in costume from behind, but her stern frown was something to be taken very seriously, especially on the bench. "Five minutes," Walker said to her retreating backside. "Please."

"My docket is clogged, counselor. Perhaps another time."

"There's a pumpkin-spice latté in it for you."

"Three minutes," she answered without hesitation. "And make it caramel macchiato. I'm pumpkinned out."

God, he loved this woman. Had known her since he was a small boy following his father around the law office. She'd been Bishop Senior's colleague at the time, before he gave up the firm in favor of Puccini's payroll. Ursula and Conrad had argued a lot. Laughed a lot. Then ultimately settled things as friends.

Walker closed the door behind him while she removed her robe. Surrounded by lace doilies and sandalwood, he cleared his throat. "It's about Marcelina Page."

"What about her?" Ursula draped the black garb on a hanger, her strict bun crowning her head like the bubblegum light of an unmarked police car.

"You asked me to take her case," he said. "I'm curious as to why."

Sunlight from the single window sliced across the murky interior, illuminating a shaft of dust particles between them. Ursula pulled out her leather chair, sank down into it, and peered at him over her glasses. "She needed an attorney."

"I know, but why not Arnold Lang? He was holding his own at the time."

"You mean before he was plastered to the front of a city bus?" Behind the desk, she waved away his look of chagrin. "Sorry. I always wondered when something like that would happen to the putz."

Walker could only hope to never be on Ursula's bad side. But she was right. Lang *was* a putz. "Your Honor, I only have ninety seconds left," he reminded with a short laugh.

"Are you wanting to pull out of Ms. Page's case?"

"No, not at all. It's just that certain issues have come up that…make me wonder."

"Wonder what, exactly?" When he hesitated, Ursula reached for her smartphone. "Come on, counselor, spit it out. I'm a busy woman."

"Did my father have anything to do with it?"

As the screen filled with a grid of bright colors, she spared him a glance. "What drove you to that conclusion?"

"Give me a direct answer and I'll throw in a bottle of Hennessy."

"The answer is yes." She waved a hand toward the exit. "Now go on. This candy won't crush itself."

Walker left with a renewed sense of disquiet that had him grinding his teeth. Ursula's next command reached him through the closing door. "And I want that bottle wrapped in gold paper."

Chapter 11

It was hard doing what she was told, but Marcelina had decided on the ride home to start following Walker's advice to the smallest detail. Doing it her way obviously had its major flaws, and she was paying for them. Especially now. So, when the doorbell rang, she took extra caution and used the peephole, half-expecting to find Rand on the welcome mat with his textured haircut and starched black uniform—something Kendall consistently griped about since his visit to their front doorstep the previous night.

But it wasn't Rand. Instead, a willowy blonde waited with head down and designer purse clutched in a tight hold.

"Audrey," Marcelina breathed, her heart slamming to a standstill. The woman's features were largely hidden behind big sunglasses, but there was no mistaking the lithe stature and soft, waist-length hair she'd seen at the police station early that morning.

And hell if she didn't open the door. As far as the chain would allow, anyway.

"You know who I am?" Audrey asked in lieu of a greeting, her tempered panic showing as she removed her sunglasses.

Marcelina swallowed hard, fixated on those heartbreaking, gray-blue eyes. "Yes."

"I know I shouldn't be here," the woman continued,

"but can I come in anyway? I promise I'll do most of the talking."

Just like that, Walker's advice was pushed aside in favor of the sheer angst etched in Audrey's delicate features. After a slight nod, Marcelina closed the door long enough to unlatch the chain, then swung it wide. Audrey stepped through the threshold, her long legs covered in billowy lounge pants. Marcelina peered left then right, looking past the ever-present squad car for signs of a different set of eyes. Seeing nothing, she closed the door and turned back to her guest. The woman now held her sunglasses and purse in a limp hold at her side, appearing frail and thoroughly drained. She gave an uneasy look around at the many dolls holding court around her, as if suddenly nervous in the company of such a large, attentive audience. "First of all, I want to thank you for talking to the police this morning," she said softly. "I hope there were no conflicts of interest where your legal problems are concerned."

Feeling only a little embarrassed, Marcelina indicated the couch. "I take it Kendall told you I was living with her again."

She nodded, ignoring the invitation to sit. "I'm not here to judge. I mean…" a shaky laugh, "how could I, right? Not with the trouble Graham appears to be in."

A knock on the door had Marcelina returning to the peephole. This time, the person on the other side of it was Rand. She opened the door a crack.

"Is everything okay in there?" he asked.

She cleared her throat, still feeling a bit edgy herself around the handsome policeman who'd played such a monumental role in the worst day of her life. "Yes. Everything is fine."

He craned his neck for a sneak peek inside. "We'll be changing shifts in less than an hour. Try to keep it brief."

"We will." Marcelina pushed the door closed once again, feeling drained all of a sudden. She turned back to her guest. "Have you heard any news yet, Mrs. Metcalf?"

"Call me Audrey," the woman said from over her shoulder as she stood in front of the glass case containing Kendall's most prized dolls. "And no, I haven't. At this point I'd rather believe someone stole Graham's car and he's still walking home." She sent a wobbly smile in Marcelina's direction. "A ridiculous notion, but…"

Marcelina gave her a brief smile of encouragement. "I hope that's the case."

A spark entered Audrey's gaze. She turned to fully face her again. "But the look in your eyes tells me you don't think so." She studied the sunglasses in her hand for a moment then made a sound of disgust. "You see this is what I need to know. Who is this Armando Rivera guy? I don't want the generic description I get from the police. I want *your* version."

"What makes you think I have one?"

"Kendall told me about your encounters with him, and about your suspicions of Graham. I need to know everything."

Of course. She remembered Kendall saying as much when Walker had asked. It was her way, after all, to speak without the benefit of a filter. Marcelina gave a helpless shrug. "I don't know much about Mr. Rivera, either, just what I've learned within the last week. I know he's a high-ranking member of some Colombian cartel from the east coast who recently moved into this area. I also know he's into financing and collateral recovery."

She left out the part where he'd just attempted to hire her.

"A *cartel*." Terror sounded in the tremor of Audrey's voice. "How are you connected with him?"

Audrey's surprise ushered in a sense of unease. Marcelina hadn't thought she was connected with Rivera, but perhaps she was… "I just caught his attention somehow," she explained on her way to the kitchen. "I've been trying to shake him ever since, but he doesn't take no for an answer." She pulled two glasses from the cabinet and pointed toward the front windows with a sheepish look. "Hence the police presence outside."

"He's dangerous, then." Audrey approached the bar and plunked her purse down between them, eyes wide with understanding. "Very…*very* dangerous."

Marcelina retrieved the pitcher of tea from the refrigerator. "He scares the hell out of me."

The woman declined the offer of a drink, pausing as she absorbed Marcelina's words. "That's the most direct answer I've gotten all morning."

Detecting the melancholy in Audrey's words, Marcelina's heart cracked a little more. "I'm sorry you're going through this. I hope your husband is all right. I really do."

Audrey swallowed, looked down at her hands. "Since you're being so direct, tell me why you think Graham is involved."

Should she? If the police didn't give Audrey details, there was probably a good reason for it. "I don't think it would be appropriate for me—"

"Nothing is *appropriate* right now." Now her blue-gray eyes fairly burned, underlying the strength in Audrey's voice. "I need to know what I'm facing."

So, the woman was tougher than she looked. And

she certainly deserved answers more than anyone. With a resigned sigh, Marcelina nodded. "I first noticed your husband at Rivera's car auctions, several of them. His bidding activity raised a few eyebrows. Still, I didn't think much of it until I saw him at the restaurant last night. He was with Mr. Rivera and I could tell he was upset. We didn't interact much, but when I saw him in the parking lot a few minutes later, he warned me to stay away."

"He threatened you?"

"No…it was advice."

Audrey's face instantly fell. Marcelina knew why since her answer more or less confirmed that her husband had been involved in some questionable acts. Perhaps his stress over the matter was what caused the tension in their marriage that Kendall had mentioned before. In some ways it made her feel better about her own situation. She wasn't the only one sucked into the criminal world by way of deceit. It could happen to anyone.

Marcelina followed Audrey to the front door with a confusing mixture of sadness and vindication. When they reached it, the lovely blonde met her gaze behind a veneer of calm. "Thank you for talking to me. All I wanted was some clarity. I feel like I've been living in the dark for a while now."

Though Marcelina knew she shouldn't ask, the questions had been shooting forth in abundance since Audrey's arrival. "You suspected Graham has been hiding something?"

"Yes. Things have been rather tense to say the least. If it wasn't for our daughter…" Tears filled her eyes. "Oh, Caroline…" It was as if she just realized how her little girl would react to the news of her father never coming home again. "I have to go," she whispered, then promptly left.

Caroline. The horror in Audrey's countenance when she'd uttered the name brought it home for Marcelina. If the burnt body turned out to be Graham, Armando Rivera had just ripped a father away from his small child. How many families had he ruined? How many lives? The Metcalfs were fairly well off, not some desperate, hard-on-their-luck locals looking for a way to rise above the poverty line. It proved that no one was out of Rivera's reach.

And if Caroline were to grow up without her father, or if one hair on Kendall's head was hurt, or if Walker's life was threatened in any way…Marcelina would move hell and earth to see that the right person paid for it.

****

Several mornings later, Marcelina's phone lit up, buzzing both her and Kendall awake. Neither of them had wanted to sleep alone that night, so they'd camped out on the living room floor in front of a string of late-night TV shows.

"What time is it?" Kendall mumbled, turning away from the light.

Marcelina's phone said it was nearly 6:00 AM…and that Walker was calling. She blinked the sleep from her eyes and sat up before answering. "Hello?"

"It's me."

She didn't like his tone. Not one bit. "What is it?"

"He's been positively identified."

Marcelina rubbed a hand over her face. Now that she'd met Audrey, Graham Metcalf wasn't just Kendall's boss anymore. He was someone's husband

and father. She closed her eyes against the kaleidoscope of colors coming from the TV. "My God."

Kendall's pajama-clad body bolted upright. "Oh, no!"

Marcelina nodded and they sat there in a state of numb disbelief. It was as if the shock of it was brand new, like they hadn't been waiting for days with bated breath.

"Marcelina?" Walker's voice reached her over the phone.

"What?"

"Do I need to come over?"

Kendall was now sobbing uncontrollably, causing a wealth of emotion to gather in Marcelina's eyes. She hadn't known Graham, and his death certainly wasn't her fault, but her visit from Audrey the day before and the despair of Kendall's tears made it oh-so personal.

"No," she finally managed. "Kendall isn't handling it so well, but I'll take care of her."

"Are you sure?"

No, she wasn't. In fact she could really use the backup right now, but Walker had enough on his plate. "Yes. We'll be fine."

A half hour later, she and Kendall hovered over the kitchen counter in silence, staring into their coffee mugs. Every light in the small apartment was on. The TV was off, preventing any kind of distraction from Kendall's mournful reverie and Marcelina's quiet reflection.

"I can't believe it," Kendall murmured. Though her voice was still nasally from her earlier breakdown, the tears had at least dried up. "I worked for him for over a year and he was always so nice. Poor, poor Audrey. I can't imagine…"

Marcelina clutched the mug, allowing the hot ceramic to sear her palms. "This is why I want you to leave town."

"No way." Kendall sniffed. "I'm not leaving you."

Spoken to a woman she'd kicked out eight months prior. Marcelina dropped her palm on the counter. "Dammit, don't you see? People like Rivera don't discriminate. They don't feel, or care who they hurt as long as they get their way. *You* could be next, Kendall."

A knock on the door interrupted her mini tirade, making it clear that their apartment had become quite the hotbed of activity. Kendall checked the peephole, then began the systematic chore of unlocking chains and deadbolts. When the door finally came open, there stood Walker in a charcoal suit and tie. "Mr. Bishop," she greeted.

"How are you doing, Kendall?"

"Not so good. I'm going to go to work today. Be there when they announce Mr. Metcalf's…death."

Fresh tears spilled down her cheeks. Walker put a hand on her shoulder and Kendall took it as the invitation it was. She leaned in and allowed the comfort he offered, softly crying against the lapels of his suit as he held her. His gaze met Marcelina's through the kitchen's opening. And she nodded her emotional thanks.

After a few moments, Kendall pulled herself together again, stepping out of Walker's embrace and wiping her nose with a tissue that had been bundled in her fist. "I'll finish getting ready." Then she disappeared into her bedroom.

"I thought you weren't coming," Marcelina said to him as they met in the middle. Without warning, he pulled her into his arms and held her tight. Was this to comfort her, too, or did he just need an excuse to hold her? Something told her it was the latter, a realization that melted her heart. She burrowed in, filling her lungs with the scent of him.

When Marcelina lifted her face, Walker kissed her forehead. His lips lingered a bit, surely longer than he'd planned for a chaste kiss. "Thank you," she whispered.

"All you have to do is say no, we're not fine," he said.

She gave him a reluctant smile. "You could tell that, huh?"

When his eyes darkened, she could sense more turmoil behind them than first imagined. He pulled away and held her out by the arms, leaning down to pin her with one of those drilling looks. "It may be in poor taste, but I have to use this as an example. Don't let this happen to you, Marcelina. Graham Metcalf made a series of bad choices, which led to his death. It's unfortunate, but it happens to the most unlikely people. Ones you'd never suspect."

And as a criminal defense attorney, he would know. Probably saw it every day. But as *her* attorney, he was warning her away from a deal that continually rolled through her mind despite her earlier assurances that she wouldn't take it. Yes, the thought of exchanging a thug like Rivera for her freedom was looking better every day—and evidently Walker was afraid she would. Had he detected her underlying conflict when they'd spoken earlier?

"Coffee?" she asked in a lame attempt to throw him off course.

"No." When she moved away, he dropped his hands, those blue eyes assessing her soul as if she'd spoken her thoughts out loud. "I'm on my way to the precinct to act on your behalf. Offer condolences to Mrs. Metcalf. Make sure there isn't anything else they'll be needing from you."

Marcelina's attempts at refilling her own mug came to an immediate halt. "Can I go?"

"No."

She calmly replaced the decanter. "If you're going to offer condolences to Audrey, I'd rather them come from me personally, not my lawyer."

"Which is admirable, but I need to at least test the waters first."

Taking a tentative sip, she let the silence stretch for a moment. "Walker…she came over yesterday." When his face showed no hint of surprise, she remembered the police car sitting outside their window. "But I guess you already knew that."

He gave her a lazy smile as he palmed his keys. "We'll talk about it later." She put her mug down and followed him to the door. "And no fraternizing with the men in uniform," Walker added. "They need to stay focused."

Marcelina raised a brow as he turned to face her one last time. "Careful, Mr. Bishop, or I'll think you're jealous."

"I only have my client's best interests at heart."

Spoken in a husky timbre that belied the words. That alone put some warmth back into her heart, but now he was leaving her with a need for him that made her want to take chase—a need that was slowly taking over all other priorities. She swallowed hard. "Thank you for coming over. It was very gallant of you."

He answered with a wink. "I'll call you later."

After the locks were back in place, she leaned against the door with eyes closed. She wanted him to stay and comfort her. Share a meal with her. Make love to her until all her demons were dispelled, just like last time. The brief respite from them was worth more than anything money could buy.

How could she handle it if her need for him got worse? Walker certainly displayed a lot more willpower, making it more and more apparent their night would only be that. One night.

"I smell sexual frustration," said a voice from the bedroom.

Marcelina opened her eyes and sent a pleading look to the heavens. "How can you joke at a time like this?"

"Because it's not a joke and I need the distraction." Kendall appeared with brush in hand. "Your lawyer is delicious and off limits which means you have no choice but to want him."

"He's going to see Audrey." Marcelina went back to the kitchen. "I want to go with him, and I know you do, too. This sucks."

Kendall followed her and was at the counter with arms crossed. "I can see why that would be a bad idea. Audrey may have come to you, and everything may have gone fine. But if they just identified her husband's body, she's really suffering right now. She'll need time and space."

And just like that, the sadness was back. Marcelina considered things over the reflection in her coffee. "You're right. Let me know what happens at work today."

Kendall took her bottom lip between her teeth. "I'm sorry, Marcelina."

"For what?"

"For giving you such a hard time about Jonah." She left Marcelina with an odd sense of disquiet. Yes, these things could happen to anyone…as long as the deaths ended with Graham Metcalf and not someone closer to her.

Moments later Kendall reappeared with her purse, keys, and a pair of white platform sandals in hand. The sun was beginning to peer over the horizon, lighting up the curtains with an amber glow.

"What about breakfast?" Marcelina asked her.

"No time. I'm going to throw my shoes on and go."

Her makeup was three layers thick again, hiding the effects of her earlier breakdowns. They said their goodbyes and Kendall slipped out of the apartment. Moments later, a feminine yelp was heard from the direction of the parking lot. Shouts ensued and a loud bang rent the air. Marcelina ran for the door, threw open the locks, and darted outside to look over the railing. There, down below, was an active tussle going on…and Kendall facedown on the asphalt. Terror took hold. Marcelina made a mad dash for the stairwell. Once on the ground floor, she was by Kendall's side like a shot, relieved that her friend was propped up on her elbows and watching the scene before them.

Two cops were wrestling with a man in a hoody, yelling at him to stop struggling and give them his hands. When he finally complied, things settled to a more controlled kind of chaos complete with heavy breathing and the click of handcuffs.

"Ow, man, you're on my face!" said a muffled voice.

"That's what happens when you struggle," Rand

replied smoothly as he and the other officer hauled the scraggly looking perp to his feet.

"I only asked her for a light!"

Rand picked something pink up off the ground beside them. "So this is *your* purse? Not really your color, dude."

Marcelina watched the scene unfold in a state of awed disbelief. Cop number-two spoke into his shoulder mic, requesting an ambulance and another unit while Rand searched the thief's pockets. By then, Kendall was sitting up, though in no apparent hurry to get off the ground.

Finally, Rand walked the perp to his patrol car and his gaze locked with Kendall's. His mouth was set in a grim line. "Are you okay?" he asked her.

Kendall nodded, her gaze a bit hazy. Marcelina helped the woman to her feet, took her face in her hands and studied the state of her pupils. "Are you sure? You look dazed. Did you hit your head or are you just in shock?"

Kendall's lips were parted as short breaths passed through them. "He came out of nowhere."

"It's okay." Marcelina pulled her into a fierce embrace. "They caught him. He can't hurt you anymore."

"No, I—I mean Rand." Kendall pulled away, her blank expression replaced by one of sheer wonder. "That thief didn't get two feet from me before he was slammed against a car and taking an elbow to the windpipe. It was…"

Oh, the woman was in shock, all right, but not from any sort of *physical* impact. Marcelina let out a relieved laugh. "You're fine. Thank God."

"...It was *incredible*."

Chapter 12

While his partner commenced with the perp's background check, Rand was back at Kendall's side with blue gloves and a first-aid kit. "Sit down over here," he ordered.

Marcelina moved out of the way and Kendall followed Rand, blinking at him like a star-struck groupie. "I'm fine."

"You have a scrape on your elbow."

Hell, even Marcelina had missed that. She stood back and watched the two with ardent curiosity. Kendall lowered herself to the curb while Rand crouched before her and opened the kit. He asked her questions and tended to her very small wound, leaving Marcelina with a strange feeling of invisibility.

A smile curved her lips.

Just then, the screech of tires drew her attention to the entrance. Walker's black Infinity went dark before coming to a stop right behind her. When he got out, she met him halfway, noting the intense worry in his eyes and in the firm set of his jaw.

"You didn't have to come back," she said.

"I tried calling but you wouldn't pick up." His voice lowered. "I thought Rivera had gotten to you."

"My phone's upstairs." Feeling a reprimand coming on, Marcelina indicated the scene before them. "I was kind of in a hurry."

His eyes softened as he took everything in. "What happened?"

"She got mugged." Marcelina jerked her head toward the black-and-white. "With a cop car right there."

"Is she hurt bad?"

He would think so with the distant sirens approaching and for all the medical supplies littering the ground around Rand and his patient. "It's a boo-boo on the elbow," Marcelina explained in a serious manner. "Very small."

Understanding lit Walker's chiseled features and a chuckle escaped. "Which one of them is milking this?"

"I think they both are."

An ambulance turned into the lot followed by a back-up squad car. The sirens were cut, but lights still flashed red and blue. A few spectators had gathered in the walkways of the building, watching the show with coffees in hand. Walker drew her aside. "Do you want me to stay?"

"No, you need to get to the police station. I'll go back inside with Kendall once all the excitement dies down."

Paramedics hefted red trauma bags toward the patrol car—where the real patient sat bleeding in the back seat. Walker faced Marcelina again, his eyes warming with appreciation. "I like this cooperative you."

Marcelina hugged her arms, rubbing the uncomfortable vibes from her body. Vibes even Walker's presence couldn't dispel. "Actually, I'm not sure I want to leave the apartment at all anymore."

His look told her he understood. "Have Kendall call me if she needs anything."

She followed him to the driver's side of his car.

"Thanks for coming to my rescue again."

"Did I?"

"You thought so," she came back with a smirk as he lowered himself behind the wheel.

After the ambulance and back-up patrol car left with the criminal in tow, cop number two opted to stay on the ground to keep watch while Marcelina and Rand took Kendall back upstairs via the elevator.

"You're still shaken up." Rand forced her onto the couch. "Maybe it would be best if you took the day off."

Marcelina rolled her eyes. Kendall's only problem was her raging hormones, but she played along as the concerned friend. "He's right. You should stay home."

"No." Kendall perched on the edge of the cushions and checked out the small bandage on her elbow. Her cheeks still bore a slight flush. "I have to go, especially today."

The couch cushions dipped as Rand sat down beside her. "I'll go for you, just to explain things to your supervisor."

Marcelina could appreciate the man's willingness to help, but did he even know that her boss had just been murdered? When Kendall began to tear up again at the reminder, she jumped in. "Maybe Rand could drive you," she suggested. "He could leave his partner here and take your car. You still look pretty shaky."

Kendall sniffed, dabbed at a corner of her eye. "If he takes my car how will I get home?"

"Well…" She turned to Rand. "You'll be off duty by then, right? You could pick her up. Maybe take her out for a drink since she obviously needs one."

They both nodded as if it were the most practical thing they'd heard all morning. Marcelina left them on the couch so they could go over Kendall's statement. Yes, there was no mistaking the pheromone cloud hovering over those two and she didn't feel a bit ashamed for stirring it up. Though the irony of Kendall falling for a cop—no, *the* cop who had played the most pivotal role in their day of shame—made her smile. It was exactly what the doctor ordered despite their recent, exuberant toasts to being single.

But if said cop hurt Kendall, Marcelina would scoop his eyeballs out with a spoon.

She went into the kitchen to grab her phone off the counter. A splash of color instantly caught her eye. Something new and largely out of place on Kendall's beige, dated countertops. It was a single rose, its perfect peach-colored petals resting just inches from her cellphone. It could have only been placed there sometime after she left the apartment…because it certainly wasn't there before.

Marcelina approached the flower, her steps slow and cautious. What was normally a symbol of affection shouted at her like an ominous message.

I am always here.

Armando Rivera was sucking her in whether she liked it or not. The thought would have made her laugh if not for the overpowering urge to run screaming for the hills. Careful not to touch the rose, she snatched up her phone, took a snapshot of it and sent it to Walker as she made her way back into the living room. "Someone was in the apartment while we were outside," she said to Rand and Kendall, her voice giving away the amount of nerves now assaulting her system.

Rand stood up, looking around with the honed awareness of a cop. "What makes you say that?"

"There's a rose on the kitchen counter. I'm pretty sure it's from Armando Rivera."

"You didn't touch it, did you?" he asked on his way to the kitchen.

"No."

Kendall rose up on unsteady legs. "He wouldn't come here with the police right outside."

"I'm sure he wouldn't," Marcelina answered, her own blood settling down into her toes. "But he'd have someone do it for him."

Rand was back, sweeping the front door and its shadows with a small Maglite, its narrow beam illuminating every dust particle and smudge on the knob. "Did you leave the door open?" he asked.

"It was closed but unlocked."

"We may be able to get a print, but if the intruder put that much thought into breaking in, they would have worn gloves."

He moved the flashlight's beam to the carpet, searching for signs of footprints other than their own. With as much activity as Kendall's apartment had seen lately, and with Rivera himself having visited a few days prior, it would surely end up a futile effort.

Moments later, Marcelina was closed in Kendall's bedroom with Walker on the phone. "Rivera somehow got past our security detail this morning," she told him, her face hot with angst. "He left a peach rose by my cellphone in the kitchen. It was something he tried to give me at the restaurant but I wouldn't accept it."

There was a brief silence as Walker processed it all. "And you think he set up Kendall's mugging so he could gain access to her place?"

"Well, really…who would steal someone's purse

right in front of the police?"

"Depends on how high they are, but in this case I'm afraid you're right."

Why did his voice sound so strange? That same feeling she'd had in the police station parking lot seeped into her pores again. The one that told her he was holding something back. "What are you thinking, Walker?"

"I'm thinking you should have Officer Sorrick call someone in to sweep the place. Make sure there wasn't anything else left behind like cameras or listening devices. We may even get lucky and lift a print."

"Rivera is too smart to leave fingerprints."

"Maybe, but the people who work for him aren't always. Is Kendall still there?"

"Yes."

"Good. They'll need her permission. Let me know what they find out."

****

Later that morning, the investigative team left the apartment looking much like the site of a natural disaster. Dolls were everywhere. Black dust mottled everything from doorknobs, walls, furniture, and highly prized collectibles, despite Kendall's desperate pleas for them to be careful. Marcelina's few belongings had been unpacked and rifled through, as well as all cabinets and drawers. Nothing had been left out, yet nothing more than the rose had been found. The two women stood in the midst of it all, wrapped up in bad déjà vu, their sense of privacy shattered once again.

"I'm sorry, Kendall." Marcelina looked sadly over at her friend. "I guess this is what you get for letting me back in."

The woman's shoulders hung in listless fashion.

"It's okay. Really."

But it wasn't. Never before had Marcelina seen Kendall look so defeated. "I'll clean it all up. By the time you get home you won't know a thing was ever out of place."

Kendall rounded on her. "Of course I'll know, Marcelina. This Rivera guy is forcing himself into all our lives, not just yours."

Marcelina blinked back her surprise. "You're right. It would probably be better if I left."

"Really?" Her eyes narrowed beneath the thick mascara. "Is that your solution to everything? Abandon your friends when they need you most?"

Despite the absurdity of that statement, Marcelina's body went awash with sympathy. Things were too off kilter in Kendall's world to handle a fight. And why would she want her to stick around, especially after this? "I've brought you nothing but trouble," she reminded softly.

"Yes, you have. For some reason you're a magnet for it." Kendall closed her eyes, took a deep breath. "But I love you, and I really need you right now. Okay?"

Her outburst ended with a dramatic exit. Marcelina was left alone in the midst of hundreds of misplaced dolls, their state of disarray mocking her with the irony of it all. To her, these dolls represented real people—all the ones who could be affected by her unwillingness to help the DEA. They represented her and Graham Metcalf and every innocent out there who would be sucked in next. This jaded, dangerous world of drugs was getting out of control, and the truth was…Kendall could be next.

The DEA's deal was looking better every day, and her list of reasons for taking it was growing. Despite her faith in Walker and his unquestionable talent in the courtroom, this was a bull-by-the-horns moment in her life where she needed to step up and wave her own red cape. Rivera was making this personal—throwing down a challenge she *wanted* to accept in order to preserve her future. Kendall's future.

And if there was a chance Rivera's pursuit of her centered around some vendetta against Walker, there was nothing she wouldn't do to protect him, too.

****

Walker waited with a tumbler of scotch within reach, his fingers lazily turning the glass in order to not give away his inner turmoil. He was at a table in a bar, surrounded by big screen TVs, casual conversation, and a wait staff that seemed to genuinely enjoy their jobs— as if the world were spinning on its axis in standard fashion. He took a breath, absorbing the normalcy through osmosis, waiting for that moment…

A presence loomed at his side. He glanced upward and beheld his father's imposing form for the first time in exactly four and a half years. Walker pushed back his chair, stood up and engaged in a brief, stiff handshake. "Thank you for meeting me. I didn't think you'd come."

Conrad Bishop looked good. Well-dressed as usual. Healthy despite the deeper age lines around his eyes and the gray in his trimmed mustache. Walker always felt like a slouch in comparison, possibly due to the many behavioral lectures he'd received throughout his childhood.

Conrad pulled out a chair and sat. "When my only child contacts me for the first time in four years, I can't help but get curious."

Four and a half. Walker dismissed the usual

bitterness that always accompanied his father's presence in favor of the possibilities. A lot of time had passed. Surely they could get through one drink without bloodshed. "I found out from your housekeeper that you were on the west coast. What are you doing here?"

"Vacationing."

"You hate Naples."

Conrad raised his hand for a waiter. "I wanted to walk on a beach without getting tar between my toes."

Since when had his father ever walked on a beach? Or enjoyed one? Or made love on one, for that matter? Walker pushed back the memory of his own recent dalliances with Marcelina before the ensuing smile reached his mouth. The woman had opened up a whole new world to him whether she knew it or not. But she deserved his professionalism right now, not his lewd thoughts. "I had a talk with Ursula Dickens yesterday."

His father's mustache tilted with a smile. "Ursula? How is the old bat?"

Walker smiled back. "Still taking bribes."

A chuckle. "That woman has no shame."

"You're right. A bottle of Hennessey was all it took to get the answers I wanted." Walker's smile waned a bit. "I just wonder what it'll take to get the truth out of you."

As if on cue, Conrad's eyes went blank. "Regarding what?"

"Marcelina Page."

He gave a casual shrug. "Throwing random names across the table won't get you answers, son."

But Walker already knew she wasn't a random name. Judge Dickens had confirmed that much. "Are you saying you've never heard of her?"

"Is she a client?"

Walker cocked a brow in challenge while managing to match his father's blasé attitude. "You should know. You're the one who asked Judge Dickens to appoint her case to me."

Though the first torpedo had just been fired, Conrad took the hit with little reaction. He sat back. Regarded him with a thoughtful gaze. "Yes, I remember now. How is it going?"

Now that they were past the bullshit, Walker felt the steel in his spine soften a bit. "Marcelina hasn't been the easiest client. She does, however, have an interesting connection with you."

"I suppose we're getting closer to the point now." Annoyance had seeped into Conrad's eyes.

Walker sipped scotch. Welcomed the burn as a much needed jab to stay on his toes. "Coincidentally enough, she knew your old boss, Puccini."

"Her and many other beautiful women."

He never said she was beautiful. Walker returned his father's bland smile. "So you *do* know Marcelina."

The smile remained though Conrad shook his head. "Not personally."

That wasn't what he'd asked. Walker leaned in, spoke low. "Puccini has been dead for six years. How is it you're still cleaning up his messes?"

The notion was waved away. "I still keep tabs on the caseload here. Marcelina's name was familiar and I knew that if Nari was alive, he would want her to have good representation."

"So instead of coming to me, you had it arranged."

"You would have said no. And I didn't see the harm."

The man was right. If Walker had sensed Conrad

Bishop's hands in it, he would have passed Marcelina's case off to the next patsy without a thought. "Tell me something," he said, wondering when he'd become so predictable. "What do you know of Puccini's relationship with her?"

Conrad looked around for the waitress. "He met her shortly before his death."

"And?"

"And nothing. He was killed, remember?" When his gaze rested once more on the doubt in Walker's countenance, he added, "Nari spoke of her once and it was with a smile on his face."

"Yet you knew she was beautiful," Walker stated in deadpan fashion.

"Weren't they all?" Conrad fired back.

"Puccini was a powerful man. He profited greatly from breaking laws and killing people, something he was only able to accomplish because of you."

"Switching to accusations already? My drink hasn't even arrived."

"He paid you because you were the best. Smart. Trustworthy."

"Hold on one moment." The waitress came and Conrad accepted his drink with a relieved smile. When she left, he stirred it with the tiny straw. "Lectures are best served with whiskey and bitters. Continue."

Walker plowed on as if he hadn't been denigrated. "You weren't just Puccini's lawyer, you were his friend. He confided in you more than his own family. Hell, even I was envious of your relationship."

"Are we still talking about Miss Page?" The annoyance was back tenfold.

"You both knew there was an assassination plot

brewing. You knew he expected it. Feared it."

Conrad only nodded.

Walker leaned in closer. "So what makes you so sure Marcelina wasn't the one who killed him?"

He shrugged again. "I guess I'm not."

"Yet you jump to her defense."

Ice rattled as he took a liberal drink. "She brought him comfort during a difficult time," he said through the cubes in his mouth.

So casual. But Walker knew it was a façade. Knew his father was privy to more than just theories and that the truth would never come out unless he wanted it to. A reluctant frustration laced Walker's words. "Wouldn't you have suspected her in the beginning knowing she was someone new in his life?"

The man's eyes narrowed dangerously. "Don't put me in the hot box, son. You forget who you're talking to."

A sardonic smile. "Sorry. Habit."

"I can appreciate your desire to lure the truth out of someone, but in this case it isn't necessary. We can be frank with each other. You want to know why I didn't name her in the investigation of Nari's death?" Conrad turned up a hand. "It's simple. Her background didn't support the notion that she was a threat."

"Hmm. All the more reason to suspect her, wouldn't you think? Especially for a woman you'd only heard mentioned once?"

Conrad took another drink, emptying most of the glass. "It was a judgment call on my part. I didn't get to be the best by being wrong."

"Or sloppy."

The older man sat back in his chair, his gaze locked

on Walker's in a silent battle of wills. "I raised a lawyer through and through," he murmured. "Incapable of intimate conversation and suspicious to a fault."

Walker barked out a laugh. "And you're still so quick to underestimate me."

"Meaning?"

"I think you know more about that assassination plot than you're letting on. Who knows, you may have even had a hand in covering it up."

A moment of silence passed. Conrad's face tightened with a scowl. "I'm going to pretend you didn't say that."

"Marcelina has been living in fear for a long time, waiting for someone to call her out as a suspect. And if we get a guilty verdict in this case against her, it's only a matter of time before they enter her DNA into CODIS and a match is made with those hair samples from Puccini's crime scene." Walker stood up and threw a few bills on the table. "I won't let her go down for something she didn't do."

Having all but accused his father of participating in Puccini's death, he exited the bar with a casual stride. But on the inside he was a wreck, wondering what the hell he'd just done.

As soon as the sun hit his face, his cellphone rang. A brief check confirmed the call was from Captain Ross. In no mood for anything more at the moment, he answered with a bite to his voice. "What?"

A brief pause. "Who is this?"

"You know who it is, you called me."

"You're in a bad mood. What happened?"

Walker thumbed the key fob and his car unlocked with a flash of headlights. "Meeting with Conrad."

His answer was met with stunned silence. Then, "Well, hell."

Exactly.

"You have court this afternoon?" Leonard asked.

Walker yanked the door open, got behind the wheel and was instantly met with a litany of texts from Judith on the dash screen. He briefly scanned them in the oven-like heat. "No. Just some scheduled meetings, some prep work, and a lobby full of anxious clients according to my paralegal."

"Good. Check your email."

The line went dead, leaving Walker with an apocalyptic feeling he'd rather avoid with another drink. But "check your email" meant business, the kind that needed to stay off the radar. As he raised his phone and brought up the account in question, his feeling of dread intensified.

—The mall, closed bay on north side, 13:30. Access through employees-only by restrooms.—

Again with the employees-only entrance. At the very least, the man could give him a heads-up of what he was walking into so he wouldn't be waylaid like last time—when he'd found Marcelina in the back office of a greasy diner.

The sick feeling in his stomach gave way to panic. Walker threw his car into drive and he peeled out of the lot. By the time he arrived at the mall, his mood had gone from bad to worse. Mall traffic had died down since the holidays were over, but was still buzzing with post-season returns and exchanges. He found the bay with paper-covered windows and a sign that read *Coming Soon!* He ducked into the next hallway, bypassed the restrooms, and pushed through the "Employees Only" door. As soon as he found the right entrance, he walked through it and was standing in a wide, darkened area littered with tarps, paint buckets and ladders. The place smelled like exposed concrete and new drywall. Two dark figures stood up from folding chairs at the far end of the room. One was wearing a suit. The other a dress.

"She came to me on her own," Captain Ross said. "For the record, I asked if she wanted you here and she said no."

"Because you'd only tell me not to do what I'm about to do," Marcelina added softly.

Her words amped up the anger within Walker. This was not what he needed right now. "I'm your fucking lawyer, Marcelina. It's my job."

Leonard held out his hands with a plea for understanding. "In this case I don't think you're going to change her mind. I can't say I'm upset about it."

Walker's gaze shifted between them. When it rested on Marcelina, his jaw set with a prickly reality. "Tell me you didn't just take that deal."

Chapter 13

It was Walker's worst-case scenario coming to life. Recent memories rose to the surface, like the mangled, bloated body of their last informant being uncovered in the morgue. Of Armando Rivera challenging him from across the parking lot. The phone call days later that proved Walker right—this *was* about him. And now the drug lord was about to get what he wanted: another chance to turn the knife.

Marcelina approached him with the caution of a lion tamer. "It was my decision to make. I want to end all of this."

Walker stood his ground, fighting the urge to reach out and shake her. "You won't come out of it on the winning end."

"I have to try. Whatever the reason, Rivera *invited* me in. Like you said, he thinks I'm corruptible, and after that job offer, I *have* a reason to go to him."

"You already turned him down," he reminded through his teeth.

"A girl can think about it," she shot back.

Leonard broke in, the only one with a fair amount of calm in his voice. "We have ways to keep tabs on her without wires, Walker," he reassured, "or anything that could give her away. We'll take good care of her. We'll always be close and we'll make contact enough times to keep thoroughly apprised of her progress."

Was that supposed to make him feel better? "You think just because you changed her background he won't suspect her of working with the cops?" Walker harrumphed. "They've been camped outside her door for days."

"At Kendall's request according to record," Leonard said with hands on hips. "She felt threatened after Rivera's visit, and the police presence has driven a wedge between her and Marcelina."

It was just plausible enough to throw Walker into a panic. He was losing this battle, and all because of Leonard and his propensity to bow to the DEA. "Rivera won't give her anything," Walker argued. "His only objective is to stick it to me. He wants to turn her against me."

Marcelina rolled her eyes. "I know you two have a past, but you're reading more into this than you need to. He offered me a job. I'm going to take it, work for him, make him trust me—"

"You know he wants more than that from you," he snapped.

Her response was calm and controlled. "And I *know* what I'm getting myself into."

When Walker's gaze shot back to the captain, the man only shrugged. "She knows the risks."

And so did Leonard. His blasé attitude was misleading as hell and Walker didn't like it.

"I'm tired of being scared for my future," Marcelina continued, her voice a plea for understanding. "I'm tired of being scared for Kendall, for you…for people like Graham Metcalf and his family. We're all drowning in Rivera's world, and it's time someone took that power away from him. You already tried it your way, remember? I want to try it mine."

She was right. His way hadn't worked and she had every reason to accept a deal that could buy her freedom. It would solve all her problems, even keep her DNA out of the system and keep her secret from coming out. So why did it feel like his heart was breaking into a million shards of glass? "That doesn't mean you should jump in the deep end without a float," he argued, his attempt to reach her weakening with every discounted word.

She gave a helpless shrug. "I'm already there, Walker. You said so yourself."

The tension that stretched between them was downright palpable. Leonard hung his head. "I'll leave you two alone." He turned to Marcelina. "If you still decide to go through with this, time is of the essence. We need to get you in there quickly, and we have a lot to go over beforehand. I'll be close by."

Marcelina spared him a glance. "Thank you, Captain Ross."

When the man left, Walker ran a hand through his hair, struggling to sort through the logic of it all. It was there, but so much harder to grasp with all the emotions blocking his way. What the hell was Marcelina doing to him? "Don't go into this thinking you're protecting anyone," he said to her. "All it will do is make you lose respect for yourself."

She was walking back to the windows, her skirt swaying with each step. "Why is it so hard for you to understand?"

Walker paced out his frustrations with hands on hips and a fierce need for more liquor. "You know what Rivera wants," he pointed out. "He'll expect you to sleep with him. Are you prepared for that?"

She swung around to face him. "I'm prepared to do whatever it takes to get him to trust me." She approached him, her expression softening in the suffused glow of the paper-covered windows. "Don't look at me like that. We aren't a thing, remember? You made it quite clear why we can't be. But if all of this goes away, we might actually have a chance to—"

"Don't do it, Marcelina." She was standing close enough to touch. Walker fisted his hands, determined not to. "Don't say this is for us, because if you sleep with him, it will destroy any chance we'll ever have."

Her brows drew down. "You yourself have been trying to convict him for years."

"But I won't cheapen myself in the process."

As soon as the words left his mouth he regretted them, especially when her eyes clouded with hurt. "If that's how you feel," she said, "it looks like I'm damned either way. At least with Rivera I can get screwed on my own terms, instead of in prison by a gang of women with broomsticks."

Her return blow hit below the belt. It meant she had no faith in his abilities as her lawyer. Probably never did. It was a foul that sparked his anger anew. "What am I even doing here?" he returned hotly. "If I can't save you from yourself, why am I wasting my time?"

"Maybe you shouldn't."

But he'd invested too much in her already, *way* more than what was required or even allowed. He wasn't going to let her blow off his efforts because of some misguided belief she could out-con a con like Rivera. She needed to know what was at stake. She needed to choose *him* over Rivera. A heady mixture of anger and desire was already swirling around them, growing so potent that there was no resisting the challenge in her fiery eyes. The swollen mouth that dared him to resist it.

Ignoring the dusty voices that told him not to, he crushed his lips to hers in a soul-wrecking kiss. Her fists were bunched in his shirt, and suddenly their world was melded together once again. Walker could tell by her soft moans that she was falling into the same dark hole with him, ready to risk it all for one more shot at coming together. "Do you feel what you do to me, Marcelina?" he rasped against her mouth.

In answer, she arched into his touch and at the same time pushed against him. They were both riding that jagged edge of reckless passion, only she was the one resisting this time. "We can't. Remember?" she said breathlessly, her brow furrowing with the battles going on inside her head. Her thick, disheveled hair half-covered her face. When she lifted her eyes, they were glassy with tears.

Walker thought she never looked more beautiful than at that moment. "Christ." He shook his head to clear it. Suffering from a major case of blue balls, he turned away in a desperate bid to pull himself together. "That wasn't fair to you." It was as much of an apology as he was willing to give.

"Captain Ross said you had a rough day." When her observation was met with silence, she tried again. "This may not be the time, but do you want to tell me about it?"

He could feel her probing gaze on his back, expecting answers. "I'd just left my father when Leonard called. It wasn't a good time."

"Your father? What happened?"

"We talked about you." When he finally turned back

around, he waved away her look of surprise and sat on one of the folding chairs. Elbows on knees, he stared at his hands. "He was Nari Puccini's best friend and lawyer. I may have failed to mention it before."

"No way," she breathed, sinking down onto the other chair, hunkering with him in the dark face-to-face. "Nari and your father were close?"

"Very."

"Why didn't you tell me?"

It was a good question he didn't have a good answer for. As he searched for one, she continued to watch him. "I guess I needed time to think. I was worried you would run if you knew how connected I was to it all. And I also knew I was the only one who could possibly defend you against Conrad Bishop—if he went after you, that is. But it turns out he knew about you all along." Walker looked up and met the confusion in her gaze. "I'd just found out he asked a judge to give me your case."

She sat back with a look of shock. "Why would he do that?"

"He said Puccini would have wanted you to have good representation."

As Marcelina absorbed the news, she nodded in understanding. "You're upset because he played you."

A humorless laugh shook his chest. "No, that's not why I'm upset. The only time Conrad resorts to charity is when guilt plays a role. He must have known without a reasonable doubt that you hadn't killed his boss. And I wanted to know why."

After some thought, understanding dawned on her face. "You don't think he had something to do with it?"

Walker shrugged. "Puccini would have never suspected him."

"Oh…" Marcelina covered her mouth with her hand. "Walker, no. What did you do?"

He produced a dull smile. "I bought him a drink. Then I accused him of conspiring to murder his best friend." For the first time in his career—in his life—Walker was about to admit something he never had before. "This is hitting too close to home for me, Marcelina. With him, with you, with Rivera… I'm not used to operating out of bounds. It's all I seem to do anymore."

Her lush features smoothed out with something akin to dread. "You're scared, aren't you?"

It was as if she'd just realized her rock had crumbled. That he wasn't superhuman after all, a realization that horrified him way more than it horrified her. But the facts were the facts and he had to face them. "If my father has something to hide, I'll never uncover it. And he won't hesitate to let you take the fall."

Her eyes were like saucers. "You mean his conscience only goes so far."

"If we can't keep your secret under wraps," he answered, "things will get bad for us. Your deal with the DEA may solve that problem, but it'll create others." And he would lose her either way. "I need to take a breath. Regroup."

Marcelina straightened a bit. "Are you saying what I think you are?"

Though throwing in the towel seemed like the best recourse, Walker didn't want to. Instead, he whispered, "Come home with me."

Emotions swirled around them until her eyes welled up with tears once again. She shook her head. "No."

The force of that small, two-letter word hit Walker

right in the throat. His reply caught there, came out strangled. "Why?"

She wiped at the tears before they could fall. "If I go home with you, I won't want to leave." But she *would* leave. The harsh reality of it was written in the misery etched on her face. "I'm letting go of my fears, Walker. I need to do this because we both know it's my only chance. I hope you can someday understand that."

"What if Rivera sucks you in? He'll make you promises that may or may not be bullshit."

Marcelina took his hands in her own. Squeezed them tight. "I won't lose my way. At some point you have to trust that I'll make the right decisions."

But he didn't want to. Why couldn't she just do what he said? "This isn't about trust, Marcelina. He contacted me the other night." Damn it, just telling her this meant he was getting desperate, and he hated himself for it. "Rivera confirmed that this is a personal attack against me, and you are the collateral damage. He won't lose focus. He won't back down until he has you where it hurts *me* most, which is either in his bed or in the ground. And if you go to him, there is no coming back from it. Not for you. Not for me."

She was so still, absorbing what he'd just told her even though it wasn't all new. She looked down at their joined hands. And then what he had feared most—the very reason he'd kept that phone call a secret—became reality in her next words. "You just gave me another reason to do this, Walker."

He closed his eyes against the blackness that washed over him.

"It's good that you told me," she continued in a sullen manner. "I'll be more aware. Maybe even work a different angle."

That wasn't what he'd gone for, but the bitch of it was…she was right. If there was no changing her mind, it was better that she go in armed with as much information as possible. That she knew all the risks, even the ones that had nothing to do with the DEA's deal.

Despite the fact she had just ripped his heart out.

Reclaiming his hands, Walker got up and paced the room in an attempt to focus on the business end of things, but it was hard to do with a fresh, hot cloud of rejection hanging over him. He needed to focus on that. Follow her lead. Knew that putting distance between them was the right thing to do since she was bound and determined to move forward with this insanity. "Rivera will expect you and I to stay in contact at first," he said with cold detachment. "A complete cut in ties would look too suspicious. He wants a fight and he wants to win."

"Okay."

His change in tone had made her blanch, but he didn't care. His only motivation for helping at this point was her safety. "Don't ever underestimate him. I showed you what happens to people who cross him. Any time you start to get comfortable, remember those pictures. Remember he's watching. Listening."

A trace of fear finally entered her eyes. Good. She needed to be afraid. Cautious. "He'll try and convince you to fire me and go with his own team of lawyers," he continued. "They're good, obviously. They'll win this conspiracy case for you if not make it go away altogether. In doing so, they'll render the DEA's deal obsolete, but keep in mind they are every bit as dirty as Rivera is. They'll bribe, threaten, anything they have to in order to end it quickly and in their favor."

"Who would they bribe and threaten?" she asked with a frown.

"Witnesses. Cops. Jurors. Maybe even Kendall." When she opened her mouth to argue against the notion, he cut her off. "Anyone can be bought, which is why we lost our last source. And why your meetings with Captain Ross are on the sly and in shitholes like this."

Her lovely face lost some of its pallor. "Yes, we already went through the non-disclosure talk. Even though it would kill me to let Kendall believe the worst."

"Kendall talks too much. Even if she remains loyal to you, she may slip in front of the wrong person." Walker let that one marinate for a while, his apprehension building until she gave a reluctant nod of understanding. It was that reluctance that put the fear of God into him since there was no room for it in this case. "It's very important you don't screw up, Marcelina," he said with force. "You either go all the way or you go home, because half-ass will get you killed. Rivera needs to think he's taking something away from me. He'll want you in his debt. He'll want you in his bed. And he doesn't like the word no." His brow went up as his words added a chill to the air. "Whatever it takes, right?"

****

Though he hadn't said the words, Marcelina couldn't shake the feeling that Walker was done with her. That everything from this point forward would be for show. She knew she'd screw up somehow before her court date, but never thought it would be by doing the right thing. She supposed his feelings for her had something to do with it—the kind of feelings she'd wanted from him. The realization he had them was a thrilling one, but had only come after she'd committed herself to the deal. But would it have mattered? If what Walker said was true, Rivera was gunning for him and she would do what it took to diffuse the situation before things got dangerous. And if the DEA was right, it was only a matter of time before Rivera supplied her with her ticket to freedom. Either way, the outcome was worth it. Killing two birds with one stone? Even better.

So, after a quick debriefing by two DEA agents, and having just packed up and walked out on Kendall, Marcelina was headed down a defiant path toward what appeared to be her last option.

Rivera.

A uniformed officer got out of the squad car to question her. She put on a good show, telling him to go fuck himself and whatever poor hooker he could find to harass. As she marched down the sidewalk, she got out her phone and made a call. A half-mile later, a white sedan pulled up beside her. Knowing what it meant to open that door, to climb into the back seat, to forfeit her last chance to back out of this…she got in.

They drove to a posh gallery on the south side of the city. Facing a well-lit entrance of marble architecture, Marcelina left her suitcase in the back seat and exited the vehicle.

"He's waiting for you in the front room," the driver said before she closed the door behind her.

Trying to ignore the fear in her stomach, she entered the place feeling sorely underdressed in her jeans and blouse. The sophisticated woman inside her revolted at appearing in less than her best, but her choice of clothing indicated an unfortunate, unplanned chain of events.

She spotted Armando's thick-bodied form as he observed a large piece of art through a pair of wire-rimmed spectacles. Standing out in his tuxedo, he mimicked the art he admired in living form. She approached, wondering if he knew she was there, and then saw the evidence of it in his profile.

"You can lose the smirk," she said beside him.

"There is no smirk." He glanced at her, amusement clear in his countenance. "I'm just glad you changed your mind."

"I need a job."

He brought a glass of red wine to his lips, sipped it. "You need more than that if the suitcase you brought is any indication."

Though Marcelina could use a glass of wine herself, the waiter with a tray of them ignored her attempt to gain his attention and walked right on by. Having showered before she left, she smelled better than the last time they met, but her brief, hot walk had made things notably sticky. Somewhat annoyed that the waiter's snub had escaped Armando's notice, she blew hair from her face. Straightened her top. "I was hoping you'd give me an advance so I can afford a hotel room."

Instead of acknowledging that, Armando extended his glass toward the painting he'd been admiring. "What do you think of this piece?"

She looked at it, her brow creasing as she contemplated what appeared to be no more than a plain black shape. "It's…a rectangle."

"Look closer."

Marcelina released an impatient breath and leaned in squinting. Beneath the black, a series of darker lines formed a pattern of some sort. She followed them, realizing a whole compilation of designs loomed there. "It's sort of a puzzle, isn't it?"

"One that can only be solved by looking past the obvious."

Ah. So there was a reason he'd been camping by that piece when she arrived. It was a lesson of sorts, about his character and her so-called incorrect perception of it. "Are you going to buy it?" she asked, slightly annoyed.

"It's a little too dark for me." He looked at her again. "I prefer color. Something bold, perhaps?"

They moved to the next painting. When he stopped to study it, she asked, "Is this a decision you need to make before answering my question about the advance?"

"You won't need an advance." He removed the spectacles and stepped back. "You can stay in one of my guestrooms until you can afford a place of your own."

She pushed air through her lips. "I don't think so."

The amusement was back as he regarded her. "It's a whole separate floor, Marcelina. I'll be a perfect gentleman, I promise."

They walked some more, looking at ridiculously priced paintings and contemplating the possibilities. "Just for tonight," she conceded finally. "I'll figure something else out tomorrow."

"If you wish."

Now at the front doors, he handed his empty glass over to the same waiter who had blown her off before. The forty-something year-old man was immaculately groomed and carried an air of stiff disapproval over her appearance amidst such a formal affair. She gave him an impudent smile. "Your barn door is open."

The waiter's face fell and he bent to check the state of his zipper, toppling several of the empty glasses on his tray. It was good enough, though a little "roughing up" by Armando's heavies would have been much, much better.

Once they were safely tucked inside the limo, the front passenger door opened. In came the bodyguard whose presence Marcelina had failed to notice, same as before at *Le Marée*.

Damn, he's good.

Which was probably why he could kill for Armando without getting caught.

When she returned her attention to Armando he had his cellphone to his ear. "Your server, Mr. Solomon," he said. "He treated my guest poorly. I trust you'll remedy the situation. Good." He disconnected the call, ignoring her wide-eyed gaze as he pulled a dark bottle from the rack of the mini bar. He opened it. Poured a glass of red wine and handed it over.

She took the glass with numb fingers, suddenly regretting her ill wishes against Mr. Solomon. Just as she'd been about to get comfortable, one phone call from Armando had let the chill back in. It was a reminder that she was in the company of some very evil men. Alone. Small. Armed with only her wits and a sheer desire to get through this alive. She took a liberal drink from her glass, unmindful of the expensive wine's flavor.

When the car started rolling, Armando loosened his bowtie. "Can I assume you left the police escort at Kendall's apartment?" he asked her.

Marcelina looked out the window at the ritzy shops they passed and infused a good amount of concern into her voice. "She's the one who wanted them. I always thought it was rather pointless, something you pretty much proved yesterday morning." She spared him a glance. "By the way, you didn't have to hurt her."

"I did no such thing."

"She kicked me out."

"And you didn't call your lawyer?" When she didn't answer him, he considered her with amusement. "Mmm. Whatever will Mr. Bishop do with you?"

Probably nothing anymore. The mere possibility amplified her growing sense of abandonment, but she had decided not to let on that she knew of Rivera's threatening phone call to Walker. It was best that she play it dumb for a while, at least until she found her footing. "He can be a bit…tyrannical," she said. "I didn't want the lecture, but I trust him."

"Trust is a two-way street," Armando answered. "Especially between lovers."

She flashed him a look of annoyance. "We aren't lovers."

His answering smile said he simply didn't believe her. "Trouble in paradise?"

If he meant to piss her off, it was working. Marcelina handed her wine back, leaned forward and spoke to the driver. "Just let me out at the next stoplight. I'll find a hotel."

"I didn't mean to upset you. No more talk about Walker Bishop, then. Okay?" It was a much kinder Rivera, his voice soothing behind her.

She glared. "Seriously, let me out. I don't know what I was thinking, coming to a *drug lord* for a job."

"I see you're still pondering the lies he told you about me," Armando said in a much-too-jovial manner.

"Just stop…the *car*."

"You came to me for help. Besides, it would be ungentlemanly to let you fend for yourself at this time of night."

As she brooded out the window, the car maintained

its steady speed. Of course the driver would ignore her. He was paid to obey the orders of one man. She was as good as trapped whether she wanted to be or not…with no recourse but to push forward with this insane plan of hers.

Chapter 14

Just as the wine had begun to take effect, her rush of anger washed it away. Tense again, the man beside her expelled a patient breath. She heard the clink of glass as he disposed of her wine, and the creak of leather as he sat back in his seat. His hand brushed against her forearm. "Just relax, Marcelina," Armando said. "Let me ease some of the burden, at least until you get some rest."

As exhausted as she was, Marcelina doubted she could possibly find sleep with the mother of all problems lurking under the same roof. "What if I wake up tomorrow and want to leave?" she asked grumpily.

"I won't stop you."

And he was full of it, but she managed to look at him then with a bit of trust in her eyes. "Okay. I'll stay at your house, but just for tonight."

His smile was brilliant and infused with a good amount of charm. "It's quite beautiful where I live. Peaceful. You may decide to stay."

"On the beach?" she asked, telling herself to ignore the slight jump in her heart.

"No, I don't like the sand."

She harrumphed. "The whole state is made of sand."

He laughed as the car rolled through a gated entrance, the guard saluting them as they drove by. It was a private community with lots of houses and pristine lawns, but the grand dwellings thinned out as they put some distance beneath them. Finally, they turned right, driving through another gated entrance, this one complete with wrought iron swinging doors. They glided down a path of cobblestones flanked by massive banyan trees and thick cypress that hid the mansion she knew was somewhere behind it all. They rounded the last bend and there it was—the estate her DEA handlers had described complete with manicured lawns, fountains, and an abundance of full, royal palm trees. The lighting was spectacular, bringing every nook and cranny out of darkness and showcasing the security cameras mounted on every corner. It was a compound, the beige adobe structure boasting two separate garages, a dark tiled roof, and light stone accents.

But it wasn't the house the DEA was interested in. When the car swerved toward the garages, she craned her neck and caught a peek of a large bow in the distance.

Bingo. There it was, Rivera's own private yacht where it was suspected all the juicy stuff happened…and where her assignment would ultimately lead her.

Armando followed her gaze. "I spend most of my time on the water."

Of course he did. The privacy would be essential to his operation. So far it was anyone's guess as to how many illegal activities went on in the middle of the Gulf of Mexico; what kinds of deals were made, how much money was exchanged, how many men were killed—information she would collect if she were fully accepted into his fold.

When, she told herself. *When* I'm fully accepted.

Only when they were safely parked in the garage did they exit the car. "This way." Armando cupped her elbow and ushered her toward the entrance of the house…a house that was every bit as impressive on the inside as it was the outside. Marcelina looked around, taking in the mixture of old-school elegance and rustic beauty, which combined wood floors and ceilings with carved marble fireplaces and trim. The warm colors and interior archways fused the two styles together with a Mediterranean flare.

She stopped in front of a metal door that looked suspiciously like… "An elevator?"

His warm breath skimmed her ear. "Comes in handy when moving all the drugs from one floor to the other."

Suppressing her shudder, Marcelina leaned away from him and answered his clear amusement with a narrow look. "You're laughing at me."

"Maybe a little."

"So, you're saying I shouldn't believe what everyone says about you."

"You're the one who came to me for help. Does it matter at this point?" Her tight-lipped silence was his answer. He stared at her mouth with a curious smile. "I'm beginning to wonder if Bishop even told you…"

She cocked her head. "Told me what?" That you taunted him via AT&T, you son-of-a-bitch?

The confirmation was there, she could see it in his eyes. He was assessing her actions, trying to determine if she'd *truly* come to him on her own, or if she was that good of an actress. In that moment, Marcelina knew the truth; this was all very much a twisted game. Every move she made would be closely scrutinized before Rivera made the next. He would crush her if he sensed she had come out of loyalty to Walker, something he'd expected. Maybe even counted on.

"I guess he cares for you more than I realized."

Rivera's words were spoken in a low, thoughtful tone, almost as if to himself. Before Marcelina could react, his hand was on the small of her back and he was coaxing her forward. "Come on. I'll show you to your room."

As they turned toward a curved staircase, an angry feminine voice met them from behind. "*This* is what I get for leaving the gallery early?"

Already skittish, Marcelina whirled around to encounter a pair of violet eyes set in an uncommonly beautiful face—a woman so soft-boned and lovely that she could only stare. Her gaze travelled down the length of a tan torso, sculpted to perfection from the roots of her long brown hair down to her slender, red-tipped toes. She wore nothing but lacy underpants, lots of gold and a men's black dress shirt, which was hanging open and barely concealing the details of a spectacular set of breasts. Marcelina had to check the urge to swallow.

Bracelets rattled as the obvious woman of the house flounced toward the kitchen with an empty champagne flute in hand. It never occurred to Marcelina that Armando had a girlfriend. Wife? Someone he shouldn't be cheating on with other conquests?

Armando lifted a hand in the woman's direction, instructing Marcelina to follow. When they, too, reached the kitchen he introduced them. "Marcelina, I would like for you to meet Jade. You will learn quickly that she is my top employee as well as the most important woman in my life."

Jade's ass-length hair shimmered as she threw back her head and laughed. "If that were true, you would have chased after me when I left the gallery, not brought home another slut."

The verbal slap—coming from whom Armando referred to as an *employee*—was effective in awakening Marcelina's fight. "You're the one skulking around in your spray tan," she retorted.

The woman answered with a cat-eyed smirk that somehow put the fear of God into Marcelina's bones.

"Jade, show some manners," Armando scolded.

"I would if you hadn't stolen her from the cleanup crew after I left." Jade whirled back around and lifted the champagne bottle for another pour.

"This is the woman I hired for Lance and his team," he explained, "which means you need to apologize."

She turned back around while taking a long pull from her glass. When it was half drained, she licked her lips and aimed a sarcastic smile at Marcelina. "Sorry. He doesn't normally bunk the hired help."

Marcelina cocked a brow. "Like he does you, apparently?"

With slow deliberation, Jade put a hand on her hip, an act that moved the shirt aside to show off one of those spectacular breasts. "That's right, bitch. And soon you'll be skulking in your spray tan, too." Then she sauntered off with her champagne glass, long legs, and upturned nose.

"She's a real class act," Marcelina said, not knowing whether to laugh or cry.

Armando's chest rose and fell with a troubled sigh. "She's my personal cook."

Marcelina barked out a laugh as they once again headed toward the stairs. "Is that what you call them these days?"

"We aren't romantic—more like siblings, actually. She's the only woman I fully trust."

Siblings my ass.

Armando must have read her mind because he shrugged a shoulder. "She likes to feel the air on her skin. Her nudity does nothing for me." When they reached the second floor, he guided her to a room at the far end of the hall. "Your suitcase will be brought up shortly."

She stopped in the doorway, peering into the room. "Why the delay? Is it being searched as we speak?"

"A standard precautionary measure." As she absorbed the honesty of his answer, he preceded her inside, stopped, and threw her a patient smile. "You aren't the first to bring your suspicions into my home."

It was a big suite complete with sitting area and minibar. She crossed the threshold in a complete state of wonder, and was caught off guard when he grabbed her hand and halted her progress into the room.

"Now," he said. "When I search *you*, will I find anything that doesn't belong?"

A snort escaped until she met his gaze and realized he was serious. Her amusement faded. "Really?"

He gave her a no-nonsense kind of smile and circled his finger, ordering her to turn around. "According to your record, you should be familiar with the act of being frisked. Arms up, please."

Just how many misdemeanors did Captain Ross add to her record? She complied, rolling her eyes as his hands skimmed along her body. "Shouldn't this have been done *before* I entered your home?"

"In front of my men? I wanted to spare you the humiliation."

"How very thou—thoughtful." She jerked away when his touch skimmed the length of her backside. "How could I possibly hide anything there?" she snapped.

"You'd be surprised. The police have become quite resourceful. Your phone, please."

She stared at his outstretched hand for a moment then dug the phone out of her pocket. Handed it over. "Awfully paranoid for a guy with nothing to hide."

"Passcode."

She ripped the phone out of his hands to punch in the 6-digit code and handed it back with a scowl.

He looked at the screen. "Ooh, your lawyer wants you to call him right away." When she reached out to snatch it again, he held it away. "You'll get it back shortly." And handed it to another man that must have been waiting in the hall. As he disappeared with it, Armando said, "In the meantime I don't think Mr. Bishop is happy with you."

Marcelina backed away, ran a hand through her hair. "I'll call him tomorrow when I find a hotel."

"You aren't afraid of him, are you?" He closed the distance she'd put between them and stood dangerously close. "Why not tell him you're here?"

Such an imposing figure Armando Rivera made, all tall and wide and menacing, in constant control of a second-nature kind of rage. He thought he hid it beneath the loosened bowtie and tuxedo jacket, but she could tell in the way his eyes never seemed to settle. She swallowed hard. "We both know how Walker feels about you. He thinks you're out to get him for his many attempts to prosecute you. But I always thought that was ridiculous or you'd be out to get *half* the judicial system. Right?"

"Marcelina." He took her by the shoulders. "I'm not interested in Walker Bishop. I'm interested in *you*. As long as you're here, you'll be well cared for." He patted her shoulder as if the matter was ended. "Get a good night's rest and we'll talk more tomorrow."

When he moved away, Marcelina asked, "Will I start the job tomorrow?"

He paused at the door with a look that said *not so fast*. "You need to get comfortable here before I put you to work. Then we'll start with some training."

Comfortable, huh? "That wasn't the deal," she reminded through her teeth. "I need work and I need money."

"You won't need money as long as you're a guest in my home."

He left her then, cutting off any further argument. She supposed that's how drug lords worked—men who have manipulated and thrown around orders long enough for it to be commonplace. Yes, Armando Rivera was accustomed to getting what he wanted.

It was the very flaw that would give her the same in return.

****

Walker sat at his desk surrounded by case files, dim lamplight, and a heightened sense of gloom. He removed his wire-rimmed readers, plopped them down and rubbed at tired eyes. She would be inside by now, probably in awe of her surroundings and already drunk on something alcoholic. But it was impossible to see past the worst-case scenarios when she refused to call him.

It was 9:32 PM. Among the many folders on his desk, a thick one was splayed before him and beside it was a tumbler of scotch. It wasn't Marcelina's case he pored over, it was one that was scheduled for court next week and needed some last-minute attention. But the pages failed to come into focus in lieu of a face that wouldn't fade away.

His phone rang, and there again was Marcelina's face. Thank God. He took another burning sip from his tumbler of scotch and answered. "Bishop."

"It's Marcelina."

Yes, he knew. "Where are you?"

"Staying with a friend."

The script ticked through his head as it surely was hers, as if they were both playing a part in a horror film that would end with lots of blood and dead people. "Kendall said you two had a fight. Are you okay?"

"I'm fine."

Or, if Marcelina played it safe, it could end with only one dead person. Rivera. In the Florida gas chamber. Or riddled with bullets. Walker really didn't give a damn how the drug lord went down. "Don't forget our meeting tomorrow. We need to go over your deposition."

She hesitated. "I don't think I can make it."

That hadn't been a part of the script. "It's important. Don't blow this off, Marcelina."

"I don't have transportation."

"I can come to you."

"No…" He heard a troubled breath move over the receiver. "Don't worry, I'll keep in touch."

She really wasn't going to meet him. Was she held so tightly in Rivera's clutches already? His defenses cracked and the worry washed over him without benefit of a way to stop it. "Make sure you do."

****

The next morning, he paid a visit to Audrey Metcalf to see how she and her young daughter were doing.

Kendall and another woman were there as well, helping make funeral arrangements.

"Mr. Bishop." Graham's widow was a mere deer in the headlights as she stood in the doorway without letting him in. "What are you doing here?"

He acknowledged the others with a respectful nod before narrowing all his attention on Mrs. Metcalf. "I've come to see if you need anything."

A wooden smile slanted her lips. "The truth would be great. But there seems to be a shortage of that lately."

The woman was hurting but also angry. He could tell by more than just her words, or the dark circles under her eyes, or the picture frame that had been turned down on the fireplace mantel. "In my experience, it usually comes when least expected," he told her, his words as solemn as the air they breathed. "If at all."

Audrey's look dulled even more, but she seemed appreciative enough of the honest answer. "Would you like to come in?"

He considered the other women behind her, watching him with expectation. By the look of Kendall she was ready to shake him down for information about Marcelina. "I was just passing through," he said, "but I wanted you to know I have extensive knowledge of the man your husband was last seen with, from when I was on the prosecution side of the aisle." He handed her his card. She took it with notable reluctance. "I'm available if or when you want to talk. No soliciting, I promise." The last was said with a respectful nod.

Audrey kept her gaze on him. "Kendall is worried about Marcelina. Do you think she's next?"

God, he hoped not. Though he knew Audrey's direct approach was of the harmless variety, he still couldn't discuss it. His gaze rested on Kendall. "I'm doing what I can to help her," was all he said.

"Are you?" Kendall asked, coming around to stand beside Audrey with arms crossed. "Because you don't look as worried as I am right now."

It was the Bishop mask, love it or hate it. At the moment he hated it, and felt doubly resentful of his legal obligations. This was too personal for him, and it went against the grain to discount the genuine terror in Kendall's countenance.

"She's with Armando Rivera, isn't she?" Kendall pressed when he remained silent.

"She isn't…*communicating* with me very much right now," he answered.

"Kendall said Rivera was behind her attempted mugging." Audrey tilted her head, her eyes coming to life with loathing. "We know he's been pursuing Marcelina, which is how she encountered my husband in the first place. *She's* the one who told me how dangerous Rivera is. Why on earth would she go to him?"

Walker was still trying to figure that one out. According to Marcelina, Puccini had taught her how unstable the players of organized crime could be—something she seemed to take seriously until now. "All we can do is hope she stays out of trouble." He turned to Kendall. "And that she comes back soon."

As he said his goodbyes, Kendall watched him, her unanswered questions written in the harried lines of her brow. But he turned away, his shoulders like rocks beneath the weight of his suit as he walked down the corridor. At the elevator, Kendall appeared at his side.

"Is she doing this to help herself," she asked, "or to protect me?"

The elevator doors opened, and Walker stepped into it. "I guess you'll have to decide that on your own."

When he turned back around, they stared at each other in silence while the doors closed between them.

****

Marcelina reached the bottom step of the stairs just in time to hear a thump in the kitchen followed by a string of angry shouting.

"You're being reckless, all because of her big tits and pretty face!"

She hovered in the archway, soaking in the scene before her as Jade stormed out of the house and onto the lanai. Armando was leaning against the sink with a wet spot on the back of his mustard-yellow shirt. A head of cabbage lay on the floor surrounded by a few wayward leaves that had been broken off.

Marcelina couldn't help but laugh. "Did she just throw a cabbage at you?"

He turned around, his look satirical behind a pair of black-framed glasses. "She's upset you're here."

"Thanks for the warning." Marcelina walked over to the cutting board and eyed a cucumber with speculative dread. "Am I next?"

A deep chuckle. "There will be no objects thrown at you, I promise. She knows better."

But Marcelina had no doubt Jade was her biggest threat so far. "It doesn't look like she fears you much."

"She's spoiled. I treat her very well."

Marcelina picked up the cucumber and took a bite out of it, not bothering to hide the insolence of her act. To show she wasn't afraid. "Since she prepares your food, maybe *you* should fear *her*." Lord knew breakfast had been an interesting challenge for Marcelina.

212

"I have a special bond with my women." A devilish sparkle entered Armando's eyes. "Perhaps someday you'll understand."

She narrowed her gaze. "Not likely." Then took another bite. "Catch." She tossed the cucumber in his direction. He caught it with heat in his look. Just as she thought, the man loved a challenge.

"So what are we doing today?" she asked as she entered the great room.

"How about we start with a swim?"

She whirled around and met his approach with a frown. "How about I meet this team I'm supposed to be working with?"

"They have a full schedule today. Tomorrow will be better."

"Oh." She took out her phone and checked the time. "Okay, then I'll have time to make that meeting with Walker."

He gave her a look that brooked no refusal. "We'll swim. Afterward, I thought we'd go car shopping."

"Rushing things, aren't we?" she murmured as he turned her toward the stairs.

"Your job requires a vehicle. You'll have plenty of time to pay me back later."

They walked slowly, his hands gently cupping her shoulders from behind. "Walker doesn't like to be blown off," she said, wary of why they were headed to the second level. Where the bedrooms were. "He's a busy man."

"I'm sure he'll live."

She paused on the second step and looked down at him. "You know, you and he are a lot alike."

A wolfish grin turned his dark features into

something almost…attractive. "Oh, I'm much more exciting. Go on, now. Change into your swimsuit."

She ascended two more steps before she stopped again. "I don't have one."

"Go look on your bed."

With a small flutter in her belly, Marcelina entered her room. There on the bed were two bikinis of vastly different styles. The first was a gorgeous two-tone peach with scalloped edges and a matching wrap that covered plenty. The second was a skimpy white thing with only a sheer wrap for the bottom. When she held that particular article of clothing up, there was just enough lace in the front to cover the details, but nothing to hide the back. It appeared Armando was daring her to be daring.

"Not today," she murmured, choosing the peach. Again, why was she doing this? Sure, he was a compelling man, daring anyone to deny him in that authoritative way of his. But something inside her knew it was the right move. She knew men, and this one liked a challenge but needed enough give to keep him generous.

So, she'd give.

Just enough.

Chapter 15

When Marcelina emerged on the lanai, it was to find it complete with plush furniture, lots of greenery and even a fireplace topped with a flat screen TV. Beside the lanai was the entry into a curvaceous, sparkling blue infinity pool. Of course, there was a hot tub built in and an elegant backdrop of fountains. Beyond the pool was a boathouse complete with lift and large cruiser. The view would have been that of other distant, splendid homes across the intersecting waterways—if not for the huge yacht blocking it.

Water splashed. She looked over to find Armando making a grand exit from the pool. His curly hair was dripping, his big body streaked with water. The man was in good shape. Not fat so much as barrel chested and meaty. Not a single spark of interest lit within her.

Though there was an inferno burning within him if the look in his eyes was any indication. "Marcelina, you are even more perfect than I imagined."

She dipped her toe in, testing the temperature. "You imagined a lot by putting that white lacy thing on my bed." Yet she sensed his victory over her willingness to wear peach for him once again.

"A man can dream." He backed up, beckoning her to follow. "Join me. The water is perfect."

It was then she spotted Jade lounging at the opposite end of the pool. The woman sat up slightly, propping herself on elbows. She was completely naked with only a slender gold chain around her waist, and not a single tan line in sight. Long dark hair spilled around her shoulders, framing her breasts as if to command admiration from anyone lucky enough to view them. They watched each other as Marcelina entered the pool. "I see now why you thought I'd go for the lace. It's actually modest compared to what you're used to."

"Ignore her," Armando said. "She's more upset with me than with you."

Ignore her? As if Marcelina wasn't flustered enough, adjusting to a dangerous, opulent world where naked people threw produce at each other? "Are you sure your relationship is what you think it is?" she asked him.

"She cares for me and for my safety. She's suspect of anyone new, especially a beautiful woman such as yourself."

When Marcelina's gaze sought out Jade again, she found the woman standing by the pool with the towel thrown over her shoulder. Jade gave a casual shrug. "I say if you don't fuck him, you're with the police. And as far as I know, *I'm* the only one who got off last night."

The accuracy of her statement put a sliver of fear in Marcelina's gut. But she squashed it behind an award-winning poker face. "Guess we can't all be overpaid hookers, can we?"

Jade licked her bottom lip, effectively delivering a visual promise that they would go toe-to-toe sooner rather than later. Then she walked into the house, her bare cheeks jiggling with each dramatic step.

"You'd do well to tread lightly with her," Armando said behind her. Marcelina whirled around to find he had drifted oh-so close. "She can be dangerous."

She backed away from him, reaching more shallow waters in case she needed to make a hasty exit. "I thought you said she wouldn't hurt me."

Amusement found its way back into his countenance. "I said she wouldn't throw anything at you. Very specific."

Well, that was anything but reassuring. "And if she did? Would you punish her?"

"That would be between me and Jade." He floated on his back, his arms swirling beneath the water. "My best advice would be to give her no reason to hurt you."

****

That night, they sat at a small dinner table on the lanai. The air was perfect, cool with barely a soft breeze rustling the palm fronds around them. Candles flickered, casting Armando's features in a gentle glow that almost made him appear harmless as he watched her. The top buttons of his paisley shirt were open showcasing the gold he liked to wear and the barrel chest it rested on. For any other couple, it would have been considered romantic. So, Marcelina spent plenty of time admiring the lights from across the waterway, sparkling beyond the stern of the yacht. "You were right," she said on a sigh. "It *is* beautiful here. Peaceful."

"Safe," he finished for her. When she sent him an inquiring glance, he smiled. "Relax, Marcelina. Despite your obvious misgivings, you *are* safe here."

She allowed a small smile in return. "Oddly enough…I feel like it."

"Then you won't mind staying until you can afford a place of your own."

With the mood effectively killed, her mouth flattened in disgust. "Guess that's a 'no' on the advance."

"I told you before, you don't need one. Just relax and let me take care of you."

How easy it would be to say yes. But to do so would be to sell her soul to the devil. Nari's warning would always be embedded there, protecting her. Walker's warning only strengthened it. "Maybe just one more night."

She could feel his triumph from there. That one concession would turn into many until he had her right where he wanted her—as his mistress. She knew there was no job. He was playing her every bit as much as she was playing him, and it was only a matter of time before her moves became more labored. Her resolve tested. But all she had to do was imagine Graham Metcalf's burnt corpse, and her drive to avoid the same fate kept her priorities firmly in place.

A plate was put in front of her. She looked down at the beautiful display of veal Marsala with cremini mushrooms and mashed red potatoes, then looked up at Armando's cook.

Sequins sparkled from Jade's red bustier. "Hope you're hungry," the woman purred.

When she left, Marcelina stood up and switched plates with her host. Armando's shoulders shook with mirth. "Now is your chance to show me how much you trust her," Marcelina challenged, indicating his plate with her fork.

He picked up his own fork and immediately downed a bite of potatoes. Watched her throughout the process. "Are you seriously going to wait to see if I keel over?"

Her answer was to glance at the clock beside the stone fireplace. An open laugh was her reward and he picked up his wine glass next. "Eat, Marcelina. I guarantee you won't die tonight."

She reluctantly picked at a mushroom. Put it in her mouth. It was divine, perfectly marinated with a buttery-soft texture that flooded her taste buds with goodness.

"See?" he said. "It doesn't all have to be tainted by suspicion."

Marcelina looked up from her plate. "You should tell *Jade* that."

Silence followed as he processed that one in the manner of someone mesmerized. "Touché."

****

Across the waterway and down a bit, Walker entered the interior of a dark, empty condo lit only by whatever came through the sliding glass doors. He headed toward the back, narrowly missing the step down into the living area. The place reeked of cheap Italian food and was outfitted with no more than a few lawn chairs and some high-tech surveillance equipment situated by the glass doors. Empty cases doubled as work surfaces and were littered with typical bachelor-pad paraphernalia. He took a seat beside Captain Ross, who shoved aside some food containers and produced a pair of binoculars. Walker took them, put them up to his eyes, following where Leonard pointed. Through the dew-streaked glass of the sliding doors, he found the couple he searched for in the distance, sitting outside and enjoying a meal by candlelight.

Laughing together.

Yes, Marcelina looked way too comfortable, not to mention way too sexy in an off-the-shoulder dress Walker had never seen before. A foreign emotion grabbed him by the nuts. Never before had he wanted to skin another man alive and then feed his pieces to the fish off the coast of some barrier island.

The DEA had this condo for six days. Could he hold out that long? Or should he get out now?

Though their location was too far for audio, it offered a clear enough side view of Rivera's back yard from around the enormous yacht that was constantly docked there. Which was okay with Walker. Sound would probably put him over the edge.

"She's doing good," Leonard said beside him. "Holding her own. Has she contacted you today?"

He only shook his head, knowing his time there was limited while the DEA agent assigned to the stakeout was napping on a cot in the next room. And that Leonard was pushing his luck allowing him access. "You said there's another woman?"

"Mmm. Another Latina. She's a bold one. Orders the muscle around and struts in the nude like she owns the place." Leonard paused, frowned. "But we don't think she's the lady of the house. There's no physical contact between her and Rivera."

But Walker wouldn't put it past the man to bring home multiple conquests. Rivera was arrogant enough to enjoy a good catfight, especially if he were the prize.

"Her and Marcelina have exchanged some angry words, though," Leonard continued.

Walker just bet they did. Though he was confident that Marcelina could hold her own against any female rival, he didn't like the idea of her having to defend herself without him. How long would she hold out? Was she miserable? Scared? Enjoying herself like she appeared to be doing through the spyglass? "You only have this place for a week?" Walker asked.

"Yep."

"We'll have him by then."

It was said with enough confidence to hand the binoculars back. Leonard took them, his expression curious. "You have a lot of faith in Ms. Page."

Walker had no choice. It was the only way to keep himself sane throughout this torturous process of watching her cozy up to Rivera. "I'm not worried she'll turn, if that's what you mean."

"But you're worried about *something*," Leonard observed.

He sat back in the lawn chair and scrubbed his face with his hands. "Her determination scares the hell out of me."

Leonard smiled. Popped a pretzel into his mouth. "Sounds like we finally have the right person sharing a meal with Rivera."

Even if it meant sharing his bed? Walker doubted even Leonard could make that right in his head, but they were all so damned desperate to see Rivera go down…

"I can't watch this." With a full head of steam, Walker rose from the chair and headed for the door.

"Where are you going?"

"To the gym. Keep me posted."

"You got it."

Two minutes later, Walker was back in the living room lawn chair peering through the binoculars. "What is that? Dessert?"

Leonard squinted through his own spyglass. "Looks like Cherries Jubilee." Then Walker felt the man's gaze rake over him as one would assess a lost cause. "Damn, man. If I didn't know better, I'd say you're in love with Ms. Page."

He may be a lost cause, but he definitely *was not* in

love. Couldn't be. Walker was many things, but a masochist wasn't one of them. "Kiss my ass," he grumbled.

A deep sigh. "That's not a denial."

****

It had been a long, fruitless twenty-four hours and Marcelina hated wasting time. She realized from the get-go that she didn't have the patience to be a "source," or a detective for that matter. As she laid in the blessed privacy of her room, taking in the rich furnishings and expensive art surrounding her, all she wanted was to scramble out of there as fast as her feet could move. Through most of the day, she'd had to tamp down the desire to mash Rivera's face into the ground and demand answers like some rage-driven, TV show detective. Anything to cut through the bullshit and get this over with.

On the other hand, she could understand why women wanted him—women who liked to be dominated, taken care of, and pampered. Women who were willing to do as they were told in order to experience the good life—if only for a little while. Armando had his sex appeal. There was mystery in the man, a bit of humor, and even a streak of kindness that made him seem more human than previously thought.

But he had no light in his eyes. They were dark. Soulless. Only coming to life when evil was at play. She'd gotten a taste of it earlier that afternoon when four cars had arrived at his home. They were all brand-new, all variations of sex on wheels, and all her favorite color. Purple. How the hell did he know that, anyway?

He'd asked her to choose one of the cars. While she allowed herself to do so this time—for the sake of her role as corruptible pawn, of course—one of the drivers went up to him and spoke low. Armando had then politely excused himself and walked with the man into the nearest garage bay. Closed the door.

Moments later he walked out alone, wiping his bloodstained hands on a cloth. There was renewed life in his eyes…and a different shirt on his back.

"Have you decided?" he'd asked her with more energy than usual.

Shaken to the core, she blinked at his new attire, wondering how many shirts he stored in the garage for moments just like this. Her gaze lifted again, meeting his with some faux fire of her own. Then she skirted around him and headed back to the house.

"Which one?" he shouted behind her.

"I'll take the purple one," she'd answered through her teeth.

Giving her no time to think, he'd caught up with her on the lanai as she watched a boat putter by, its small wake lapping against the seawall.

"They're all purple, Marcelina." His hands closed around her upper arms. "What's wrong?"

Everything. The fact he knew her favorite color. His ability to throw her off course. That he'd just beaten a man and enjoyed it. That she was there instead of with Walker. "What did you do to him?" she'd asked him straight up.

He'd turned her around to face him. "I taught him greed doesn't pay." The disapproval must have shown in her eyes because he smiled and took her chin. "Don't worry, I didn't kill him." The smile faded a bit. "That's what I find most attractive about you, you know. Beyond the beautiful shell, you have a certain integrity I don't see often."

She focused on his mouth, anything to avoid the soulless gaze. "And that's something you admire? Integrity?"

"It gives me hope. Having you in my home, here with me…you have the power to make me a better man."

He'd kissed her then, a bare touch of lips she'd backed out of before he could take it too far. As he'd watched her, she'd given him a breathless, puzzled frown, one that told him he was right to hope. Right to pursue her.

Then she'd left, contemplating his moves with every step toward her room. He'd pulled off one of the oldest tricks in the book with the "I'm a project, fix me" routine. Women went nuts for it, and he knew how to play *that* game better than most.

But he'd chosen the wrong woman to play with, and now that her first horrible day had ended, Marcelina was experiencing some serious withdrawals from normalcy. She picked up her phone, checked the time. It was past ten o'clock, which meant it was too late to call Walker. Not that she could tell him what she'd seen that day, because her phone was probably bugged just like her room.

I'll call him first thing in the morning.

Turning out her light, she pulled the sheet up to her chin and lay wide-awake for what seemed like an eternity. Hours later, she was floating far off in the warm gulf waters, letting the current carry her away to uncharted territory. Far from reality. Far from her problems and far from her uncertain future.

Something touched her leg. When she shifted her gaze, it was to find Walker standing beside her in his suit and tie, waist deep in the small, lapping waves. It was then she realized she hadn't drifted at all, and that he was there to keep her from going out too far. At the sight of him, her belly began to quiver with warm desire. He was broad-shouldered and steely-eyed, his dark hair impeccably combed, which only made her want to mess it up. She loved him messy. She loved him all buttoned up, too.

She loved him.

Marcelina blinked at the realization. Smiled. Yeah, it was quite possible she'd had it bad for a while now.

As she lay there, the water skimming over her body, he let go of his briefcase. It floated away while his hands began to roam. His striking blue eyes were alight with the life she so craved, the heat she so desired, the want she so needed. He parted her legs and moved in, touching her where her own fire burned. She wanted him so badly she ached. As he held her gaze, he bent low and trailed small kisses down her belly. Cupped her bottom in preparation to lift her to his mouth. "Walker," she breathed.

The very real sound passing through her throat brought about a terrible sort of reality. Only in dreams did men in expensive suits frolic with their lovers in the Gulf of Mexico. Without another soul around. On a normally crowded beach.

Her eyelids fluttered open. Reality descended as she searched the dark and registered the black rectangles of expensive art on the walls. She wasn't in the Gulf of Mexico. Walker wasn't between her legs.

But someone was.

With a choked gasp, Marcelina shot to the head of the bed and turned on the light to find Jade camped at the foot of it, her dark hair pooled over the white coverlet. With a cat-like smile, she ran her tongue over her lower lip. "But we were just getting started."

Marcelina performed a quick body check. Her panties were still on, thank God, but how far would Jade have gone if she hadn't woken in time? She shot off the bed and lowered her nightgown. "What the hell are you doing?" she asked in horror, feeling much like a little girl who'd been sucked into an angry mob without an adult.

Jade slinked onto the bed and struck a pose, her body sleek and curvaceous beneath the sheer black fabric of her robe. "Since Armando is sleeping alone again, I thought you might be into girls."

Rage took over at the thought of what almost happened. The woman had been between her legs, of all the… "Get out of my room, bitch," Marcelina growled, fisting her hands at her sides.

"Who's Walker?" Jade cocked a perfectly plucked eyebrow. "You sighed his name when I touched you. Maybe Armando needs to know you have the hots for another guy."

Did this mean Jade wasn't privy to Armando's vendetta against Walker? The evil grin made it really hard to tell… Marcelina swallowed. "What do you want from me?"

The covers rustled as Jade got to her feet, her robe parting in the process. Fully bared to her, she approached with swaying hips and attitude. Marcelina forced herself to stand her ground when Armando's "cook" met her nose-to-nose. Her words were low and smoky. "I want you to leave here and to never come back. You're dangerous. I know this deep in my gut. And if you're with the cops, I *will* gut you, Princess. Slowly."

The woman sauntered out of the bedroom leaving Marcelina more traumatized than Armando's garage beating earlier that day. She fisted her hands to still their trembling, hating that Jade could affect her that way. Could she stay knowing that she would be tested at every turn? Threatened even in her sleep?

What would she wake to next?

Feeling more alone than ever, she picked up her phone and brought up Walker's number. All she wanted was to call him. Hear his voice. Lose herself in his arms until people like Armando, Jade, and their sick, twisted world no longer existed.

"I'm sorry, Walker." Tears blurred her vision in the lamplight.

Chapter 16

The next morning, feeling proper in a smart blouse and skirt ensemble, Marcelina descended the stairs to find Armando waiting for her in the sitting room with a man who wore the look of an attorney like a second skin. It was his shuttered manner more than the suit and polished shoes. Both men stood when she reached the landing. As she passed the kitchen to her right, a fully dressed Jade ran a knife through the belly of a fish. She then reached inside and pulled out a long strand of intestines. Marcelina stopped in her tracks and met the woman's wicked smile. "Little early for fish, isn't it?" she asked in a breezy way that masked her sudden onset of anxiety.

"It's never too early, Princess." Jade then took up her glass of orange juice with a gore-coated hand. Drank with her sultry gaze and bloodstained apron.

Disgusting. Gross. Ick.

Armando approached with guest in tow. "Marcelina, good morning." He leaned in, kissed her cheek. "I'd like for you to meet Dan McDonald."

Dan was also observing what Jade left on her glass with a horrified look that disappeared quickly when he held out his hand. They shook. "Nice to meet you," Marcelina said.

"Dan is my most talented attorney. His track record is the best in all of southern Florida."

They walked deep into the sitting room, out of view of Jade and her gruesome display. "Armando has been filling me in on the details of your trafficking charges," Dan said, his navy-blue suit swishing with his steps. "And I think, with my help, you have a legitimate shot at beating them."

Reaching the bar, Marcelina took the glass of orange juice Armando handed her. "I already have an attorney."

Dan declined the drink. "Not one who can guarantee an acquittal."

She looked at Armando who stood amongst the Mediterranean décor, holding his juice as if posing for a portrait. "No one can do that. Can they?" she asked him.

He quirked a smile. "With Dan on your team, it's as good as done."

It was playing out just as Walker predicted it would. Rivera wanted him out of her life, and apparently sooner was better. She put her glass down on the bar's granite surface. Cleared her throat. "Armando, can we talk in private, please?"

With a mild nod, he excused them, indicating the door to the study. She went that way, feeling his nearness and his forced patience as he humored her. When he turned to slide the doors closed, Marcelina scoped out the loaded bookshelves around her, along with the dark, cherry desk that could very well house some kind of useful information. She made a mental note to visit later and have a look around under the pretense of finding something to read. The shades were pulled down in this room, lending a legit godfather feel to her cage-like surroundings. Still, she crossed her arms and oozed impudence. "What are you doing?"

He gave her a lazy blink. "I'm helping you get out

of these unfortunate drug charges you've been saddled with."

"My legal problems are none of your business."

"It is when you're residing under my roof."

"Something I didn't want in the first place."

His gaze travelled down the length of her. "You seem pretty comfortable to me."

Then her ruse was working, but it didn't make the insinuation settle in her stomach any better. "You know Walker is my attorney," she argued.

"If that's all he is, you wouldn't be calling his name in your sleep." His voice was slick as clarified butter.

Marcelina had already prepared herself for this and Jade didn't disappoint, which meant she had resigned herself to owning it. She narrowed her gaze. "Did your most trusted employee tell you *everything* about last night?"

Armando approached her, his big body emanating power and protection. "She did. If it makes you feel better, she was punished for her lewd treatment of you. But *you* should have come to me the moment you were able."

Which would have landed her in his bedroom in the wee hours of night, something she would try to avoid as long as possible. Marcelina lifted her chin. "I like to handle my own problems."

"Yes, I know." He was close now, gazing down at her like a Colombian Daddy Warbucks in heat. "It's one of the reasons I must have you on my team. You are a rare example of strength and loyalty. This Jonah King person was careless in his handling of you, yet when you caught a case, you were willing to take your hit. Not point fingers and lay blame."

Caught a case? Took her hit? This was language she didn't understand, but sensed she should learn it if she were to play a convincing loyalist. "I'm not a rat."

"You aren't a good judge of men, either. You need to let Walker Bishop go. He became a threat to your case the moment you two exchanged the first kiss."

Since Armando had been there to witness their first kiss, his logic was hard to deny.

"I'm offering you a way out, Marcelina," he continued. "That's all."

Bullshit. She knew what a *real* threat looked like, even when wrapped in false concern. Chewing her bottom lip, she peered up at him through her lashes. "Give me time to at least think about it?"

He considered her request with the thoughtfulness of a statue, probably because he wasn't used to being challenged. After a moment, his shoulders relaxed a little. "Of course. But not too long or I may have to take matters into my own hands."

She cocked her head. "What's that supposed to mean?"

The look entering his eyes reminded her of a California wildfire: eager to do damage to anyone or anything that got in its way. "It means you're in my world now," he said in a low, meaningful voice. "I know what's best for you. And if I decide Bishop is too much of a liability, well…let's just say I never did tolerate much of that."

Feeling as if he'd knocked the wind out of her, Marcelina blinked. Swallowed. Nodded in understanding. It wasn't until they left the godfather room that she took her first recuperative breath. She sat with Dan, listened and nodded like a good girl. Asked some questions. Looked genuinely impressed. The man could argue a good case, enough to justify the costly suit and six-figure Cartier watch he so proudly wore.

Not long into their session, the doorbell sounded with the ominous chime of a Roman cathedral. In a far-off part of the house, the door was answered. Voices could be heard, one deep and unfamiliar, the other too low to recognize. Regardless, Marcelina knew who it was by the sheer amount of energy heating her blood. *Please, no…not Walker.*

The bulldozer bodyguard appeared. "Walker Bishop here to see Ms. Page."

Armando's gaze shifted to Marcelina, lingered in that cool way of his. "Invite him in."

Surely he could see her heart thumping from where he stood. And surely he was aware of Walker's arrival ahead of time since no one could enter this fortress without permission. Despite her nerves taking yet another hit, she would play this off to everyone's advantage. So, with scruples firmly in place, she stood when footsteps approached from down the hall. But Marcelina's knees nearly gave out at the first blessed sight of Walker since falling into this dark underworld of insanity. He was the most beautiful thing she'd seen in days, his all-business attire and stern countenance virtually glowing with goodness and light. But she managed to regard him as if he'd done something horribly wrong. "What are you doing here?"

Armando stood by the carved marble fireplace with hands in pockets. Walker met and kept the suspicious glare he received until he dismissed it altogether as if to say *yeah, I'm in your home. Choke on it.* "We rescheduled for this morning. Did you forget?"

Under the cool shell, Marcelina knew her lawyer boiled. "Right." She went to Armando, worrying her bottom lip between her teeth. "I need to leave with him for a while."

The man's tough features planed out. "Why, when you can conduct your business here? In fact, Dan may be useful to you and…Mr. Bishop."

It was as if he used the name as a reminder of his earlier threat. She took Armando's hand, gave it a reassuring squeeze. "This is something I need to do on my own," she said, her words slow, encouraging and loaded with meaning.

His mouth finally moved with a hint of approval. "By all means, then. But don't be long. Dan has other business today as well."

"Let me get my purse." She left the room—left the two men alone to do whatever it was men did when they vehemently wanted to kill each other but couldn't.

Except Armando would, and very well could. The possibility had her rushing back in record time, with purse in hand and a clear need to hurry along. Walker followed her out of the house without a word.

In the car as he drove in silence, he ignored her subtle glances, which she knew he could feel. It was a short yet very long time later when he turned into the entrance of a parking garage of a beachfront condominium. He stopped at the gate and punched in a code. The arm lifted to grant them entry.

They went inside and the car's interior went dark. As her eyes adjusted, Marcelina watched the smattering of parked, high-end vehicles they passed. "Where are we?"

He pulled into a vacant space and shut everything

off. Then he took her purse from her lap and threw it in the back seat. "Leave that in here. I don't trust the son-of-a-bitch as much as you do."

His look told her to play along. Marcelina did so without missing a beat. "Armando wouldn't bug my purse."

He got out, circled around, and opened her door. The joy of being with him was much like reuniting with a long-lost love after days of searching for each other. They walked to the stairwell. He opened the door for her and ushered her inside. As soon as the door closed behind them, he turned her around and waved a black device all over her clothing. An electronic "frisking" of sorts. This was becoming commonplace since the last time she'd been frisked was two nights prior. Now that they were out of the car, out of range of possible listening devices and surrounded by concrete, she spoke candidly. "Is it me you don't trust? Or *him?*"

"If there's anything in your clothes, this will detect it," he said. "Looks like you're clean."

His lack of an answer made it clear he doubted her already. Tears sprang to her eyes, and she forced them back before they could pool. "Your timing makes me wonder who is bugging who?"

Hands on hips, he paced like a caged tiger. "You're being monitored," he confirmed. "I'm not really sure how."

"So you know about everything Armando and I discussed this morning?"

"Captain Ross heard it and he called me. We have to play this smart." His switch in gears was smooth and mechanical. "It's too soon. You need to tell Rivera we talked about it and I convinced you to keep me as your attorney."

His proven knowledge of such a private conversation scrambled her thoughts for a moment. Had they heard *every* word exchanged? Or just the ones in the study? Willing her heart to slow, she took a breath. "He'll never go for it. He wants you out."

"Okay, then we'll work as a collaborative team, even if I'm bumped down to advisory status. I've built your case from the ground up. You trust me. It's not an unreasonable request."

Her mouth fell open. "You want to *work* with Armando's lawyer? The one who bribes and cheats to win cases? Wouldn't that be cheapening yourself, something you said you'd never do?"

His wry smile lacked humor. "Assuming, of course, you want to go back."

Which meant yes. The thought of letting him do it went against every fiber of her being. He must have detected her internal struggle because his look softened. His shoulders relaxed, and his voice dropped to a husky timbre. "Don't go back."

The Walker she wanted was offering her another chance. Her eyes began to sting and blur again.

And before she knew it, she was in his arms.

No other sounds echoed through the stairwell except for the heady rush of their mingled breaths. Marcelina held on to Walker so tight she wondered how he could breathe at all. "I'm okay," she whispered, sniffing loudly. "Really. My biggest problem is this woman named Jade. She's sicker than Armando is."

"What did she do?"

She shook her head briefly against the warmth of his neck. "Left a hell of an impression, that's all. I'm fine."

"Did she threaten you?"

"She's suspicious."

He leaned away just enough to brush her hair back from her face. Wipe a streak of moisture from her cheek. Then he gave her an incredulous laugh that also scolded. "Captain Ross said you mentioned my name in your sleep." He closed his eyes as if contemplating the wisdom of locking her away despite her wishes. "I wanted to laugh and cry over that one." When he opened them, they were burning, begging her to do what he wanted. Then he took her face in his hands and kissed her, a desperate kiss she sank into with equal fervor. She held him tight, needing the feel of his body against hers, never wanting to let him go.

"Don't go back, Marcelina," he repeated against her mouth.

His breath was warm honey and soft encouragement. Loath to break away, she looked down, resting her forehead against his chin. It was smooth from his morning shave, a routine she would die to see him perform in his wet skin and towel. "I have to." She swallowed against the foreboding in her voice. "I already have a car, several swimsuits, and a new lawyer. I'm this close to having Rivera where I want him."

Her attempt at humor was completely lost in translation. Walker held her out by the shoulders, his eyes burning as he looked down at her. "You're seriously going to fire me?"

A deep sigh. "I won't let them bribe or threaten anyone. It's still up to me how they handle my case."

"Tell me you don't really believe that."

"He'll take you down eventually, Walker," she hissed, suddenly angry that he held his own safety in such low regard. "He has that much resentment toward you, and he is so—*So* dangerous. He beat the hell out of one of his own drivers, all for wanting a raise!"

"Don't say it." His look warned. "Don't say you're cutting me out for my own good."

"For your *safety*. You were right about Armando. He *needs* to win this one or *you* could end up in Captain Ross's pile of photos. I couldn't bear it, Walker."

They stood there for a moment, watching each other until she finally threw her head back and turned away.

"This isn't worth it," Walker said behind her, his words firm. "Look at me."

She turned again and met the raw determination in his eyes, in the set of his jaw.

"I'm in love with you. I think you love me, too. It's important enough for me to put you first."

The impact of his words blew through her like a sonic blast. He loved her? Coming from a man who professed his love of winning cases above all else, this was the rarest of gifts being offered to her on a platter of pure humility. The importance of it sank in to meld with her own love for him burning deep within her heart. The fierce need to choose him was crippling her resolve, but it couldn't happen. Now that she knew the extreme workings of Armando's mind, she couldn't endanger Walker more than he was endangering himself. She began to back away. "I admit if I'd have known just how twisted his world is, I wouldn't have gone in. But it's too late now. I have to see it through."

His nostrils flared. "No one wants you with Rivera. Kendall is terrified. She thinks you're doing this to protect her."

Yes, that was part of it. But more than anything she

Jules Parker

was doing this for a chance at happiness. "I don't ever want to feel the way Audrey does, Walker," she said softly. "I hope you can understand that someday."

In other words she loved him, too. She could tell by the softening of Walker's brow that he interpreted her words correctly, but she couldn't say them out loud. Not yet.

"There are ways out of this," he said with a hint of the sadness she felt down to her very toes. "But I'll just be wasting my breath, won't I?"

This was it, the moment she must sever their ties. It was a gamble that—with any luck—would end in big rewards. Regardless of his threats to end things for good, she would always carry the hope that he would forgive her one day.

The door was behind her. She took a step back, then another as the severity of her choice lodged in her throat. "Like I said, it's too late." She gave a helpless shrug. "I'm in this until the end. I have no choice now."

The fire in his eyes dimmed as the door to that heart he'd just offered her closed. In came a feeling of doom like none she'd ever felt before. "If you really believe that," he said, "then I guess this is goodbye."

He was back to the Walker she first met in that little interrogation room at the police station. An impersonal stranger, indicating the door. Her heart drumming a million beats per minute, she yanked on the handle.

And braced herself for an even longer car ride back to hell.

****

Walker returned to his office with the weight of deep bitterness in his soul. He'd tried to shut it out, something he'd been good at before, but his proven methods had failed him this time. The wound was too deep, inflicted by a woman he'd known better than to fall for. The fact it was for all the right reasons had no bearing in this case. Rivera had won, which was wrong on all levels.

His waiting room was occupied by one stranger, two clients, and a baby. To Walker, all of them looked pissed, even the baby. Before the door swung closed behind him, they all began talking at once, their voices melding together into a gaggle of panic and petitions. Judith stood up from behind the reception counter with a fistful of pink slips. "Mr. Bishop, you have—"

"I know," he snapped. Fifty million messages, same as damned usual since he'd failed to forward his calls before he'd blown out of there with his cellphone plastered to his ear. He snatched the pink slips from Judith's grasp, broke through the small mob coming at him, and very politely asked them to make an appointment, leaving them with a very frazzled looking paralegal.

His office door was open and when he charged through it, the sight of his father sitting behind his desk stopped him short. It was another slap of reality he didn't need—Conrad Bishop lifting his leg on Walker's professional space. "Perfect." He laughed as he closed the door behind him.

Because laughing was better than losing it altogether.

With his jaw propped on a hand, Bishop Senior closed the file he was browsing through. "Want me to move?"

Walker waved away the notion as he advanced toward a wooden hutch in the corner. "No, you belong there. Always did." He opened a cabinet, pulled out a heavy box giftwrapped in gold paper. "In fact, I'll buy you a drink."

He took out some red plastic cups and placed them on the desk, then ripped open the paper.

Conrad watched with what looked like amusement. "Isn't that Ursula's bribe?"

"It was. Now it's my road to karma." He broke the seal, twisted the cap off and poured three fingers of Hennessey in each cup. Without replacing the cap, he took one of the drinks and sat down on the client side of his own desk, opposite his father. He lifted the pricey booze to his lips and downed a liberal portion of it while Conrad took a reasonable sip, watching him.

"I hear you're looking to expand," Conrad said.

Walker's throat rallied and burned, but it wasn't from the booze this time. "Yep."

The simple, piss-free answer seemed to surprise his father, who continued to scrutinize his mood from across the desk. "You seem lost, son."

Considering the contents of his cup for a moment, Walker replied, "I'm not lost. In fact I see more clearly now than ever." Then he drained the cup, swallowing loudly.

"The liquor won't make it any prettier."

"It's worth a shot." He reached for another pour.

"Does this sudden epiphany have anything to do with Marcelina Page?"

The cognac began to numb the path of fire to his belly. If all went according to plan, he'd make his one o'clock arraignment in a better mood.

Or not at all.

"I never noticed it until now, how people like us operate," Walker said, staring at nothing in particular. "I didn't see it so clearly until she looked at me with that same mechanical drive. As if everything carefree and alive within her had been ripped out." He looked up to see his father watching him and pointed. "Yeah, just like that. We aren't so different from men like Rivera, men who have no purpose but to conquer. It's how I remember you. How I've dealt with my own clients."

Conrad sat back in the plush leather chair, considering him with the deportment of a psychiatrist. "You love her, don't you?"

Walker rubbed his eyes with frustration, unwilling to deny it. Conrad wouldn't believe him if he did. "I *loved* her." An incredulous laugh escaped his throat. "I loved the woman who broke into my house; showed me that water can light up in your hands; who made me find a whole new appreciation for cooled seats. And just when I realized I don't want to live on the dark side of the duplex anymore, she ripped my cord right out of the socket. So here I am, back in the dark again." He held up the cup for a bitter round of *cheers* then drank to karma.

"Sounds…interesting."

Walker glanced up at his father, too miserable to care that he was making a fool of himself in front of the man. "She made everything interesting."

"You don't think she'll want you when this thing with Rivera is over?"

The flare of surprise over Conrad's knowledge of Marcelina's whereabouts quickly left him. Of course the man would keep tabs. He probably even suspected she was outsourcing for the DEA. "I can't be with a woman who has no faith in me," Walker said.

"Or who may have crawled into bed with the cartel." The bitter, plastic-cup-salute Conrad got in return had him sitting up, crossing his arms over the desk. "It's not too late."

Walker closed his eyes, let the Hennessey work its magic on the tension in his shoulders. But his chest was still tight and his head...well, there'd never be enough liquor for that. "She knew my limits going in. The hell of it is she's not just doing it to stay out of jail. She has this misguided belief she's protecting me. Protecting our chances for later. Either way, you and I both know it's only a matter of time before she loses her soul."

"Like us."

Walker raised his cup again. "Like us."

A crooked smile formed beneath Conrad's slim mustache. "Then you'll want to pour another drink. Because I just may have a solution to your problem."

Chapter 17

"You're back."

When Marcelina finally entered the sitting room she'd abandoned an hour ago, Armando approached her with a look of encouragement. "I'm surprised you didn't take your new car."

He shouldn't be surprised by anything with all the security around. Having been searched and wanded upon re-entry, Marcelina felt even more oppressed than before now that Walker was out of her life. Needing the time to think and to regain her bearings, she'd asked him to drop her off a mile out. Which he did without question. Without acknowledgement. Hell, without even a final goodbye. It was too much to hope that he would be there for her when it was all over. "I didn't think about it," she answered him. It was the truth. Her new car, as sexy as it was, held no fascination for her whatsoever. She couldn't even remember the make and model.

Armando took her hands, enfolding them in his large warm ones. She noticed the bruises under his rings, still colorful from the "lesson" he'd doled out the day before. "What did you tell him?" he asked her.

Unable to answer, she pursed her lips and then gave him an uncomfortable smile.

"So you fired him?"

The joy in the man's eyes made her want to dole out a lesson of her own. Instead, Marcelina took a breath.

"Yes."

With a deep chuckle, Armando pulled her against his big, beefy chest and held her tight. "You won't regret it, Marcelina. This was the best thing you could have possibly done for yourself." He pulled away, held her out by the arms. "And it shows me you're capable of making tough decisions, no matter how conflicting. I'm proud of you."

She looked around, noting the lack of an audience. "I thought you said Dan would be here when I got back."

"He had an important meeting to get to. We'll discuss all of that later. For now, I have business in Miami, something that came up this morning. I want you to come with me."

A rivulet of shock zinged through her system. "To Miami?"

"I prepared a suitcase for you. We'll fly over and then take the yacht back to Naples in the morning."

Marcelina leaned to the side, peering around Armando to confirm that, indeed, the dock was empty. No yacht. As she processed the speed in which his fastballs were coming, she blinked and gave herself a mental shake. It was important to keep up or she'd do the DEA no good whatsoever. But still… "You want me to go on an overnight trip with you?" When his smile faded a bit, she explained what must be a poorly masked look of horror on her face. "Armando…when am I going to start work?"

"Relax first, then work." He patted her shoulder and turned her toward the lanai where the table was set with two covered dishes. "When my business is done, we'll have a short vacation. I'll show you all the pleasures Miami has to offer."

With no choice but to head that way, she stepped through the open glass doors, her gaze trained on the covered dishes. What sort of surprise was underneath that lid? "Is Jade coming, too?" Where *was* Jade, anyway?

"She has other plans. It'll be just the two of us."

He pulled her chair out. She sat, trying to sort out the dangers of being alone with him. At least Jade provided a distraction. The lids came off. As she studied what looked like crab salad on a thick bed of Romaine lettuce, she said, "Separate bedrooms?"

Armando paused halfway down to his seat. "If you want."

"Because I'm not sleeping with you." She picked up her fork and poked at a succulent hunk of white meat.

"A challenge I have happily accepted."

When she looked up, it was to see a sparkly-eyed cad wolfing down his first bite of food. "Armando…"

His throat rumbled with a laugh, his loaded fork pausing halfway to his mouth. "I love it when you're annoyed with me. We leave immediately after lunch."

And he wouldn't tolerate any more argument over the matter. She was to do as she was told and enjoy herself. Let him "take care of her." The man certainly was a charmer, loved his challenges though it was clear why he expected to get his way since he was a man of power. He knew what turned women on, what made them pliable, how to manipulate them with softly spoken orders and just enough give to keep the difficult ones happy.

But two could play at that game…and Marcelina was no ordinary woman. She, too, knew what made the opposite sex tick. A spark of life ignited inside her hollowed heart. Yes, it was time to focus—focus on taking this man down, and offering a challenge was just the beginning. Letting him win would feed his ego. Then as he crested that misplaced wave of victory, she'd throw him off balance by asserting her own dominance. Once he realized she was his equal in every way, he would become the pliable one, yielding to her power in just as many ways…

If she survived that long.

After lunch, she entered her bedroom and stopped short, staring at the perfectly made bed where Jade had invaded her "privacy" the night before. Walker's words slammed into her chest like a fist full of brass knuckles.

I'm in love with you. And I think you love me, too.

They were the last words she'd ever thought to hear from him. Their fling was just that, an outlet they'd both needed to vent their frustrations. He was most likely using the L-word to get her to abandon her mission. All men ever did was manipulate, and it would piss her off greatly to find out she'd done this to be with a man who was just like all the rest.

"Have fun in Miami, Princess."

Marcelina's heart jumped at the unexpected presence behind her, but this time she managed to keep her cool. "Still lurking in dark corners, Spray Tan?" Without turning to confront the danger, she advanced toward the bed where an open suitcase lay in wait.

"You got some balls, I'll give you that." Jade followed, stopping close enough to brush skin as she reached past her and lifted the white lacy bikini out of the suitcase. "Looks like Armando prepared you for romance."

Refusing to back away, Marcelina snatched it out of

her grasp and threw it back in. "You would know better than me since you've already gone through it."

"I was curious to see how you'd repack this thing." Jade lifted another item up by the shoulder straps. Admired it. "Look at that plunging neckline. He'll surely get a peek at those pretty titties in this." A husky laugh. "But don't worry, it's Miami. You'll fit right in."

With her no-fear attitude still in place, Marcelina held out her hand. Jade placed the silky mini-dress in it, surely expecting her to toss it aside as a reject. So when it was placed back on top of the pile, a slow smile spread across the woman's mouth.

Marcelina closed the lid and channeled her inner bitch, which did much to burn away what little fear was left. This was war now, a fight that would surely end in someone's bloody demise. And she vowed to be the one still breathing when it was all over. "From now on, Jade…" She turned to face her adversary with a mean tilt to her mouth. "You stay out of my room, out of my things, and out of my way."

A dangerous spark accompanied the amusement in Jade's eyes. "Or what? You think Armando will kick me out for you?"

She stepped closer, looking down a bit on a flawless face worthy of the devil's bride. "He isn't the one you need to worry about."

Laughter bubbled up from the woman's throat, growing louder until the bedroom rang with cackles. "Armando has had many whores under this roof." Still amused, she walked over to the dresser and picked up a silver comb from a vanity set that was displayed on a silver tray. Marcelina was pretty sure its sharp, pointy end could do worse than part hair, and was more than relieved when it went back on the dresser.

"You wouldn't be the first one to threaten me," Jade continued. "He is too kind to his women. Makes them feel important. His last bitch tried to throw me over the side of the yacht. You know what happened to her?" The woman was back by her side, invading her personal space once again, so close that her breath fell on Marcelina's lips. "He *gave* her to me as a gift." Her tongue darted out, made contact. "I tied her to my bed and cored her with a hand mixer until she had nothing left for Armando to desire. But for you, Princess…my filet knife is ready and waiting."

****

Miami. As soon as the jet's wheels touched ground, Marcelina's senses were overwhelmed by the city's sheer energy, its heat, its passion. A lot went on here, too much for her to grasp. And that was all before she left the plane.

Or maybe it was the newly discovered fear of flying that had her sweating bullets…

"You've never flown before?" Armando asked as he helped her down the small flight of steps to the tarmac.

"First time." Marcelina thanked God as soon as her feet hit solid ground. "Then again, I've experienced a lot of 'firsts' since meeting you."

His body brushed against hers. "And there will be many more to come."

Always someone wanting to get too close…but personal space was sacred ground in this world, to be constantly battled over until one gave in and the other rose up the victor.

However, two could play at that game. Though she'd been a wreck the whole flight over, Marcelina had managed to down some cocktails, pretend sleep and "accidentally" lean on his shoulder—a subconscious gesture that implied trust. He'd been very pleased by that, having woken her with a kiss on the forehead and a tender smile that was genuine this time. She was sure of it. It was the first sign of a real pulse beating somewhere inside of him.

Her first victory. A small one that came with big promise.

Once they were safely inside the limo, Armando relaxed. She imagined the bulletproof glass had something to do with that. "The yacht hasn't arrived yet," he said, dabbing a linen kerchief across his forehead, "so I've booked a suite at the Four Winds Resort. You can catch up on your rest there while I conduct my business."

As the view outside her window turned from airport to city traffic, Marcelina sat back with him. "When will you be through?"

"Just plan on dinner around six o'clock." He handed her a plastic keycard. "There are a few dresses waiting for you in the closet of your room."

She took the card, marveling over the efficiency of his world. "Are they all as modest as the outfits in my suitcase?"

His shoulders shook with a silent laugh. "So I enjoy clothes that enhance a woman's assets. Sue me."

The delight emanating from him was contagious. Marcelina smiled, shook her head as if she were discovering more and more about him every day. Which was the truth. "You're hopeless."

The scenery outside was getting more colorful by the mile, but it went largely unnoticed as their gazes remained locked. Armando's was hot. Burning with promise. "Yes," he said. "I am hopeless."

****

That afternoon, Marcelina was surrounded by five-star luxury, reminding herself once again not to get used to it. As soon as they'd entered the sparkling glass tower that stood tallest among all of the buildings on Miami's coast—which had only ever been on the horizon for Marcelina—she was in a continuous state of awe. Armando had failed to mention his suite was more like an apartment complete with corner balcony, multiple bathrooms, and a nosebleed view of the Atlantic Ocean. Her private room was a creamy haven of retro furniture and ocean-blue floor-to-ceiling curtains that blocked out the overwhelming light from the balcony. She had gone from pauper to princess so fast, there was no time to see past the glamour, though she continually struggled to do so. She was exhausted, her mind and body overwhelmed by the tumult of her morning, as well as a gross lack of sleep.

After donning a sheer black chemise and panties set Armando had supplied for her, she'd crawled under the sheets with the intent of going over her carefully planned seduction of a major drug trafficking syndicate. For once she didn't mind wearing the sexy clothes he was forcing on her. There was no lawyer to obey. No rules according to Captain Ross. She was free to conduct this operation any way she chose, and the thought of using her body as a means to an end wasn't so daunting anymore. With Jade out of the way—albeit briefly—Marcelina could use that excuse to relax and enjoy her time in Miami. It would only serve her purpose to let go. Get swept away. Let Armando Rivera in so he would do the same for her in return—a task that was nearly impossible when Walker's image would repeatedly break through her well-laid plans of seduction, rising up to punch the joy right out of her first time in a five-star hotel.

She finally succumbed to exhaustion by forcing her thoughts away from what troubled her most. Later, she woke as a door opened and closed somewhere beyond hers. Feeling much better, she opened her eyes. Stretched. The sun was shooting through the slightly open curtains at a late afternoon angle. Her sheets were all over the place. She looked down at the sheer undergarment she wore, knowing if Armando was back, it would be an opportunity she couldn't pass up.

A light knock sounded on her door. Marcelina lay back down and pulled the sheet over her waist, leaving one breast slightly exposed. Her eyes were closed when the door opened without the benefit of another knock.

She could feel his approach; his open perusal of her disheveled state; sensed his need for her as he hovered over her bed. Her breath skimmed evenly through parted lips as she feigned sleep. Then, much to her shock, his lips were on hers as he delivered a gentle, wake-up kiss.

Her eyelids fluttered open. "Armando?" she whispered.

"Marcelina," he whispered back. "The most revered portrait artist in the world could never capture how beautiful you look right now."

As if realizing her risqué appearance for the first time, she backed away and lifted the sheet up to her chin. Blinked the sleep from her eyes. "Is your business done?"

The mattress sank as he lowered himself to the edge of the bed. "Yes."

His desire to touch her lay heavily between them. But the timing wasn't right yet, so Marcelina prevented it by sitting up and keeping herself well covered. "Okay. I'll get showered and dressed."

"Marcelina..." His mouth lingered open as he continued to look at the outline of her body. Then he blinked, straightened. "Yes, of course. I'll do the same."

It was almost six o'clock by the time she stepped out of the shower. Surrounded by decorative soaps, thick linens, and scented mist, she padded across the cloud-like carpeting and opened the door. As the humidity escaped, she took a blow dryer to the mirrors. Her reflection appeared, freshly scrubbed, pink-cheeked, and fresh. But there was something sad about the way her dark eyes stared back at her—something missing in them that took away a layer of her old self.

She put the finishing touches on her makeup and styled her hair so that it fell in thick, silky waves over her shoulders. All set, she turned toward the scrap of lavender hanging on the back of the dressing room door and removed it from the hanger. Held it against her body. It was the least revealing dress of the three that had been waiting for her in the closet, yet the scalloped neckline would surely fall halfway to her navel. If there was ever a need for double-sided tape, it was now, but a thorough search of all drawers and cabinets turned up nothing.

At least the back fell short of revealing her ass crack. "Hope it's warm tonight," she muttered to herself. She slipped out of her silk robe and into the dress, straightening the thin straps over her shoulders. Since the style would show any and all undergarments, she wore nothing beneath it. Metallic lavender fabric draped over her generous breasts, the folds at least thick enough to hide the shape of her nipples, though the opening showcased her natural, unbound cleavage. The skirt stopped halfway up her thighs, not even allowing her to sit without risk of showing all she had. Damn that man.

The silver heels that were placed in the closet beneath the dress added at least five inches to her height. Feeling very naked, Marcelina went to the jewelry box and peeked inside. Diamonds sparkled in the lamplight, inset with smaller amethyst stones, as if he knew exactly which dress she'd choose. Smooth. Very smooth.

Another knock. "Marcelina, are you ready?"

Ready as I'll ever be. She gave one more adjustment to her hair, pulling it all over one shoulder. Then she opened the door.

Armando Rivera stood there in a satiny shirt that damn-near matched her stilettos. It was unbuttoned enough to reveal the usual—a variety of precious metal and lots of chest hair. They were a matching pair, even with his darker dress slacks.

"You totally planned this," she accused with hands on hips.

The man couldn't seem to speak as his gaze swept down her body. He closed his mouth and swallowed. "Then again maybe we should order room service. I'm not entirely sure I want other men ogling you."

The husky tenor of his words gave away his full intent to get her out of that dress before the night was through. "You should have thought of that before leaving me with no underwear or dignity whatsoever," she retorted haughtily. Her silver clutch was still on the TV stand halfway into the room. She turned to go get it, gracing him with a sexy walk and a view of her bare back. It did much to turn up the heat, or so she felt from the doorway.

In the elevator, they stood side by side. He brushed a knuckle against her hip ever so softly. Her breath hitched. "Stop it," she admonished.

"I can't help it. That dress is like a thin layer of frosting I want to lick off before devouring the rest of you."

His boldness was going where it hadn't before. Did he sense that she was caving, or was his patience simply running out? "There will be no devouring."

"I like the room service idea," he replied, ignoring her last assertion altogether. "Start with dessert first."

She firmed her voice. "No dessert. At all."

He chuckled, turning toward her, boxing her in with a hand against the wall beside her head. Ever so slowly he gathered her hair up and moved it off her shoulder, uncovering all of her cleavage. He traced the valley between her breasts with a fingertip.

The skin there crawled, yet Marcelina managed to soften her gaze. "Please don't do that."

"I feel your heart pounding. You may as well give in now."

The doors opened and another couple stepped in, giving her the blessed excuse she needed to move away. Every time the man got too close, it was dread that made her heart race. Fear that this was the time he'd force her to the next level.

Throughout their walk down a crowded causeway along the beach, Armando behaved for the most part. When he touched her, it was with a hand at her lower back; however, his fingertips would sometimes dip below the fabric, grazing the top of her rear end. She would suck in a breath, knowing his entourage was following them and most likely watching the show. Unable to publicly chastise him without giving his actions away, she would simply elbow him in the arm. He'd chuckle and draw her close to his side, but only long enough to place an affectionate kiss on the top of her head.

There were people of all sizes and colors, dressed in a variety of styles from the elegant to the seriously odd. Marcelina supposed they blended well and was relieved to learn that she was not the only one barely dressed. Girls strutted their stuff in skintight things that bared the bottoms of their butt cheeks. Some dresses had more holes in them than fabric. Some were no more than straps covering the naughty parts, making Marcelina's own attire feel quite sophisticated.

They walked to a glass-covered courtside full of people, all while their shadow-bodyguard kept close. Brilliant lights bathed them in colors as they moved through it. Greenery and flowing water reminded the tourists they were in Florida. A salsa band played music on a stage. A man completely painted in silver walked the crowd, taking pictures with pedestrians at their request.

Armando knew a lot of people, was in fact a very popular man. He introduced Marcelina by name alone, not as his girlfriend or his woman. The men were appreciative of her appearance and the women looked at her like she was trash. Of course her boobs were beckoning to every Tom, Dick, and Harry within range, so how could she blame them?

They sat at a table and ate lobster by candlelight. Her attention was all over the place while Armando's remained fixed on her. "Too much?" he asked.

She took a bite of tender meat, barely tasting it. "Hmm?"

His smile was sympathetic. "You look like a deer in the headlights."

Yes, it was all painfully overwhelming, but she apparently needed to either relax or hide it better. She gave him a wide-eyed smile. "I'm fascinated. There's a lot to see."

He put a napkin to his lips and sat back. "Finish your drink."

She'd been picking at her food for a good few minutes, something he also must have noticed. She cocked her head. "Are we leaving?"

"We're going to dance. Then we'll go back to the hotel."

Dance. Now, that was something she loved to do, but not in a thin drape of sparkly lavender with a cartel scumbag who only wanted to see her out of it.

But, alas, this was another opportunity she couldn't pass up—an excuse to let her guard down. She gave him an uncomfortable smile over the rim of her wineglass. "I don't think I'm up for dancing." Then she drained it.

He stood, extending his hand over the table. "Come on. I'll even let you stand on my feet."

It was another challenge thrown out ever so smoothly. "Oh, really?" She threw her napkin on the table and stood. As she passed by the bodyguard, she whacked her clutch against his chest, knowing he'd hold it for her without question. She sauntered out onto the dance floor, closed her eyes, and let the music sink in and penetrate the bundle of nerves she'd become. Ever so slowly her body relaxed and her hips began to sway to the beat. Salsa was something she was good at—was taught the dance by a pro she'd dated right out of high school. She opened her eyes, raised her arms and made a dramatic turn to find Armando close and already moving with her. His eyes shone appreciation for her skill as he grabbed her hand and began to throw her around in a series of gyrating twists.

"No dipping," she warned, knowing her loose breasts would never stay under wraps.

"How about a warning beforehand?"

"A compromise?" she asked with a half-smile.

"You're obviously no stranger to the dance," he pressed. "I believe you know a dip is unavoidable."

Her smile widened as she shifted her weight from foot to foot, artfully turning and swaying in her heels to add a simplistic sex appeal without showing off.

He yanked her against him. "You're holding back," he said in a rough voice. "Don't." Then she was twirling. He held one hand high, and she tucked her free one close to her chest to keep her dress closed. She let go of his hand and gave the man what he wanted. With seductive grace, she moved everything from head to heels, twisting her hands in a way that beckoned. Throwing her hair. Shaking her ass. Before long, she was out of breath and laughing.

"Dip!" he warned loudly.

She put a fist to her chest and let him toss her over one arm. As her hair brushed the floor, people clapped and whistled. It was then she realized they'd cleared the dance floor, at least enough for some in the crowd to have their phones out and cameras going. The band struck up another song. People began to dance around them again, but she was still in Armando's arms. Her own arms were between them as he held her close, his fast breath moving her hair.

"Another?" he asked.

She shook her head. "I'm tired."

Without a word, he kept her hand in his own and pulled her along as he cut a path through the crowd. Once they left the glass-covered courtside, a shiny black sedan pulled up. He opened the door for her.

What? No limo? "Where are we going now?" she asked.

"Back to the hotel. I have a surprise for you."

Though she dipped into the back seat, her heart was once again racing, but not from the exertion of their dance floor dalliance. She sank into soft leather that surrounded her with a fresh, new-car smell. Slid over to make room. Armando settled in beside her, throwing off a heat that was downright radioactive. "I don't think I can take any more surprises," she declared with skepticism.

The car began to move. "Trust me. You'll like this one."

Chapter 18

The whole ride back to the hotel was as quiet as could be. It was the quiet before the storm, Marcelina knew, fearing Armando's "surprise" was the climactic ending of their cat and mouse game. To think otherwise would be catering to a naivety she had abandoned when her ex-boyfriend left her with a classic case of holding the bag.

Her trepidation grew when they left the car, only they bypassed the elevators in lieu of the pool—a huge, palm-studded body of water in the back of the hotel that was lit up like a theme park. White-draped cabanas lined the sides of it, all of them closed. In fact, no other soul was around.

"I thought it would be nice to have it all to ourselves," Armando said behind her.

As she wondered how much it had cost him to have a public pool shut down, she turned around and spotted the cabana behind him. It was closest to the hot tub, its front flaps tied back revealing a dimly lit interior and an elaborate table topped with all things romantic—chilled champagne, rose petals, a plate of chocolate covered strawberries…

But it was the double bed behind it that captured Marcelina's attention. More like a poolside lounge for wet, post-swim naps, but it was adorned in silk sheets that were turned down and ready for use. An abundance of pillows were added, surely more than the usual quota. A black speedo and white bikini waited on the bed's quilted spread, inviting a nighttime dip before sex. And, of course, the bikini was the lacy number she'd been avoiding.

"I'm dying to see you in that," Armando admitted as she gaped at the display. "Are you ready to wear it for me, Marcelina?"

It was hard to answer with the blood swiftly draining from her face, but she managed to look up at him through her lashes. "I don't know."

Her answer was the honest to God truth. He must have sensed it because he took her hand and flattened it against his chest. "Feel that?"

There was plenty of movement beneath the fabric of his shirt. A strong heartbeat. Some muscle that flexed with her touch. She nodded.

"I've never had a woman capture my heart the way you have," he declared, his gaze filled with raw heat. "I want you so badly I physically ache. I know you want me too. I've seen it on the dance floor. When I touch you. Look at you." To prove it, he skimmed his knuckles over the curve of her shoulder. "It's time to say yes, Marcelina."

It was an order, something he was simply born to give. Couldn't help. Armando Rivera was used to being obeyed and he was testing her. Was her capitulation real enough to sleep with him or was there cause to suspect her? Still, she knew he expected somewhat of a challenge. After all, that's why she had gotten this far while maintaining a modicum of his respect. "And if I say no?" she whispered through shaky lips.

The intensity of his gaze didn't change. "Then we'll

swim, drink champagne, and go to bed in our separate rooms." His voice lowered in pitch. "But I won't like it."

There was a hint of danger in those last words, like they were a warning not to test him beyond that point. He was done humoring her. She was done playing hard to get. Marcelina accepted it as if a judge had just handed her that five-year sentence—with a bone-deep sense of dread. She needed a moment of mental preparation, a staunch reminder of what she was working toward. She managed a small smile. "Why don't we start with the swim and go from there?"

Armando wore the look of a confident man as he jerked his chin toward the cabana. Marcelina walked into it and began to pull the flaps closed, but he stepped in with her and took over the job. Soon they were both behind the privacy curtain, leaving her to wonder if the swim was even an option. He came up behind her and hooked the straps of her dress with his fingers, lowering them down her arms.

She closed her eyes as the dress slid off her body, leaving her more vulnerable than she had ever been in her life.

"You've been seducing me from the start," he rasped. "Don't think I haven't noticed." His lips brushed kisses over the shoulder he'd touched earlier. "I've already seen enough to know what lies beneath the dress. I'm tired of small glimpses. Let me see all of you now."

Stepping on the dress in her five-inch silver heels, Marcelina allowed him to physically turn her until she faced him. She stared at his chest, unable to look up at him as he finally got his fill.

"Marcelina." Her name slid out in a pained voice. "Don't make me wait any longer."

The man was getting desperate, which meant the longer he waited the less gentle he may be with her. But she couldn't help it. Just a little bit longer... "Swim first," she repeated, her chest constricting through the words.

The air crackled, his body stiffening slightly. Marcelina was the one testing her boundaries now, something she hoped would earn her a bit more respect as they moved to this very important step in their relationship.

It was a gamble that paid off.

"Of course." He kissed her forehead, though he had a death grip on her shoulders. When he released them, he began to unbutton his shirt, removing it while she watched. Then he went for the clasp of his trousers, unzipping them slowly. She swallowed, reached for her own swimsuit, and turned her back while she donned it. Changing together was an indication he simply expected her to follow him down this path toward romance. He expected her to obey with no further argument. He would give her this swim, but then she was his.

Before her fears could give her away, she switched off her feelings and mentally prepared herself for sex. Unwanted sex. She removed her shoes, tied the lacy wrap around her waist, knowing he watched her every move. When it came time to put on the top, he stopped her.

"Let me help you with that." Armando hooked the tied strap over her neck and lowered the cups down to her breasts. When she reached up to take over, he batted her hands away. "I'll do it."

His fingers brushed the undersides of her breasts as he tucked them in place. She knew he'd done it on purpose, as an excuse to feel her up. Once the clasp was finally connected, he turned her around again, stepped back and stared. "You look stunning in white. Just like the peach, it sets off that lovely dark skin of yours."

He'd removed his jewelry and stood before her, bare-chested and hairy with an erection that pushed upward against his speedo. There wasn't much fat above the hips, but the man lacked the definition that Walker possessed. She looked at the outline of his penis, trying to get used to the idea of it probing at her crotch.

He moved to the flaps. When they came open, they were greeted with something other than a spectacular view of the pool.

For there was Jade, wearing a pair of black leather shorts, matching bustier and an evil grin. Marcelina stopped in mid-stride, her eyes going wide as the woman looked her over. "Nice," Jade purred. "Makes your tits really pop."

"What are you doing here?" Armando growled.

Undaunted by his obvious anger over her untimely interruption, Jade continued to take in her fill of Marcelina's body, though her words were for her boss. "I have something for you on the boat."

"Can't it wait?"

"No, it can't."

Never in her life did Marcelina expect to feel relief over Jade's presence. Maybe this was a blessing after all, earning her more time to mentally prepare herself for sex with Armando. She turned toward him, knowing Jade was getting a clear view of her poorly concealed posterior in the process. "I'm tired, anyway," she murmured. "Can we do this tomorrow?"

"Come with us," Jade answered for him. "We'll

have a nice little threesome in the state room."

Armando's mouth flattened with chagrin. "She's teasing of course."

"No, I'm not." Marcelina felt the woman's body heat as she sidled up behind her. "He likes to watch me pleasure his women."

"Jade, that's enough."

Instead of moving away from her, Marcelina turned back around. They stood there exchanging looks that dared the other to react. Jade finally smiled, bit her lower lip. "And I can't wait to get between your legs again, Princess."

The image of a hand mixer popped into Marcelina's mind. Suppressing a wave of resultant shivers, she sent Armando a look of disgust. "Tell me again how much like a *sister* she is to you."

Again Jade answered for him. "We've never fucked if that's what you mean. But what man doesn't like a little lesbian action, especially if he gets to take part?"

Looking extremely pissed, Armando grabbed a robe with one hand and Jade's arm with the other. Before they disappeared around the cabana, he bestowed Marcelina with a look of apology. "Lincoln will escort you back up to our suite. Wait for me there."

The bodyguard appeared out of nowhere, nearly startling her out of her skin. She backed up, bumping into a chair as she made her way toward a bench without showing *Lincoln* her ass. She picked up a second bathrobe from the bench and donned it before preceding him back to the hotel.

It was the first time she'd been alone with Armando's bodyguard. There was lots of muscle standing beside her. She looked down at his hands—big hammy things that probably caused all the damage in those gory photos Walker showed her. But now that he had a name, she wondered if casual conversation was an option with the man. As they rode the elevator up in silence, with his gaze trained on the doors, she decided to test that theory. "I suspect there's more between Jade and Armando than what they claim," she said. "Am I right?"

A brief pause. "I'm not at liberty to say."

His voice was deep, something she expected. The intelligence in it was something she had not. "Which means yes," she tested, but when he didn't take the bait, she chewed her bottom lip. "It's much too strange. He puts up with her crap way more than one would expect."

"He trusts her." Lincoln looked down at her. "He trusts me, too."

Message received. Marcelina knew trust was a rare thing in Armando's world. Beautiful women were a dime a dozen, just temporary distractions for a powerful crime lord…or so she'd learned from Nari. Now she was one of those dozen. Not in the same sense, but still a glorified whore with every intention of taking the untouchable Rivera down. Jade *was* right about her, after all. In every way. But as long as she could hold Armando's fascination, Marcelina knew she had a little power over him, too. Hopefully enough to get through this with her skin intact.

****

"Kendall is missing."

There were words in Walker's ear, coming through a telephone receiver he held in the dark. He felt the cold plastic against his face, in his hand, but he couldn't remember answering the phone. Alcohol-induced sleep continued to battle with the name that was rattling through his head like a spinning quarter. *Kendall.*

He rubbed at tired eyes then blinked up at the ceiling. "Who is this?"

"It's Rand. Sorry, *Officer Sorrick.* Kendall and I were supposed to meet for dinner at seven but she never showed. Her car is here and her door is unlocked, but she isn't home. Have you heard from her?"

Who the hell were they talking about again? Oh yeah. "Kendall has barely spoken to me since Marcelina left."

"Well, I got a text from her when she left work but nothing since then."

Slowly but surely, the fog cleared from Walker's brain. As the wheels began to turn, he sat up beneath the sheets, wishing Leonard hadn't called off that security detail so soon. "Do you suspect foul play?"

"She wouldn't have stood me up."

Shit. The man sounded worried, but how much did he know about Marcelina's new deal with the DEA? How much could he say? "I'll make some calls."

"I'll knock on some doors and get back with you soon."

They hung up. Walker turned on a light and rolled out of bed. On his way to the kitchen, he dialed the last number he'd called before turning in.

"Hello," came Leonard's voice over the line.

Apparently he hadn't gone to bed yet. What time was it, anyway? A quick check of the microwave clock confirmed it was only a hair past nine, meaning Walker must have tied one on earlier than he'd thought. "I just got a call from Officer Sorrick who thinks Marcelina's roommate is missing. Have you heard anything?"

A muffled curse as kids screamed in the background. "Forest, get my keys out of your sister's mouth!" The sound of chaos was replaced by the sliding of a door, then silence. "Sorry, the wife is working late. Now what is this about someone missing?"

Kids. Barbeques on Sunday afternoons. A healthy family to enjoy them with. They were fleeting thoughts that Walker pushed aside, along with the sudden shaft of envy that accompanied them.

Since when?

Swallowing back that slap of reality, he briefed Leonard on the few details he had. "I'm assuming Rand Sorrick doesn't know what's going on with Marcelina."

"No one knows but you and me, though I'm assuming by the sound of your voice you think Rivera has the roommate."

He hoped to hell not. "If he suspects Marcelina, he could be using Kendall for leverage." Another call beeped in. The same number as before was showing on the display. "Hold on." Before toggling over, he turned on the faucet, stuck his mouth under the stream, swished and swallowed. With dishtowel in hand, he answered. "Have you found something?"

Rand's voice again. "Her neighbor says she saw a man knocking on Kendall's door about an hour ago. Tall, well dressed, short hair, and a full beard. He left with someone from her apartment. It sounded like a woman but she isn't sure if it was Kendall or not. I don't like this."

Neither did Walker. "I have Captain Ross on the other line, I'll be right back with you." He toggled again. "Leonard, one of Rivera's men might have taken Kendall. Until we know for sure, we need to make plans to extract both her and Marcelina from his house."

"Marcelina is in Miami with Rivera."

What? "Since when?"

"Since noon."

Well hell. That meant she left town shortly after their underground garage breakup. Walker could see her and Rivera now, romancing the night away as Kendall lay trussed up in some warehouse, waiting to be used as a lesson in loyalty. Rivera—the merciless son-of-a-bitch—would kill them both if Marcelina didn't pass. "Don't you have contacts in Miami?"

"We have two agents keeping an eye on their hotel," Leonard said, "but word is Rivera's yacht is anchored offshore and they plan to board it in the morning. Once they do that, we're as good as blind."

"Then keep them off the goddamned yacht!"

"The DEA won't risk blowing Marcelina's cover over some woman who may or may not be missing. Besides, if Rivera does have the roommate, *he'll* be watching *us*."

"It won't look right if we just sit it out."

"Twenty-four hours, Walker. If Kendall hasn't turned up by then we'll shove a probe up Rivera's ass."

If she didn't turn up by then, it would be too late. Leonard had already hung up leaving Walker alone with Rand, the cop who seemed to care enough to break a few rules. "You still there?"

"Yeah," came the man's voice. He sounded worried, pissed, and ready to go renegade on the first asshole who crossed him. "The more I think about it, the more I smell Rivera's stench all over this."

The guy was smart. Knew at least why he'd been camped in Kendall's parking lot for the past few days eating protein bars and flipping through magazines. Walker was impressed. It was enough. "I take it you went inside Kendall's apartment."

"Yeah, but I didn't notice anything out of place other than the unlocked door and her keys on the counter."

Which was odd as hell considering the hardware on that door. Whoever left from Kendall's apartment with the man either thought she was coming right back…or it wasn't Kendall. Either way, it definitely stank. "I'm going to make another phone call," Walker said. "See if you can find any other leads."

They hung up and he ran a hand through his hair, fisting it painfully while he searched out another number. This was going to hurt.

After a few rings, his father's amused voice filled the line. "Two times in one day. I'm almost afraid to look up for all the flying pigs I may encounter."

Walker reached for the overhead cabinet, pulled out a dusty bottle of pink bismuth and began to shake it with vigor. "Is that offer still on the table?"

The silence that followed was the most deafening moment of Walker's life. He heard a faint puffing of smoke, then a long, slow exhale. "I take it you would like for me to make some calls."

Despite the long-past expiration date on the bottle, Walker turned it upside down and swigged a good portion of its contents, swallowing with a shudder. "Do it."

When he hung up, he knew he'd just signed away the part of him that resented everything his father stood for. Because now he was no better.

****

269

The nights were cooling faster, coating everything outside in an early dew that signaled the coming of a mild Florida winter. Walker drove the streets with his windows down, searching every sidewalk and stopping to ask the occasional night crawler if they'd seen a petite blonde wearing a light-yellow dress and heels—the outfit she'd worn to work that day. It was a futile effort that could possibly get him mugged, but knowing an off-duty Rand did the same on the other side of town amped up the urgency. He hated this feeling. *Helpless* was never in his wheelhouse before, and he didn't like it. Didn't like blending with the nightlife since his career specialized in the bad choices commonly made during those wee hours.

His dash display showed an incoming call from Rand. He answered. "Bishop."

"I know where she is."

Any hope Walker garnered from that was overshadowed by the grimness in Rand's tone. "Where? Is she okay?"

"She just called my cell. Asked me to come pick her up at this bar west of Golden Gate."

It was better news than he expected, but the celebration would have to wait until Kendall was proven to be safe and unharmed. "That's way out there. Do you know what happened?"

"She said a woman ambushed her when she got home and shoved her in the back of a car. Next thing she knew, she was dumped on the side of the road out in the middle of nowhere with no purse, no phone…she's been walking this whole time."

Which meant Kendall had never made it into her apartment at all, and whoever this woman was had taken her purse and keys. That would explain why there was no evidence of a break-in. "Son-of-a-bitch!" Walker hissed, realizing that this also changed the motivation behind Kendall's kidnapping. There was something behind it, he just had to figure out what. "Tell me where I can meet you."

"If she isn't hurt, I'll take her back to my place. But I don't know…she sounded pretty shaken up."

The text came nearly an hour later. Walker drove to the ritzier neighborhoods on the west side of 41 Highway. By the time he got to Rand's house—a Spanish-style stucco he shared with two other cops—it was past midnight. Beneath a tall arched entryway, the door opened and Rand's grim face appeared. "Before you see her, you should know she refused to go to the hospital."

That didn't sound good. When Rand moved aside, Walker entered a tiled foyer that opened up into the main living area. It wasn't a huge house, but the neighborhood alone warranted a hefty rent. The roommates were on duty and had left the place with the lingering odor of barbeque sauce and—Marcelina's favorite—a "lived in" feel. Most of the lights were out except for the two lamps flanking a long, sectional couch. He found Kendall curled up there, scared and hurting. She had a bruise on her face, bug bites all over the place, and her bare feet were wrapped in gauze. A first-aid kit sat opened on the floor, papers and refuse scattered everywhere. When she sat up, Walker was by her side in an instant, just in time to catch her sobs against his shoulder. "Shhh, you're safe now," he soothed, feeling incredibly thankful after the tumult of the last several hours.

"Sh—she hit me." Kendall brought a fistful of

271

tissues up to her nose as fresh tears formed. "I didn't even know her and she totally knocked me out."

When Rand sat down on her other side, Walker shared a look with the man. "Can you describe her?"

Kendall pulled away from him and plucked another tissue from the box beside her. "She had long brown hair, like really long. She was pretty but with no fashion sense at all. I mean, who wears a maxi dress with combat boots?"

Leonard had given the same description of a woman residing at Rivera's home—minus the clothes. "Did she say anything?"

"Aside from asking me for directions to the nearest hookah lounge?" A spiteful laugh. "No. I was tied up in the back of her car with a gag in my mouth. She didn't say anything when she dumped me on some abandoned road with the snakes and mosquitoes. After I got the ropes off, I had to walk forever with no shoes, no purse, no nothing." Tears gave way to anger. "The bitch stole my *shoes!*"

At least it hadn't been earlier in the day when the sun was most brutal. Kendall's fair skin would have cooked right off her bones.

"Kendall also thinks Rivera is behind this," Rand said. "Is there anything I should know about that?"

Yes, there was. Walker trusted this man, needed a colleague with the same kind of skin in the game, but he was also bound by secrecy. "Marcelina is staying with him now," was all he said about that. It was all he *could* say since even Kendall only knew that much. "This woman Kendall described sounds like someone who lives with Rivera. She's suspicious of Marcelina. This stunt tonight was probably her attempt to get into the apartment and search it for anything damning against her."

Her emerald eyes big and glassy, Kendall looked up at Rand. "One time when Marcelina thought she was alone, I heard her mumble something about whoring herself out for the DEA."

Kendall's words ricocheted throughout the room like a cartoon bullet, causing Walker to blink uncontrollably at the floor. How many times had he coined her the dummy of the two? He felt Rand's piercing gaze on him.

"And you let her, didn't you?" the man said in an accusatory tone.

Since there were no longer any secrets to be kept, Walker pushed out a bitter laugh. "I did everything short of lock her in my closet." Told her he loved her. Asked her to come home with him. God, what a fool. "She wasn't in any position to listen to my advice."

Rand was back at Kendall's feet, checking out the bandages that were already dotted with blood. The man was suppressing a new level of anger that rivaled Walker's, despite his efforts to conceal it. "If this was about searching the apartment," he said, "why didn't it look searched? Would someone like that care about leaving everything in order?"

"Maybe she was interrupted." Walker replied. He turned to Kendall. "Your neighbor says she saw a man knocking on your door, and that he may have left with this woman." He looked at Rand who fed Kendall the description of the man. Tall, well dressed, short hair, and full beard. "Do you know anyone like that?"

She searched her mind, shook her head. "No."

Then Rand said, "The neighbor also noticed a tattoo

on his wrist. Could have been part of a full sleeve, but he was wearing a shirt with long sleeves."

Kendall blinked once or twice, then her eyes lit with dawning. "I suppose if he grew a beard, it could be Marcelina's ex-boyfriend, Jonah." Her gaze flitted between Rand and Walker. She must have noted the fresh wave of alarm in Walker's expression because her eyes widened like beach balls. "No way. Do you think Jonah King is working with Rivera?"

At this point, it was too late to matter. The mere possibility that King was back in the picture—revealing what he knew about Marcelina's past with Nari Puccini to the wrong people—made Walker's veins crystalize with cold.

Chapter 19

Sitting alone on the balcony over forty stories above the beach, Marcelina soaked up the view of the Atlantic Ocean and the many boats that floated like glowing specs beneath the sunrise. The air was chilly, but she didn't mind since the grapefruit and dry toast on her plate—something Armando thought she would enjoy—didn't exactly require temperature control. It was okay. Her appetite wasn't there anyway, and she enjoyed the solitude as long as she could have it, knowing the next time Armando appeared he would most likely expect to take up where they'd left off.

Through the open sliding glass doors, she heard someone enter the suite. Lincoln appeared in his collared short-sleeve shirt and muscles. "Where's Armando?" she asked him.

"On the yacht." He eyed the one bite she'd taken from her toast. "He wants you to join him there."

The yacht…it would be her first close-up look at what the DEA referred to as *the* suspected location of illegal activity. She had privately named it the "boat of doom" since it was likely that many a killing had taken place there. Shaking off her sudden onset of heebie-jeebies, she asked, "Did he even come back last night?"

Lincoln's stiff countenance showed little more than a hint to get moving. "Don't worry about your things. Someone else will get them."

The man was a machine, not giving up anything she didn't need to know. Willing her hands to remain steady, she emptied her coffee cup and rose from her chair. "They aren't really my things anyway."

The airy white blouse she wore had no top buttons, leaving her cleavage open to the wandering eye. The bulldozer's eye never wandered, though. Marcelina knew because she paid attention as they rode the elevator down to the ground floor. Armando's muscle was loyal, all right. She wondered what the penalty was for ogling the girlfriends. A beating? A date with Jade's filet knife? A bullet in the head?

Ding.

When the doors opened, Lincoln touched her arm slightly, directing her toward the lobby. "We have a car waiting."

Of course. She walked with him, wondering what he'd do if she were to detour to the gift shop. What was the penalty for making Armando wait? A black eye? Starvation? Sexual torture?

No, he didn't hurt women. He had Jade for that.

They rode in silence, Lincoln beside her with his hammy hands flattened calmly on his bulging thighs. He wore lots of rings and she wondered how much damage they inflicted when throwing a punch. Had they mangled Graham's face before he was burned? Because Lincoln had made it quite obvious in the parking lot of *Le Marée* that no one crossed Armando Rivera without paying the ultimate price. The image of him leaning against the restaurant's pillar with that "I'm watching you" look about him would be seared in her brain for an eternity. Or was it a "you're already dead and don't know it" look?

She breathed through the shudder that nearly racked her shoulders. It was a good image to keep in her mind—the reminder she needed in order to stay on track.

The car pulled up to a busy boat dock bobbing with sleek powerboats. Locals and tourists flooded the area, sharing space with the abundant population of sea birds ranging from fat pelicans to bold, food-foraging seagulls. As soon as the door was opened for her, Marcelina stepped out of the car and was immediately met with the sights and sounds of fun and sun. In the distance, the stretch of taupe sand was littered with lifeguard shacks, umbrellas, sun chairs, and waste containers. Vendors were here and there loading up their folding tables with jewelry and clothing. The ocean waters had been surprisingly teal from way up on her forty-something-floor balcony, but down here it was an olive green dotted with the occasional whitecap. Aside from her bucking nerves and the random wave of sulfur assaulting her olfactory system, she could get lost in this for a day or two. But the chaos made her appreciate Naples' quieter side all the more.

Her gaze skimmed over the horizon, searching out the big black bow of Armando's yacht. Huge freighters could be seen in the distance along with a closer variety of large cruisers, but she couldn't point his out among them. They headed to the end of the docks toward a small runabout. Lincoln helped her climb aboard, then climbed in himself, tipping the thing dramatically. A man in uniform, who stood behind the wheel, nodded politely to her before starting the engine. Lincoln shoved off, then they motored toward the line of buoys indicating deeper waters. Once past them, the driver gunned it.

Marcelina held her hair back as the wind cut across

her skin. The boat skipped over waves, carrying her toward whatever awaited her on Armando's yacht. Then she saw it, the black 128-footer she recognized from his private docks. It was sleek and modern, built for speed as well as luxury.

The Boat of Doom. That damnable nickname surfaced once again, almost like a warning that she was about to face *her* doom next. Regardless, there was no turning back. She could only hope Jade's surprise for Armando wouldn't result in her becoming the yacht's latest casualty—especially before she had a chance to give the DEA its layout and crew estimations.

The driver idled up to the side of it where a man waited at an open gate, holding out his hand to help her board. The transfer was surprisingly smooth despite the waves.

"Mr. Rivera is expecting you in the galley."

Great. The kitchen. Jade's domain…

Lincoln followed Marcelina, his oppressive presence heightening her sense of danger. They passed through a smoked set of sliding glass doors and she was once again ensconced in luxury. Nothing spelled wealth like polished veneer, which was everywhere as was the eggshell seating, buttery pillows, and recessed lighting. She was led toward the front of the boat, down a side hallway and into another open room that was meant for dining. Windows offered a panoramic view of the Atlantic, and they surrounded a large table decoratively set for eight.

And then there was the galley, open to it all and every bit as equipped as Armando's kitchen at home. Jade leaned against the island's counter with a champagne flute in hand, her violet eyes twinkling while

Armando filled two more glasses. He put the bottle on ice, turned toward Marcelina and handed her one of the flutes.

She took it, noting above all else the spooky lack of conversation. "Good morning?"

A smile softened his mouth as he drank in her appearance. "My apologies. I'm always speechless when I first lay eyes on you."

He seemed to be in a good enough mood, though Jade continued to give off those lethal vibes of hers. Marcelina put on a good show of ignoring them by returning Armando's flirtatious look with one of her own. "I take it whatever brought you here last night has been handled?"

"For the most part." He came close and gave her a hello kiss on the cheek. "Now we begin our trip back to Naples."

Strong aftershave tickled her nostrils. "How long will that take?"

"If we stop in the keys for lunch, we should be back by late afternoon…unless you're in a hurry."

His voice dared her to deny it. She shook her head before again lifting the champagne to her lips.

This pleased him as he broke into a good-natured grin. "Terrific. I have many plans for you on this journey back to the west coast."

She nearly choked on the dry bubbles. "Plans?"

"I'll leave you two alone," Jade said in a surprisingly sweet tone. "Call me if you need me."

Since the woman's light mood alone was cause for suspicion, Marcelina took and stored her words as the usual threat. Unless Armando had disciplined her for her behavior the night before… After all, he'd looked mighty pissed by her untimely interruption of his planned poolside seduction, and even more so over her foul-mouthed insinuations that he was into kink.

"She's awfully friendly this morning," Marcelina said, watching the woman leave. "Did you two kiss and make up?"

His lips thinned out with annoyance at the accusatory nature of her comment. "We've reached an understanding where you're concerned," Armando replied.

Ah. Definitely disciplined. Would this be the end of Jade's threats? Something told her not to hope. "I still don't know why you put up with her, or why you trust her so much. She's done nothing but undermine you since I arrived."

Her words put a dire look in his countenance. "As my guest, you shouldn't feel uncomfortable or afraid. I told Jade that if she disrespects you or me again, I'll have to rethink her value in my home. I meant it."

"Really?" Marcelina doubted that, too. It must have shown because he took her chin in a gentle hold.

"Yes. She and I have been through a lot together. Hardships you couldn't possibly imagine. But I won't let her continue to challenge my authority, and she'll learn the hard way—like many others under my employ—that no one is irreplaceable."

Whether true or not, Marcelina made a concerted effort to look pleased by his explanation. He certainly sounded sincere enough. "Thank you for that." Her voice was soft and relenting. "I feel better already."

He let go of her chin. "Good." He grabbed the bottle of champagne and refilled their glasses. "We're building trust here. A step in the right direction."

They toasted. Took a sip. He continued to watch her over the rim of his flute. "I would also like to apologize for *my* behavior last night. I know I came across much too strong. Forgive me?"

She blinked at the mere thought. "There's nothing to forgive."

"It's just that I seem to lose my head after spending time with you. And that dance…well, that dance was downright dangerous."

She laughed a little. "Yes, it was."

Armando put the bottle down on the table as they crossed over to a couch that stretched along the entire length of windows. But instead of sitting, he blocked her path. "So you aren't upset about last night?"

"No, Armando." She frowned as if suffering a deep, internal conflict. "In fact…I woke up this morning wondering why you didn't come back."

He took the flute from her hand and set them both down on the side table. He drew her close, ran his fingers through her hair and gently pulled it so that her face was tilted upward. "You don't know how glad I am to hear you say that."

His lips crushed hers in a powerful, demanding kiss. Her insides recoiled at this unwanted taking of her mouth and she had to check the urge to push him away. Instead, going against everything in her gut, she opened for him, allowing his tongue to invade and conquer. Somehow, she found the capacity to respond with equal fervor.

"Oh, Marcelina," he breathed against her mouth. "I want you so badly I'm in a constant state of need, whether we're together or apart. I don't know how much longer I can wait to make you mine."

She looked up at him, her forehead damned near

breaking into a sweat. "I know. It's just…" She pulled away and circled around him to stare out the windows. Take a much-needed breather. As she looked out at the passing coastline, he put his hands on her shoulders.

"What, Marcelina?"

She shrugged. "I—I need to know you want me for the right reasons. There's this little voice inside my head that tells me you're just out to punish someone you think of as an enemy."

"You mean Walker Bishop." When she nodded, his hands slipped around her middle, pulling her back against his chest. "Is that why you hesitate?"

She closed her eyes. "Yes."

"This has nothing to do with your former lawyer. If my words won't convince you, then let me prove it in bed. I guarantee you'll have no further doubts about my feelings for you." His lips were in her hair. His hands undid her top two buttons, then dove inside her blouse. As he cupped her bare breasts, she swallowed back the building knot in her throat.

"Tell me, Marcelina…is your heart pounding because of your desire for me? Or because you fear me?"

"I don't fear you," she whispered back, her gaze wide on the view beyond the windows.

"You look afraid to me."

It was then she realized he could see her reflection in the glass. She lifted her hands, wrapped them around his forearms. "I guess I am a little."

"Of what?"

"I don't know, exactly. I told myself not to fall for a man like you, but…" She let the sentence hang.

"A man like me?" He sighed, his warm hands still holding her breasts captive. "Despite this label you have pinned on me, I am capable of loving a woman the same as anyone else."

Did he seriously just say the L-word? As Marcelina absorbed this, he continued.

"The truth is, I've loved before. Nicolette was her name."

"What happened?"

"I found her with my boss, who was powerful enough to coerce whomever he wanted into his bed. I was young and foolish. Forgiving. I didn't blame her at first, but when I began to rise in power, she tried to worm her way back into my life. It was then I saw her for what she truly was—a capitalist through and through."

Sympathy broke through her gaze as they stared at each other in the reflection of the glass. "I'm so sorry."

His smile belied the genuine heartbreak she'd detected in his story. "I believe you."

Once again she caught that rare glimpse of what might be a real person beneath the deadly paradox that was Armando Rivera. This Nicolette woman had truly broken his heart—was quite possibly responsible for his transition from man to monster. It reminded her of how powerful love was, how vulnerable even the strongest of men were to it.

And especially the strongest of women. But Marcelina refused to think about it, squaring her shoulders against the image of Walker with his own heart in his eyes. The way he looked when he told her he loved her…

She closed her eyes to Armando's reflection, then turned in his arms and tilted her face upward. His lips met hers again, taking, tasting, then devouring to the point she couldn't breathe. His arms crushed her to him so tightly her ribcage creaked.

"Tell me you won't betray me," he rasped against her mouth. Then he pulled away and took her face in a firm hold. "Tell me!"

His passion had been unleashed. "I won't," she promised softly as her entire being screamed with the lie. Her hands moved up, began to slowly work open the buttons of her silk shirt. "I do want you, Armando. Please…"

The soft plea was his undoing. With a snarl, he ripped the rest of her buttons open sending them everywhere. He reached around, unzipped her skirt and it, too, joined her blouse on the floor. All she wore now were her heels and thong. He backed up, pulling her with him, and sat down in one of the dining room chairs. He opened his legs, drew her between them and buried his face in her chest. Breathed deep. "You smell so good," he growled against her skin, cupping the outer curves of her breasts with his hands, kneading them around his face. He sucked on her nipples one at a time, taking his time.

Marcelina managed to stay still and allow him to do it. But Walker's words continued to assault her from within the deepest recesses of her heart.

I'm in love with you. I think you love me, too.

Oh, God, what was she doing? Her body was meant for him. She needed *his* mouth on her, *his* hands, *his* touch… To deny it and allow another man to have her— no matter the reason—was a betrayal to herself, not just Walker. But she couldn't give up when she was on her way to becoming a key figure in Armando's life. Her mission was important, too, more so than her selfish desires. She firmed her shoulders, bit back the snarl that hovered at her lips. This man disgusted her, yet she was doing exactly what Walker said: cheapening herself in the worst way possible.

Her thong was pushed down her legs. With a huge swallow, she stepped out of it. Completely naked and vulnerable to anyone who may walk in on them, she let him touch her.

If you sleep with him, there's no coming back from it. Not for me.

Walker's vow moved out of her heart and lodged inside her chest, making it suddenly hard to breathe. "Oh, God," she croaked.

"I know," Armando murmured, moving his hand between her legs. "I feel it, too."

But he wouldn't. There was nothing between her legs that indicated she was into this. She was bone dry. Not ready for him at all. He looked up at her with a perplexed frown and Marcelina saw his wheels begin to turn—right before the half-empty bottle of champagne smashed against his skull.

Marcelina stared in horror as Armando's unconscious body teetered to the floor. Then she stared at the bottle in her hand as if it had acted alone. *What the hell did I just do?*

Was he dead? Had she just killed a crime lord…for real this time? Though blood oozed from a cut on his temple, his chest was still moving beneath his champagne-soaked shirt. The stuff was all over her, too, reminding her that she was still naked.

And in a hell of a lot of trouble.

Damn you, Walker. It was easier to blame him for her inability to sleep with Armando rather than her weak constitution. His words had haunted her since he'd spoken them, doing much to mess with her brain. Now she was in some deep shit, having just coldcocked a leading member of the Columbian cartel, stranding herself on a boat with a bunch of killers. She set the evidence of her betrayal down softly, hoping not to alert anyone. Then she bent and retrieved her clothes, donning them with haste. Leaving the heels, she tiptoed down the hall with every intention of quietly diving overboard. No one lurked in the main cabin, so she slid out onto the deck and quickly ducked along the side.

"Going somewhere?"

With a gasp, she looked up to see Jade standing before her wearing a black leather swimsuit and a sick smile. Marcelina had no time to process Jade's drawn back fist before it shot forward.

And slammed into her face.

****

Voices. The sound of the ocean. As Marcelina slowly returned to consciousness, that familiar feeling of doom came with it, as if it were infused into her bones. She opened her eyes and blinked up at the soft light coming from a recessed ceiling. A complete body check told her that one side of her face was pounding. Her muscles were weak. Her hands were bound above her head. She shifted to look up at them and saw raw metal handcuffs attached to part of what looked like a network of hardware. A brief test proved they were solid.

The bed beneath her was covered in black plastic…hammering home exactly what was about to happen to her.

As her lungs began to work again, so did her brain. She was trussed up because she had attacked Armando Rivera on his moving boat of doom and was caught trying to escape it.

She'd been on the inside for three days—not nearly enough time to gather intel—and already she was a dead woman.

Jade came into view. "Look who's awake."

A rush of anxiety cost Marcelina what little precious breath she'd gained. She was helpless to defend herself, and words just wouldn't do it this time. Not with Jade.

The woman's long hair brushed against Marcelina's blouse as she sat down beside her. "I don't know what disappoints me more," she said. "That you proved me right or that Armando had to suffer for it."

"What's going on? Did you hit me?" Not that playing dumb would work, but it was the best Marcelina could come up with in the hopes of buying time.

Jade only smiled. "Please don't continue with this charade. I'll lose all respect for you."

"Is—is Armando okay?"

She nodded, showing exaggerated concern. "Yes, he's just fine, thank you for asking." The amusement was back. "He's always had a very hard head. Wouldn't listen to me where you were concerned. But now, Princess, he has some questions for you—questions I begged him to ask you last night, but he wanted to wait until after he got you in bed."

The answers were becoming more and more clear. Jade and her good mood. Her request for Armando's attention the night before. She'd had something for him, all right, and it was proof that Marcelina was working with the DEA. "I was being set up the moment I stepped foot on this boat. Wasn't I?"

Jade shrugged. "I told him you'd never sleep with him. That part pleased me greatly." Her look darkened.

"You hitting him over the head? That just pissed me off."

And a pissed-off Jade equaled blood in the bedroom. Marcelina swallowed hard, pulled against the handcuffs, hating that she couldn't hide her fear any longer. "I didn't plan to hit him if that makes you feel better."

"No, it doesn't. It doesn't make Armando feel better, either." Jade crawled onto the bed, straddling Marcelina's legs between two silky thighs and rendering them useless. She reached behind her hip and produced a filet knife. Marcelina looked down just in time to watch its slow path to the middle of her chest. "Because this is something you've been planning for a long time, isn't it?" With the tip of the knife, she moved the folds of Marcelina's blouse aside, exposing her heaving upper torso. The blade barely brushed her skin, tracing an intricate pattern over her belly without drawing blood. Unable to look away, Marcelina watched its sweeping ascent, held her breath as the tip traced the dark outline of one, bared areola. Then it moved over a sensitive spot on her chest and she flinched.

Jade pouted. "Guess that zap I gave you left a little burn."

Zap? Jade must have used a stun gun to keep her immobile, which would explain the weak muscles.

"Unfortunately, I can't start until Armando gets here." Jade held up the knife, flipped the blade downward and sheathed it with the quick skill of a pro. "So I think I'll just play for a while."

Chapter 20

Jade shimmied down her legs a bit further, bent and took a nipple between her teeth. Then she looked up to meet Marcelina's terrified gaze before biting it. Hard. Marcelina squirmed and bucked as her panic spilled over the edge. "Get your filthy mouth off me!" she yelled.

The pressure eased. "I'm sorry." Jade flicked her tongue over the abused nub. "I didn't plan to bite you if that makes you feel better." Then, while Marcelina panted and heaved, she drew it into her mouth, sucking on it so that it popped out twice the size. Then she moved to the other nipple, sucking on that one, too, as she kept the left one extended with a pinch of her fingers. "Mmm. This is the way I like them. Nice and big. Makes them easier to grab hold of when I cut them off."

A choked sob left Marcelina's throat. Jade's evil laughter filled the cabin.

"That's enough for now, Jade."

That was Armando's voice. It was flat, lacking the warmth from earlier. Jade moved aside to reveal the man standing at the entrance to the cabin. A white bandage was held in place over his head-wound with a band of gauze. More men were behind him, but Marcelina couldn't see how many. "Armando," she wheezed. "Please don't let her do this."

He approached, holding her gaze with the soulless look of a killer. All fondness for her was gone. "You tried to kill me."

"No!"

"Jade was right about you all along."

"I don't kill people! That's what *you* do!" Her bravery came out, brought on by a cold realization that she wasn't going to be able to talk her way out of this with Armando, either.

"At first I thought you were working with the police," Jade said from the other side of the bed. Marcelina was flanked by her executioners, her trial going on at that very moment. "I even got your little blonde friend out of the way so I could find the proof I needed."

"Kendall? What did you do to her?"

"Nothing bad. I'm sure she's back at home, nursing a case of sore feet. Not that I'd know, because when I went to search her apartment, I was interrupted by a metro sexual butt-fucker who claimed to be an old friend of yours."

Confusion abounded since Jade's colorful description didn't fit any of her friends. Unless…

Oh, no.

Jade angled her body to address someone by the door. "What's your name again, honey?"

"J—Jonah."

The voice of her ex-boyfriend signaled a whole different ballgame. Marcelina's lungs froze in her chest at the thought of what he'd told these people. Her head popped up and her visual confirmation revealed the newly bearded and bloody face of her blackmailer. His hazel-green eyes were sunken beneath a mop of messy top hair, but there was some intelligence left in them. "Jonah," she said with as much calm as she could muster, "if you know what's good for you, you'll stay quiet."

"Oh, but he was the one who sought *me* out." Jade looked pleased with herself while Armando stood by and let her preen. She gave Jonah a little foot nudge on her way by. "Isn't that right, Metro? You said that Armando was in danger and that you would tell us why in exchange for protection. But all it took was a few strikes to that delicate face of yours and you sang like a bird at dawn's chorus."

This wasn't happening. Marcelina was connecting the dots now, and the resulting picture was much different, much worse than before. Her eyes widened on Jonah. "What did you tell them?"

"I'm sorry, Marcelina." His face crumpled beneath the full beard. A sob escaped, letting loose a shower of snot and saliva. "The feds were closing in on me. I had to find a way out."

"Asshole! You found it!"

"Aaahh." Armando finally spoke. "I think we're getting our first glimpse of the woman behind the charade." The bed dipped as he sat down beside her. "You had me fooled. You made me think I was pursuing you, when you were the one pursuing me the whole time."

Marcelina pulled against the cuffs, the skin of her wrists chaffing with the impractical rush of adrenaline that told her to keep trying them. "That's not true, Armando. I didn't want to have anything to do with you at first. Remember?"

He rose from the bed and walked over to where Jonah King knelt on the floor. "Repeat what you told Jade."

"Please don't kill me," Jonah begged. "I came to you

as a gesture of—"

Armando's ring-studded fist slammed into the man's face. He cried, spit out a tooth along with a lot of blood. "Oh God, oh God, oh God…" Another sob. "She's the woman who killed Nari Puccini."

The rapid nature of his accusation put Marcelina's brain in a tailspin. It was the confirmation she'd dreaded, that this secret he held over her was the one that would end—or at least ruin—her life. "Seriously, Jonah?" she railed. "If I were that clever, I would have killed *you* a long time ago!"

"It's true!" More blood showered out of his mouth.

"You see," Armando said to her, "the police noticed that a sentimental amulet Puccini always wore was missing from the crime scene while his other valuables remained. It was evidence that was kept out of the media to weed out the false leads. Tell us about that very unique amulet, Jonah."

Jonah obeyed. "It was a Coccinella charm with his mother's initials on it. I found it in Marcelina's room."

The charm Nari had given her before his death. Why didn't she think of it as possible evidence before? Because it had been kept out of the media on purpose, that's why. Nari said he never took it off. He said it would bring her luck in love just as it had brought him victory over his enemies.

What he failed to mention was how it would one day bring her death.

"I saw him wearing it at his step-son's wedding," Jonah continued. "As soon as I found it in Marcelina's room I connected the dots. Latina woman, same time, same place…it all fit."

"What puzzles me is how *you* were ever a guest at

Puccini's step-son's wedding," Armando said in amused disbelief.

Jonah closed his eyes. "I was the bartender."

And just as Marcelina feared, his so-called leverage had put her in an even worse predicament than before. There was no hope of talking herself out of this one since they all believed she killed Nari…and that she had apparently been sent to kill Armando. Her panic-driven improv with a champagne bottle didn't exactly help her on that front, though one would think it a bit clumsy of a skilled assassin.

"He's lying," she choked out in a last-ditch effort to discredit her ex. "He was obviously privy to that kind of inside information. What makes you think he actually found *anything* in my room?"

Jade reached into her bodice and produced the silver and red charm between her thumb and forefinger. With a smug smile, she replied, "Because a little lady-bird told me."

There it was—her token reminder of Puccini that had gone missing apparently when Jonah stole it from her jewelry box. A bubble of insane laughter welled up in her throat. She was going down for Nari's murder all right—only the mob would have to get in line.

Armando came back to her bedside with narrowed eyes. "It made sense to Jade, but I didn't want to believe the word of this arrogant prick so quickly. I told her if you'd been sent to kill me, you would have done it already." His expression went blank. "And then I woke up in the galley with blood in my eyes."

His dramatic conclusion was followed by enough time to make Marcelina break into a sweat.

"As I stumbled to my feet," he continued, pacing the

floor with slow, meaningful steps, "I remembered what you said at *Le Marée*. What was it? 'The romance is a lie that can only end in tragedy.' It sounded familiar to me then. Now I remember hearing those exact words years ago from Puccini himself."

"I didn't. Kill. Nari. Puccini." Marcelina's words came out in a slow growl.

"That would have made you, what? Nineteen?" Armando wiped Jonah's blood from his knuckles with a hand towel. "I don't know what surprises me more, Marcelina: That his taste ran that young, or that you slept with a man that old."

"I didn't sleep with him, either! We were friends!"

But they were just words by now, spoken from the lips of a desperate woman. Armando nodded as he approached the bed again. "I understand why you think you can continue to fool me. I let it happen once. But I am never fooled twice, especially by a dumb cunt who can't follow through on a simple hit." He held up a finger when she opened her mouth to argue. "I only want to know one thing. And before you try to deny it again, remember that your answer may mean the difference between a slow death and a quick one."

He leaned over her, flanking her body with his arms as he gazed down at her face. "Who hired you?"

She kept her mouth shut, knowing he wouldn't be satisfied with any of her answers.

"Tell me, Marcelina. It could save you from a lot of pain."

"No one hired me," she breathed as tears filled her eyes. "I'm not a killer."

"It would have to be an enemy of mine. Bishop would be the obvious choice if I thought he had the spine.

Someone from Mexico…the Jalisco Cartel, perhaps? Or was it the mob, same as who hired you to kill Puccini?"

When she bit her lip in silence, his forehead smoothed out making him look more cold and ruthless than ever before. "I'm heartbroken, Marcelina. You really were the woman of my dreams." He smashed his mouth to hers. She struggled beneath the cruelty of his kiss, knowing it was more of a kiss of death than of passion. Then he lifted up and walked away. "Jade, she's all yours. Don't stop until she talks."

Jonah was pulled to his feet by two of Armando's crew. "I'm sorry, Marcelina," he blubbered from the doorway. "I just wanted a way out, that's all."

"Who did you think these people were, Jonah?" she yelled at him with an incredulous laugh. "Low level street dealers? No! They are *Columbian cartel!* The kind who will shoot you in the balls and let the sea life finish them off before your body hits shore! My God, how stupid can you be?"

"Shut her up," Armando barked, his body blocking all view of Jonah.

When they exited the cabin, Jade began to play with her filet knife again. She studied Marcelina's heaving form, trussed up and panting with fear. She cocked her head. "Aw, look at that. Your nipples…I'm going to have to suck on them again."

Marcelina pulled herself up as best she could, her vision foggy behind the fresh tears that formed. "Don't do this, Jade. Please."

The last came out a breathless sob as the knife hovered over her abdomen. "I can cut you open just enough to pull your guts out slowly," Jade said. "Or…" She moved the knife up to her breastbone. "…put it straight through your heart. You wouldn't feel much for long. All you have to do is give me a name." Her grin deepened with malice. "But I may not believe you, in which case I'd be forced to gut you anyway."

So it would be a slow process either way and Armando's bitch was taking her time, trying to figure out the best angle to start. Marcelina's navel sucked inward as the cold metal of the knife touched it. She squeezed her eyes shut, suppressing a cry of sheer terror when the blade pressed down…

"Hey."

The bed shifted beneath her, then sprang upward. There was a shuffling sound, a gurgle, and then a faint snap. Marcelina's eyes came open just in time to see Lincoln's blurry form lower something large and limp to the floor. She blinked, realizing that the limp object was Jade.

The door to the bedroom was closed. As she watched in dumb shock, Lincoln moved toward a set of drawers and quickly sifted through them. "Here." He dropped a blouse onto her chest. "As soon as I unlock these cuffs, you need to get decent in a hurry. Got it?" He went for her handcuffs with a small key.

"Lincoln, what are you doing?" she squeaked.

"Saving your ass."

The cuffs came off. Marcelina shot upward, ignoring the urge to check out the damage to her wrists as she struggled to get out of one blouse and into another. "But why? I thought you were one of Armando's most trusted men!"

He put a finger to his lips reminding her to be quiet. "I was Puccini's trusted man first. That's all you need to know."

She buttoned up, the questions bombarding her one after the other. "That doesn't explain why you're saving me. Everyone thinks I *killed* Nari."

"Not everyone."

Her gaze shot upward. "Who?"

He was at the door with his ear flat against it. "Never mind about that," he whispered. "Now, scream."

She got off the bed. Moved toward him. "What?"

"Scream or he'll come through that door wondering why you aren't!"

It was then she saw Jade on the floor, her neck canted at an odd angle. The woman's lips were unusually pale, her violet gaze half-lidded and blank. It was Marcelina's first look at a real-life dead body. The enormity of it all hit her at once. She opened her mouth, filled her lungs, and let loose with a scream that would have curdled the blood of a goat.

"Goddamn, you're good at that." Lincoln wiggled his jaw, blinked his eyes. "Come on. Out."

A blast of warm sea air hit her in the face and she realized he'd already opened a window and punched through the screen. "What am I supposed to do?" she asked in a panic. "Swim to shore?"

There was no shore in sight since she was staring out the left side of the boat.

"You won't have to. Someone's coming down the hall! Jump, dammit!"

With no time to think about it, she wiggled through the windowsill, cutting her palm in the process. As the blood began to drip, she hit the water.

The ocean was cold, jump-starting Marcelina's system with a jolt. She surfaced, took a deep breath, and went under again, hiding as long as her lungs would allow until the yacht was a good distance away. The vibrating hum of the engines faded as she continued to hover there. And then she broke the surface with a guttural gasp.

As air filled her lungs once again, she wiped the salt water from her eyes and looked around. Her hand and wrists stung like a bitch, reminding her she was bleeding. The boat was getting smaller but was still close enough for someone to spot her if they were looking. She went under again, hoping nothing carnivorous circled below.

The sound of another, smaller engine began to grow louder. Louder. She broke the surface again, hoping to target the approaching boat and avoid getting run over. Waves swelled around her. She bobbed with them, catching fleeting glances of a powerboat as it puttered and growled toward her.

She waved her arms, hoping to God the people on that boat were there to rescue her. When she topped a swell, the glimpse she got of Armando's yacht proved that it was no longer producing a wake. It was stopped. "Oh no," she rasped. He must have found out she was missing.

Thank goodness the owners of the powerboat had seen her and were at that moment pulling close. The engine was cut. The ladder went down. She quickly swam toward it, cutting through the water with as much speed as she could muster.

When she latched onto the ladder, with barely enough energy left to climb it, a hand appeared.

"Grab on, I'll help you up!"

She must have been delirious because that sounded like Rand's voice. Summoning her last bit of energy, she reached up and clasped that arm as if it were her only remaining lifeline. A strong grip hoisted her upward and onto a platform, then she was being dragged through a small opening. When she was let go, Marcelina sprawled out against hot, course carpeting, panting in air that tasted like salt water.

"Ladder's up, let's go!" Twin inboard engines roared back to life and were gunned. They were moving fast, bouncing along the waves at a good clip. Marcelina rolled onto her back, catching her breath and watching the cloud studded sky roll by.

"Stay down. We don't want them to see you."

She lifted her head to confirm the owner of that voice. Sure enough, Rand Sorrick was positioned at the side of the boat, his T-shirt and cargo shorts a bit off character from the starched black uniform she was used to. He was keeping an eye on that yacht with his pistol pointed downward in a firm, two-handed grip, ready to fire when needed.

A quick peek at the driver of the boat ended in a double take. Salt stung her eyes, blurring her vision, but there was no mistaking that familiar broad stance. The black hair and steely profile. The determination. Walker was at the wheel, whisking her away from danger yet again. Marcelina started to crawl toward him, but a hand on her arm reminded her they weren't out of the woods yet.

"Keep still."

With so many questions but no breath to ask them, she simply obeyed and closed her eyes again. Let things happen. The last, most horrific hour of her life replayed in her mind. The champagne bottle. The handcuffs. Jade's filet knife and Armando's scathing accusations. How in the hell had she escaped such an inevitable death?

Lincoln. Armando's bulldozer of a bodyguard had turned out to be her savior. What did he say? That he was Nari Puccini's most trusted man first? The light came on and Marcelina had to laugh. Her humor, however, was quickly stifled by the realization he was still on that yacht, possibly facing a date with his own doom. Would he be okay? Something told her he would.

Then she remembered his role in Graham's death, and the conflicting emotions that followed warred with each other behind closed eyes. Soon the boat slowed, idled for a while, then the sounds of other boats and people wafted above her.

Rand appeared, his watchful gaze scouring the docks. "Are you ready to get out?"

She threw an arm over her face and nodded. "I think so."

"Your hand is bleeding. We'll get you fixed up in no time flat, but first you have to get up off the floor."

He helped her up. She wobbled to her feet, looked around for the driver of the boat, but aside from the two of them it was empty. "Where did he go?"

The docks were crowded with people. A visual search of them proved useless, but for a split second she thought she saw Walker's head among them. Before she could call out though, her view was blocked by a family of six exiting their rented boat.

And just like that he was gone. Had he been there at all? Or was she so desperate to see him she imagined the whole thing? A dockhand came up and offered to help her out. Rand was beside her also ready to give a hand. She blinked at him, still in somewhat of a daze. "What are you and Walker doing here, Rand? And how did you know I'd be floating in the ocean?"

She was lifted out as if she weighed nothing. Once Rand was also out of the boat, he guided her by the elbow through the smattering of people, spoke low. "Your lawyer told us everything. That was a really stupid thing you did."

"Where is he?" Marcelina swiveled her head in a desperate attempt to find him. "I need to talk to him."

"He didn't seem interested in talking."

But he'd come all this way to rescue her again. He couldn't just leave, not without allowing her to explain what happened since they last saw each other. His sudden disappearing act planted a seed of dread in the center of her chest. This was it. His last time…

The need to fall apart was quashed behind other fears, other unanswered questions. "Oh God, how is Kendall? Did Jade hurt her?"

"Don't worry about Kendall," Rand replied. "She's tougher than you think."

"And my ex-boyfriend, Jonah King, is on that yacht. He's a dick but I don't want him to die."

"It's being handled. For now, we need to get out of here."

"What do you mean it's being handled?"

"Just be quiet and walk, Marcelina."

They hoofed it across the sidewalk and to the edge of the street. A dark blue sedan pulled up. Rand opened the rear door and shoved her inside, then got in the front passenger seat. When the car began to move again, she looked at the rearview mirror and was met with a familiar set of green eyes.

A powerful mixture of joy and relief exploded throughout her body. "Kendall! Oh, thank God!"

She reached over the seat and wrapped her arms around Kendall's slender shoulders. Her friend was safe and breathing and driving a getaway car that smelled like an old cab. It was a beautiful moment she would never, ever forget.

Kendall kept both hands on the wheel, though the corner of her mouth lifted. "Uh…driving, here."

"She said she made you disappear," Marcelina croaked beside her ear. "I thought I'd never see you again."

"Other than that bitch stealing my favorite stilettoes, I'm fine." Kendall made a hard left, narrowly missing an oncoming truck.

As the blaring horns faded behind them, Marcelina noticed the bruise on Kendall's cheek. "The bitch had a mean sucker punch, didn't she?" And Marcelina would surely have a matching bruise to prove it.

Kendall's gaze met hers again in the rearview mirror. "You talk about her in the past tense."

The image of Jade's blank stare would forever be emblazoned in her mind. "Because she's dead now."

There was a moment of thoughtful silence before Kendall nodded. "Good."

"Yeah." Marcelina's shoulders gave way to a shudder. "Good."

An hour later, halfway across Alligator Alley—the everglades highway that would bring them home—she was curled up in the back seat fighting a long bout of nausea. It wasn't from any injuries she'd obtained from her ordeal, or dehydration from her time in the ocean since she wasn't in it for that long. It wasn't carsickness, either. It was because she couldn't fight the feeling that her whole world was about to come crashing down on her. Why would Walker help in her rescue, then leave before she had a chance to talk to him? To apologize? To tell him that she hadn't *failed* in her mission to seduce Armando Rivera, she had abandoned it altogether? She'd given up her deal with the DEA and any subsequent perks that went with it…all for a chance at love. How could he possibly turn her away once he knew the truth?

Rand's phone rang and he let go of Kendall's hand to answer it. The low spoken conversation that followed earned him more than a few curious glances. When he hung up, both Marcelina and Kendall asked, "What was that about?"

He twisted around, met Marcelina's worried gaze. "Rivera's dead."

For a moment, she thought she'd heard wrong. Armando dead? No. The man was indestructible. "How do you know?"

"The coastguard boarded his yacht shortly after you jumped overboard. He was found with an apparent gunshot wound to the chest, along with another dead passenger. A woman."

A woman with a broken neck. The sickening sound of Jade's bones popping would stay with Marcelina for a lifetime. But she didn't quite know how to feel about Armando's demise. Relief, of course, but would this be yet another "hit" pinned on a mysterious woman he'd been seen with shortly before his death? The déja vu was incredible…and uncanny.

"Well, I, for one, am happy," Kendall beamed from behind the wheel.

Marcelina found a smile. "Yes, I am, too."

"They also took into custody a guy who claimed that you were the last one seen with both Rivera and the deceased woman."

She closed her eyes, put her face in her hands. "Jonah King. And I swear I didn't kill anyone." The last time he saw her she was in absolutely no position to do so. Only Marcelina knew the truth, but no way would she rat out Lincoln, the one who'd apparently killed Armando, too. At least not until she had a chance to speak with him, make sure her instincts about him were right. Could it be he was just a bodyguard after all? Was he ever Armando's hit man, or did that role solely belong to Jade?

Rand just put his hand on her shoulder and gave it a squeeze. "If you did kill him, it was obvious self-defense. No one could fault you for it."

This wasn't happening. No one would believe her, not with Jonah and his big-mouthed accusations. He'd spill everything. In a desperate bid for sanity, she met Kendall's gaze in the rearview mirror. "Kendall, you know me. I've done some stupid things in my life, but please tell your boyfriend I don't kill people."

"She couldn't shoot a hoop let alone a pistol," Kendall told Rand without hesitation.

They smiled at each other. "Thank you," Marcelina said then frowned a bit. "I think."

Chapter 21

Walker stood in Captain Ross's office and watched through the glass as a beautiful moment unfolded in the lobby. Three women were huddled there, talking, crying, exchanging hugs…although, it looked as if Kendall and Audrey were doing all the talking while Marcelina nodded and listened. Walker couldn't help but feel good about that—as if she'd learned something from him after all.

Words are like quicksand…

"She'll be needing you," Leonard said beside him, also watching the scene in the lobby.

"No," Walker answered. "She won't."

"She's looking at hours of debriefing."

"I'm not her attorney anymore."

The man produced a sound of frustration. "Quit pouting, Bishop. You know she only fired you for show."

It took all Walker had to keep his voice neutral and his fists from flying. "She made her choices, Leonard."

"So, you're just going to leave her out there to dry, huh?"

If anything, the police captain should understand that he really *couldn't* be her lawyer anymore. Their relationship was out, especially among the agents who kept such close tabs on Marcelina. They'd heard enough to get the gist, and even congratulated him on 'nailing' a woman like that. It was nothing but charm with those guys.

Walker went for his briefcase, which was still warm from the long ride across the state in his trunk. "She'll be all right."

Leonard threw him a black look. "You sound awfully sure of that."

Because he was. Though she didn't know it yet, Marcelina Page no longer needed to fear her past or her future. Conrad Bishop had taken care of her past with a few phone calls and a pair of Marlins baseball season tickets. Good seats, too, right behind home plate. It was that easy for him, while men like Walker were bound by the system. The law. A canon of ethics. None of that meant shit to his father.

As far as Marcelina's future went, Jonah King deserved all the credit. So shaken by his ordeal with the cartel, he spilled everything to a table full of fascinated detectives, which included the two DEA agents assigned to Marcelina's case and Captain Ross. He not only admitted to smuggling drugs into the country, but also to duping a clueless girlfriend into accepting his mail. There was no mention of Nari Puccini. Walker figured it was either because his conscience had finally met its match, or he was so scared that Marcelina—skilled assassin that she was—would set her sights on him next.

As soon as the trio of women moved into another office, Walker slid out the door and made his way through the lobby. Now that he'd verified she was back and in one piece, he was done with all things Marcelina Page.

"Walker!"

It was her voice calling out to him. The urge to turn around and go to her clawed at his insides, but he ignored the pain, pushed through the glass doors of the precinct, and walked into the late afternoon sun.

"Walker, please!" he heard again just before the doors closed behind him.

As soon as he got in his car and put the air conditioning on, he dialed a number. It was answered immediately. "Hello, son."

His father sounded smug, as if Walker should be impressed by his resourcefulness. "She's back," Walker said. "And aside from a few cuts and bruises, she's okay."

"Yes, I know. I spoke with her over the phone after she was recovered. We had to…go over some things."

In other words, she had to know what story to tell during her debriefing. "You mean so the lies would coincide?" Walker scoffed.

"You opted to take that route, son. If there's a time to withhold judgment, it's now."

The man was right. For the first time, Walker had to consider what kind of wall Conrad had been backed up against when he'd first opted to cheat.

"When we have no good alternatives," Conrad continued, "all we can do is weigh the stakes. The players. The consequences. Then hope like hell the necessary evil comes out on top. Nari was a dangerous man, but he lent balance to a very volatile ecosystem. We both made sacrifices we had to live with—until we couldn't."

It was the first time Conrad had ever attempted to explain his actions. Was it possible he was trying to make amends? Walker squinted against the sun's rays flashing through the moving palm fronds across the street. He put his visor down, trained the vents to blow directly on his face. Took a moment to summon the words. "I've judged you for a lot of years now. In a perfect world, I'd take this as a lesson and let bygones be bygones. But it's not a perfect world, and all I can do right now is thank you for helping Marcelina. I never thought I'd ask you to cheat for me, but...you really came through when I needed you." Nothing like choking on a mouthful of hot crow.

"Is that all?"

And those three words reminded him why Conrad would never make father of the year. Walker glared daggers out the window. "If there's something you want in return, just say it."

"How about an invitation to the wedding?"

He opened his mouth to ask what the man was talking about when it dawned on him. "There won't be a wedding," he bit out.

"Why not?" Conrad replied. "You love each other, don't you?"

"None of your damned business."

"The hell it isn't. I didn't just have Marcelina pulled from the brink of death for a happily ever never, son."

A happily ever—what? "The brink of death, huh?" Walker threw the car into reverse and mashed the gas.

Conrad's voice sounded above the squeal of tires. "According to my source, she was a breath away from getting her guts sliced open."

The image flashed before Walker's eyes in vivid detail, putting a pained grimace on his face. "And who is this source?"

"Is that really what's important?"

Walker rubbed at his eyes before returning his hand to the wheel and tearing out of the parking lot. "Good

God, your hypocrisy knows no bounds. I *know* what's important, Dad. I'm the one who tried to preserve it. I even told her I loved her, but it made no difference. And now that I've said way more than I need to, I'm hanging up."

And he did. Why did he always end up losing his cool with that man? Marcelina was safe which was all he cared about. No one, especially Walker, needed to know the sickening details of her and Rivera's romantic night in Miami. The asshole had been taken down mob style, which deserved a resounding round of applause, but not before he'd put his mark on a woman that Walker wanted for himself.

Yes, Rivera was dead. The man had gone out, however, having won a very crucial round in this rekindled war of theirs. Whether Walker was ready to get over that remained to be seen. Perhaps he was justified in kicking Marcelina out of his life. Perhaps he was just—what did they call it these days—butt-hurt? The only thing he was sure of was that all analysis would be best saved for later.

When he was once again capable of rational thought.

****

Marcelina stood with her forehead pressed against the glass doors. The nausea was back as she watched Walker's car squeal out of the parking lot. He'd heard her call his name; she could tell by the way his spine had stiffened before exiting the police station lobby. He wasn't going to forgive her or even hear what she had to say. Just when she'd gotten her life back—partly thanks to Jonah and his weary confessions—she'd lost a key part of it again.

"Walker will get over it," Kendall said beside her.

"Come on. Rand says we're up for an interrogation."

Marcelina's thoughts went from one disastrous subject to another. "*We?* As in not just me? Why?"

"Because the DEA says he and I took matters into our own hands, even though all we did was drive to Miami and rent a boat." She leaned in, lowered her voice. "Walker put it all together. He told us what to say and what not to in case this happened."

Of course. Walker was the most capable man she knew. Up until now, though, she thought he'd just driven the getaway boat. But it was much, much more than that. Her unexpected conversation with Conrad Bishop— telling her what to say and what not to—hammered home the fact that Walker had gone against everything he believed in order to save her one last time.

There were so many questions, so much she needed to say... "I really need to talk to him," she murmured as they made their way back through the lobby arm in arm.

"He's angry. Give him time to cool down."

"I'm afraid it will take more than just time," she said sadly. "He told me he loved me. And then I pushed him away."

Kendall sucked air through her teeth. "Oooh. Not good." They reached the office where Rand waited with Captain Ross and the two DEA agents in charge of Marcelina. "I say after this, you go to Walker's place with some wine and a fresh serving of humble pie."

It was a thought Marcelina had already entertained. She was good at humble pie, something she'd learned to scrape up just like an impromptu egg casserole. But chances were his door would be locked this time.

And she was right. When she tried it the next morning, Walker's side of the duplex was closed up and dark as doomsday. So that afternoon, she went to his office where she stood in front of Judith with her purse under her arm and a white-knuckled grip on the countertop. She wore a prim blouse and business-casual slacks, something befitting of a lawyer's girlfriend. She was playing by the rules, something Walker would appreciate. "I'm here to see Walker," she said in a professional manner.

Judith's smile was sympathetic. "He's with a client right now."

Something told her Judith had been ordered to keep her out. "I'll wait."

A flash of rebellion entered the woman's eyes. Judith pursed her lips, picked up the phone, pushed a button. "Marcelina Page is here to see you … Yes, I'll tell her." With considerably more tension than before, she hung up and cleared her throat. "I'm sorry, Ms. Page, but he asked that you leave. He said if you need representation, to call the public defender's office."

His reaction wasn't entirely unexpected, but Marcelina's heart plummeted just the same. "Can you give him a message for me?"

"Sure." Judith—the intern with a chronic case of enthusiasm—looked as if she needed a vacation.

Marcelina opened her mouth, but couldn't produce a word. How did one convey her feelings in a message from the front desk? Tell him I want him more than anything. That from now on I'll do what he says. Be there for him when he needs me. Tell him I'll love him every day for the rest of my life.

"Tell him I'm sorry."

It was all she could do not to break down right then and there. Checking the urge to run for the door, she lifted her chin and sauntered to it as if it were common practice to make a complete fool of herself. Since her eyes were closed when she pushed on the handle, she didn't see the man that had approached from the outside.

A collision occurred, knocking her off balance enough for him to have to hold out a steadying hand. "Easy," he said.

The door swung closed behind her. The morning sun shined down on a large, familiar shape that damn near blocked the light. "Lincoln!" She cleared her throat, stepped back. "What are you doing here?"

He shoved hands in pockets and gave her proper girlfriend attire a brief, confused once-over. "Favor for a friend."

When he began to walk around her, she stopped him with a hand on his arm. "I didn't know what happened to you."

"The less you know the better."

She felt like telling him she was glad he was all right, but the jury was still out on that one. Instead, she said, "Well, uh…now I can thank you for saving me."

"Thank the guy who told me to." He took one of his hands out of his pocket and produced something that flashed purple and gold in the sun. "He wanted me to give you this."

By the time she recovered from her shock, Lincoln was gone. She couldn't even ask him where he'd gotten the foil wrapper of her favorite candy that had been discontinued over six years ago. The desire to know for sure consumed her thoughts like a sudden flash fire…because what she was thinking was impossible. Yes, the chocolate was no longer there. But the message she'd just received was more brilliant than ever.

Nothing is impossible.

"Nari," she breathed.

****

Walker punched the speaker button, cutting off his intern before she had a chance to say anything more about Marcelina in front of his present company. Judith had made it no secret she liked Marcelina, had probably even discussed the issue with his father.

"You should have let her come in. I can wait in the lobby."

He glanced up at Audrey Metcalf who was sitting across from him on the client side of the desk. "I'm not a fan of wasting my time," Walker replied. "I'm sure she isn't, either."

His guest had not only come with a desire to hire him, but with a squirming four-year-old that was at that moment wiggling out of her lap. Little Caroline ran to the door, opened it, and disappeared down the hall in the direction of the waiting room.

When a tired-looking Audrey started to go after her, Walker stopped her. "She'll be fine with Judith." Besides, his intern deserved a little payback for ignoring his wishes.

Half standing, Audrey hesitated for a moment, then decided to abandon the chair altogether. "I should go, anyway. I'm sure you have a busy schedule."

Walker also stood. "Actually, my only scheduled hearing for the day was postponed until next week. And no matter how busy I am, Mrs. Metcalf, you can always come to me."

Appreciation flashed in her gray-blue eyes, though it was immediately dulled by the possibilities. "I just hope I won't need you."

He smiled. "That's what they all say."

After another few minutes of banter and legal advice, they walked to the door, slowly and with the somber steps of uncertainty. "I have no idea what kind of trouble Graham left me with," Audrey said. "Something tells me I'm about to find out."

He opened the door for her. She thanked him and they advanced down the hallway. When they reached the waiting room, Walker expected to see Caroline behind Judith's desk, pushing buttons, scoping out the vast selection of writing tools, and being a general pain in the ass. But the sight that greeted him was far from satisfying. In fact, his blood ran ice cold all over again.

There was Caroline, curled up and asleep against none other than Armando Rivera's henchman.

Audrey approached him with a grimace. "I'm sorry," she whispered.

The big man held up a hand as if it were no trouble.

"She doesn't normally do this, but she's had a rough week." Audrey's eyes began to well.

"All they did was exchange names," Judith said from behind the desk with a look of adoration. "Then she just squeezed right under his arm and fell asleep."

A smile tugged at Audrey's mouth. "She must feel safe with you."

The man simply shrugged. "It wouldn't be the first time I was confused for a pillow."

Walker's incredulity doubled as he watched Audrey sit down next to her daughter. The three could be mistaken for a family if not for Graham Metcalf's blood all over the thug's hands.

"That's not it," Audrey said. "You have a look about you, like some kind of protector."

The man's gaze flitted briefly over to Walker. "I'm a bodyguard."

She let out a small laugh. "That explains it, I guess."

Walker went to Judith's desk. "Name?"

Judith looked down at her notes. "Lincoln Reyes. He's here to see you regarding a personal matter."

"Mr. Reyes, would you please step into my office?" Walker extended a hand to the hallway. Not that he liked the idea of spending time alone with Rivera's bodyguard, but he'd do it to get the damn guy away from Audrey and Caroline.

With a sigh, Audrey stood up again. "I'm sorry, I'm keeping you. Here, let me take her."

The transfer would have been comical if not for the sick situation Audrey was in. She had no clue who she was exchanging kind words with. Caroline groaned, began to whine a little. Audrey threw her over a shoulder and soothed her. The little girl's eyelashes blinked open and her sleepy gaze immediately sought out Lincoln Reyes. She waved a tiny hand. He waved back.

If Walker weren't trying to keep things civil, he would have thrown the murdering son-of-a-bitch out. But that would have caused more alarm than the Metcalfs needed. Better to hear what Mr. Reyes had to say, throw a few choice words back at him, and *then* throw him out.

Back in the hallway, Walker insisted the man enter his office first which he did without argument. Walker closed the door, watching every move Mr. Reyes made as he took the same seat Audrey had abandoned a moment ago.

"That was very sweet, Reyes," he said as he circled around his desk.

The caution Lincoln exuded was palpable, though he answered, "Cute little girl."

"I just hope she never finds out she cuddled up to her father's killer." Damn, Walker thought. He shouldn't have said that, but he just couldn't help himself. Feeling brave, he met Lincoln's gaze. It was a spooky, amber gaze, and oh so cold.

"Come again?" the man asked.

Walker gestured in the direction of the lobby. "*Metcalf.* Audrey and Caroline *Metcalf.*"

The name registered and Lincoln's eyes went from cold to steely, confirming he had no idea who he'd just been conversing with. "I didn't come here to talk about that."

"Good." All pretenses fled as Walker finally welcomed in the rage. "Because I may be for hire, but I'm not for sale. Go find yourself another attorney."

Though Reyes stiffened a little, he showed no animosity for the harsh dismissal. "I came here as a favor to someone. Someone who thought you needed to know what went down on that yacht."

It was Walker's turn to put two-and-two together. "Ah. *You're* my father's source."

The man relaxed as if grateful they'd found the same page. "That phone call from Conrad was…unexpected. Hadn't heard from him in six years."

Six years? "Since Puccini 'died,' you mean?" When Reyes gave a short nod, Walker shook his head in disgust. "You picked a hell of an occupation, moving from one crime lord to another."

"Lucky for you."

"Don't be an asshole." If Walker didn't know better, he'd think there was amusement in the eyes of the killer before him.

"Helping your girlfriend wasn't exactly a hardship," Reyes said. "Rivera was more of a loose cannon than what I'm used to, so I guess it played out the way it should. Not that Marcelina made it easy…"

It was a teaser. Walker hated teasers, but hell if he didn't want to hear more, so he motioned for the man to continue.

Reyes obliged. "I didn't expect her to need me so soon. She was getting cozy with Rivera and I thought Conrad was halfway full of shit. Next thing I know she's trying to jump ship. Gets caught. About gets herself killed, especially after that fool move of hitting Rivera over the head with a champagne bottle."

Walker sat there blinking like a dumbass. "A champagne bottle."

Reyes gave a grim nod. "All hell broke loose. Some tool bag named Jonah brought Mr. Puccini into the mix, and next thing I know I'm operating on autopilot. Hoping like hell Conrad was right about that boat tailing us."

Walker could see the picture Reyes was painting. "I'm still not buying that you're the good guy in all of this. Rivera was your *boss*. You were loyal to him."

"I've only ever had one boss. It wasn't Rivera." The man stood up. "And I can see why Marcelina was worth the sacrifice. She is…" His brows shot up. "…one hell of a woman." And he walked out of the office.

Blindsided, Walker stared at the open door, trying to figure out if that was relationship advice or if Reyes wanted her for himself. Probably the latter. But then the other words Lincoln had spoken began to churn in his mind.

She was getting cozy with Rivera.

It was something Walker had expected. Feared even. The timing of Marcelina's assault on Rivera, however, was suspicious. He already knew she hadn't supplied anything useful to the DEA. Was it self-preservation that drove her to hit him with a champagne bottle, or did she develop cold feet?

Not that he could ever know for sure. But did it really matter if she slept with Rivera? Did he even care anymore? Were his rigid standards worth losing a woman who'd taught him to live and love the way Marcelina did?

Or were his standards the only thing keeping him from losing it altogether?

Chapter 22

It was dark. All Christmas lights had been taken down. Marcelina Page emerged from the shadows in her bright jogging outfit and ponytail. Not exactly the proper attire for breaking into houses, yet that is exactly what she planned to do.

On her way up the driveway, she bent and picked up the newspaper. Since she was already privy to what was on the front page, she planned to use it as a tool for her defense. The headline read: *An Old Mystery Solved?* followed by the byline: *The hidden life of Armando Rivera's assassin.* Below it were three photos: one of the late Nari Puccini, one of the silver and red charm he'd given Marcelina before his death, and an unflattering driver's license photo of Jade.

Marcelina smiled. That charm…something she'd dismissed as a simple harbinger of luck had turned out to be quite magical after all. Not only had it brought *her* luck, but it had also brought Puccini power over his enemies. Though Jade had not killed either crime lord, the woman would earn the legacy thanks to some fancy footwork performed by Nari's loyal bodyguard. The charm had been found in Jade's possession, after all, along with her Latina DNA—something law enforcement had been searching for since Nari's "death." As impossible as it seemed, Marcelina could appreciate whoever Lincoln had found on the inside to switch her hair samples with Jade's...and their willingness to be bought.

Nothing is impossible.

She stepped up onto the front porch, knowing the door would again be locked. But much to her surprise, when she tested the handle, it opened right up. Biting her lip against the glimmer of hope she dared let in, she slipped inside and locked the door behind her. Turned around to survey the shadows. Her eyes immediately adjusted and the first thing she sought out was the coffee table. She approached the scales of justice on top of it and squinted in the dark.

That glimmer of hope instantly disappeared. Her little kid's-meal contribution was no longer there, proving what she'd already come to terms with. Walker was erasing her from his life.

Or so he thought.

A faucet came on in the back of the house. After placing the newspaper beside the scales of justice, she headed that way and entered his bedroom. It was in the same immaculate condition as the last time she had done this, with only the unmade bed to indicate the place was lived in. In the sliver of borrowed light coming from the bathroom, she walked over to the chair and sat down. Waited.

"I could have you arrested for that."

His voice startled her into an adrenaline rush that almost hurt. Heart racing, Marcelina got back to her feet and approached the bathroom, her shame of breaking into his home again gobbled up by the insatiable desire to see him fresh out of his shower. Sure enough, he was at the vanity making the final passes beneath his chin with a razor. And just as expected, he was beautiful, wearing just a towel and the last remaining traces of shaving cream. His skin was moist, firm and moving with the well-defined muscle of his upper body as he shaved.

Warm steam circulated between them while Marcelina watched, propping herself against the doorsill and folding her arms to hide the tremble of her hands. "If I didn't know better, I'd think you were expecting me," she said, her voice surprisingly calm.

He turned off the water and wiped his face with a hand towel. "What do you want, Marcelina?"

Steeling herself against the censure in his tone, she cleared her throat. "I want to apologize." He moved past her and headed straight for the walk-in closet. Marcelina decided the heady scent of his aftershave was yet another thing she couldn't live without. "I also want to tell you how I feel," she forged ahead, following him to the closet. "And beg you to give me another chance." When he continued to ignore her, her heart sank a little. "But I can see you're still in no mood to listen, so I'll give you some space."

She backed away from his closet with the hopes he would call out her name. Stop her from leaving. If not, she would loiter in his kitchen and prepare for round two. Kendall had told her to forget the "proper girlfriend" attire and go at him Marcelina-style. It was a good plan, something that wouldn't leave her feeling like such a dork if she were kicked out on her can like last time. Kendall didn't seem to think that would happen, but just in case…

Marcelina took what could be her last look at his bedroom, a masculine space yet so very simple. Bed. Dresser. Desk. Chair. Oh, look, something out of place on the end table—a couple of files with a pair of wire-rimmed reading glasses placed on top. Yes, she thought with an inward sigh. Magazine quality as always.

Except…this time there was something else out of place—a tiny burglar that had apparently been moved off the scales of justice and onto his nightstand.

"So, apologize," he said behind her.

That glimmer of hope was back, this time with an achy quality that caused her to put a hand to her heart. Close her eyes. "I've never been more sorry than I was the moment I turned you away."

"Tell me how you feel."

She turned around, opened them to find him watching her, still dressed in nothing but a low-slung towel. Waiting. Her pulse thrummed in her ears. "I love you, Walker, more than anything. And I will put us first from now on, no matter what."

He stepped closer, still cautious but without the hard edges. "I'm glad to hear that."

"You are?" She blinked, trying to put his words into place. Did this mean he was forgiving her? And if so, was it at arm's length, or the way she wanted? "Aren't you going to ask me if I slept with him?"

Without breaking her gaze, he said, "It doesn't matter."

Yes, it did. She could see it beneath his skin, hear it in the rough texture of his voice. But she could also see that he loved her enough to accept it if she had. Marcelina felt the irresistible pull of a smile. "Then I'll just tell you. I couldn't do it. When the time came it felt like I was losing a part of me, and I couldn't risk it, Walker. I couldn't risk losing you and I had no choice but to give it all up."

"You did more than give it up." This time a hint of anger broke through with his words, a sign that there was a lot more going on under his skin than first imagined. "You nearly got yourself disemboweled. It was a stupid move, attacking Rivera like that."

He was looking at the lingering bruises around her wrists. The physical evidence of her close call with death. She frowned a bit. "I know. I panicked." How did he know about her near escape from Jade's knife since that part had been left out of her statement? As far as anyone knew, Jade was the one to free her, a story she'd rolled with in order to keep Lincoln out of it.

Lincoln. She'd literally run into him outside Walker's office, and he was the only one who could have supplied that kind of information. Hell, Marcelina was still wrapping her mind around the fact Walker had "toed the other side" in order to rescue her.

"I'm the one who owes you an apology, Marcelina," Walker said, breaking through her epiphany with a humble tenor to his words. "I was blind to your reasons for going to Rivera when I should have been the one person to see them. To back them. I've been doing a lot of soul searching over that one. I had to ask myself how I would have handled you getting killed." He sighed. Gave a quick rub of his eyes as if to eradicate the image from his brain. "The answer is I wouldn't have. If sleeping with Rivera meant the difference between your death and your survival, it's something I could live with." He came closer, the tension easing off him. His voice going husky. "But knowing you didn't *does* help things a lot."

His honesty brought forth a bubble of laughter from Marcelina's throat.

"It doesn't, however, change the fact I should have trusted you from the beginning," he continued. "No matter the outcome."

"Something I'm also guilty of," she admitted, her heart in her throat.

"And now that we have that out of the way," Walker murmured, "there's only one thing left to do."

She tilted her face upward, desperately hoping it was the same thing she was thinking, and acutely aware he was still only wearing a towel. "Kiss and make up?" she whispered back.

He rolled his eyes, fed her the clue. "Beg me to give you another chance."

Sensing his playful mood, she catered to the arrogance of his remark and gazed up at him through her lashes. "Please, Mr. Bishop. I don't want to face this world without you. I need you by my side always, fighting for me."

He took another step closer. "As your lawyer or as your lover?"

Marcelina's head fell completely back as he finally wrapped his arms around her. "God, never again as my lawyer. I'd rather face prison than have to keep my hands off you."

A burning fire had entered his gaze, mixing with the blue in a heavy contrast that gave her goosebumps. "Good answer," he replied, and then she was being utterly, thoroughly, passionately kissed. She tasted his forgiveness in the way his lips slanted over hers, and in the way his tongue found its way home. She felt it in the all-encompassing hold around her shoulders and in the bulge growing harder and harder against her belly. His unconditional acceptance of her—even before her big confession—made this victory all the sweeter.

"Don't think you're off the hook just yet." Walker's words were slow and suspiciously throaty against her lips. He leaned back and threaded his fingers through her hair, removing the rubber band in the process. "You still may be facing a life sentence with no chance of parole."

For a heart-stopping moment, Marcelina felt that old fear seep in, one that told her those legal problems may not be over. But then the sparkle in his eyes put those fears to rest. Pure, unmitigated joy surged through her at the thought of such a life sentence. "As long as I get to serve it with a sexy lawyer who can rock a stiff suit *and* make love all night…I can think of nothing better."

****

Six months later

Sunday afternoons spent with barbeques, the beach, and a family to enjoy them with…this was Walker's life now. He took it all in behind the tinted lenses of his shades, then flipped another burger. Meat sizzled, which signaled the need for another pull from the ice-cold beer in his hand. Pine trees shaded him from the sun. The flip-flops were off and his toes were curled in the sugary sand.

His cell phone buzzed. He reached into his pocket and checked the screen.

"This is a work-free zone, Bishop." The phone instantly left his hand and was replaced by a cold bottle of barbeque sauce. Arms circled around his waist from behind. A voluptuous, bikini-clad body pressed up against his naked back. "And Rand likes his medium-rare," Marcelina added.

All thoughts of work instantly fled. Walker set the

bottle of sauce down on the brick beside the flaming grill and lifted his arm. The woman he loved moved in beneath it, looking up at him through her own shades with a wistful smile. He couldn't help it. He had to kiss that smile. Their lips touched in a gentle pairing that promised many more moments like this to come. "Rand can get out of the water and flip his own damn burger," he murmured.

"But it's your turn to cook."

"All bets are off when you kiss me like that."

She laughed against his mouth and took another nibble at his bottom lip. "I've completely jaded you."

As his swim trunks began to shift with something that could become embarrassing, a voice carried over the Gulf breeze. "Hey! Less PDA and more sauce!"

He and Marcelina looked at one another, then glanced toward the water where the waves gently rolled up on shore. Rand and Kendall were emerging from them, dripping wet and pink from sun. Yeah, Walker supposed they were more like family than any he'd had. And with his and Marcelina's wedding coming up, it wouldn't be long before he had the official kind. With kids and everything.

Since when?

Since six months ago when a sexy little criminal had broken into his home and turned on the lights. Before that, Marcelina Page was just another client to keep at arm's length. Now she was his world.

"Give me the phone." Kendall held her hand out and took the offensive object from Marcelina's hand. Kendall promptly threw it in an open beach bag that was by a picnic table littered with food. "That's a capital offense, Walker."

Didn't they have better things to do in the water than spy on him? "I wasn't going to answer it," he replied as he brushed the burgers with the sauce. "Even though I do have fifty million messages and a full week in court to look forward to."

Rand threw his towel down and joined Kendall on the bench of the picnic table, straddling her between his legs. "When does your new partner start?" he asked, popping the top of the beer she'd just handed him.

"After we move into the new office next week."

"It's a house," Marcelina corrected. "With three bedrooms and a patio."

Walker made a point with his spatula. "The sign outside makes it an office. The patio is a bonus." She took the loaded plate of burgers from him and stifled a laugh. "Hey, none of that," Walker admonished as he followed her to the table.

"What's so funny?" Kendall asked.

Marcelina sat down and leaned in. "Ask him what the sign says."

They all looked at Walker with expectation. Oh well, he thought. May as well get used to it. "Bishop and DePriest." Snorts and snickers were his reward. "Yeah, yeah, laugh it up."

"Sounds like an action film," Rand provided, then altered his voice to deliver the dramatic movie trailer. "Guns, clergymen, and the explosive battle between good and evil."

Kendall doubled over and smacked him on the arm.

"It could read Bishop, *Padre,* and DePriest."

All eyes flew toward the direction from where the voice came, and there was Conrad Bishop strolling toward them from the boardwalk. Walker halted before sitting down, his hand suspended over the bowl of potato salad. A bad feeling came over him, and he sent Marcelina an accusatory look. She answered before he could ask, her mouth softening with a pleading smile. "I invited him."

Conrad arrived at the table with boat shoes in one hand and a pastry box in the other. His casual linen shirt and slacks moved with the breeze. To most people he appeared relaxed—though Walker detected the underlying tension inside him. Yes, his father had been putting forth some effort to repair their relationship. Walker was even meeting him halfway by allowing him into his professional life on an advisory basis. But where his personal life was concerned, there were still many lines in the sand…and the old man had just stepped over one, invite or no.

Walker acknowledged their new guest with a polite nod, indicating the empty seat on Marcelina's right. May as well let her be the buffer since she initiated this little get-together.

Everyone else greeted him with warmth and welcome. "What's in the box?" Marcelina asked.

"Torta caprese." Conrad accepted a plate and hamburger. "From that little shop in Bonita."

Rand's astute gaze grew curious as he assessed the elder Bishop. "When you suggested the sign read 'Bishop, *Padre* and DePriest,' I took it to mean you would like to fill that third room in Walker's new house?"

"Office," Walker grumbled. "And it's already arranged, but he'll be there as a consultant only." Those people didn't get added to the sign. He could feel Marcelina's surprised gaze on him. Yes, he'd given in to the idea, but only because his father was technically retired and because he'd offered to pay rent for the office space. It was a step toward healing that Marcelina had been advocating for a while now.

The meal continued with casual conversation that just didn't reach the comfort level from before. Or was it just Walker? The others seemed to accept Conrad's presence without a problem, but until the man disclosed the truth behind Puccini's so-called fate, the trust would never come. Marcelina seemed to be okay with it. She never asked about the "deceased" mobster, nor did she question the ethics—or lack of them—of such a man skating from justice. Walker was outnumbered in his beliefs, he knew. But he could forgive it for the sheer fact that Marcelina was alive and sitting beside him.

And, despite Conrad breaking some important bonds over the years, he'd begun to make repairs by helping to fix the future.

"You walk down the aisle in five weeks," Kendall was saying to Marcelina, "and we still don't have your shoes picked out."

"Can't I just go barefoot?" Marcelina suggested through a mouthful of burger. "It *is* a beach wedding."

Kendall groaned, picking up her soda can with a look of utter distaste. "*Be my maid-of-honor* she said. *It will be fun* she said."

Conrad chuckled, patted her hand. "As long as it ends in 'I do,' I'm sure it will be perfect."

"So will you be in town, Mr. Bishop?" Kendall asked. "It's not too late to get you fitted for a tux."

Walker caught his father's look over Marcelina's head. Since he still hadn't invited Conrad to the wedding, these moments usually came with a change in subject, or a smartass comment about eloping to Fiji. But this time… "He'll be in town," Walker answered for him, staring out at the gulf while he chewed. Now, if he could swallow without choking.

A hand covered his thigh, squeezed. When he glanced down at his fiancé, it was to encounter a look of pure adoration.

Well hell.

Conrad's mouth twitched with a smile. "As it happens, Kendall, my schedule just cleared up." There was something akin to moisture gathering in his eyes, but he looked away before Walker could be sure.

Sometimes, he supposed, meeting halfway wasn't so bad. And with a true miracle, the *Padre* may even make it onto the sign. Probably not. But if Walker had learned anything over the last six months…it was that nothing is impossible.

A word about the author...

Jules Parker is a longtime lover of action movies, fast cars, and good books. She picked up her first romance novel at the age of 12 and has been crafting white-knuckle love stories ever since. Having published 10 novels under the name J.A. Dennam, she took a short break to focus on health and family, and is returning with a fresh set of ways to deliciously torture her characters. Her favorite thing is to immerse herself within the creative confines of her she-shack, though she is also known to ride motorcycles and cuddle chickens.